The Wine Jelly Murder

by

Meg Benjamin

Luscious Delights

The Wild Rose Press, Inc.
PO Box 708
Adams Basin, NY 14410-0708
Visit us at www.thewildrosepress.com

Publishing History
First Edition, 2025
Trade Paperback ISBN
Digital ISBN

Luscious Delights
Published in the United States of America

Dedication

To Bill and all the wedding planners: Molly, Josh, Ben, and Beth.

Chapter 1

"She can't come in. There's no meal for her."

The mother of the bride was wearing a green dress. I guess you could call it sea foam. It was very soft and flowy, sort of a *sunset on the piazza* kind of dress, although since it was November in the Rockies, with snow in the forecast, it was not the kind of dress you'd usually wear around here.

Still, it was an appropriate color and style for the mother of the bride. Of course, at the moment, that mother of the bride looked more like Xena Warrior Princess than someone overcome with emotion at the thought of her little girl finally getting her fairy tale wedding. The MOB was definitely pissed, and she was definitely not allowing the couple in front of her to enter the dining room at the event center.

The objects of Xena's wrath were a middle-aged man and his younger date. I judged said date to be in her twenties, and she was dressed appropriately for the wintry weather in a turquoise sweater dress. Like most sweater dresses, though, it was designed to show off the wearer's assets, which the young lady had in abundance. She was very sexy, with feathered blonde hair and some spectacular chandelier earrings. She also was very embarrassed and apparently wished she were anywhere other than where she was.

So why, you might ask, was I involved in the

question of whether Miss Sweater Dress got to join the celebrants at a wedding reception dinner? Simple. At the moment, I represented Robicheaux Catering, and I had to reluctantly agree with the MOB about the food situation. We had exactly fifty-three dinners prepared for the fifty-three reception guests, and Miss Sweater Dress would be number fifty-four.

Robicheaux Catering had done enough weddings now that Nate and I had slipped into the wedding planner's abbreviations, like MOB and FOB. They made communicating with each other a little easier.

I am not, I hasten to add, the owner of Robicheaux Catering. I am, however, his number one employee and his significant other. It was for this reason that I'd been summoned from the kitchen by our very professional but also very harried head server. Nate had gone upstairs to help get the wedding cake ready for its appearance on the dessert table, and the wedding planner, who was perhaps best equipped to handle this mess, had gone with him. But then Miss Sweater Dress had appeared with her escort, causing the MOB to go more or less postal, and someone had to step in.

I was pretty sure I knew what was going on here. According to the wedding planner, the mother and father of the bride were divorced. The mother had been very much in evidence during all the wedding planning we'd been part of during the past few weeks, but I'd never met the father. I was pretty sure I was meeting him now, along with his plus-one, Miss Sweater Dress.

"Oh, come on, Eileen," the FOB said. "You can come up with more food. Just make the servings a little smaller."

Had we been doing a buffet, always my favorite way

to serve a catered meal, he'd have been right. We always had a little extra for the buffet dishes, and Miss Sweater Dress didn't seem like the type to eat a whole lot.

But we were doing a plated meal, which meant each person got a pre-portioned plate for each course. A plate that had been paid for in advance, based on the number of RSVPs the wedding planner had received. Occasionally, people RSVPed and then didn't show up, but that hadn't happened here. There were no no-shows for this particular reception, which probably made the MOB happy, given the price per plate. We had no extra food.

Eileen, the MOB, regarded the FOB with narrowed eyes. "You had the invitation. It was for you alone. And you RSVPed for only yourself. Ergo, we have no provisions for your…friend. Unless you'd prefer to give her your meal." She raised her chin like she was Catherine the Great confronting a presumptuous peasant.

"Oh, for Christ's sake." The FOB turned to me. "Are you in charge of this thing?"

"I'm part of Robicheaux Catering," I said. "Ms. Rosenberg is the wedding planner. She's dealing with the wedding cake right now, but she should be back momentarily." At least I hoped so since I was fresh out of ideas.

"Well, if you're the caterer, you can take care of this. Just fix a plate for Sandra and we're good to go." The FOB did his own Catherine the Great imitation, although in his case it should have been Peter the Great.

I took a breath. "I'm not sure that's possible. The meals were all pre-ordered. I can't take food from someone else's meal for a new plate." I desperately wished Nate would appear. Maybe he could come up with a way out of this mess. I didn't have a clue.

"You heard her, Jeffrey." The MOB folded her arms across her chest, her eyes like lasers. "The dinners are set. There's no extra. Give her your food or go eat at McDonalds."

Jeffrey, the FOB, looked like he was ready to displace the MOB bodily and snatch a couple of plates from the waiters' trays. Miss Sweater Dress, meanwhile, looked like she wanted to crawl away. My sympathies were absolutely with her, but I still didn't have any food I could slip her.

"What's happening here?" That was the voice I had been longing to hear. If I couldn't have Nate to figure things out, I'd settle for Thalia Rosenberg, wedding planner extraordinaire.

Thalia was a friend of Nate's mom, Madge Robicheaux, which is probably how we got on her list of caterers in the first place. She was around Madge's age, but she appeared a lot younger, possibly through some very expensive plastic surgery. She had flawless platinum hair, bright green eyes, and the iron determination of a brigadier general. I'd never been so glad to see anyone in my life.

Thalia stepped in front of me smoothly, and I longed to slip into the dining room where I belonged. But both MOB and FOB were still blocking the entrance, and I couldn't very well push them aside.

The two combatants gave her competing versions of the problem, while Miss Sweater Dress got more miserable by the moment. "I see the problem," Thalia said. "Let's step over here and see if we can work something out." She took both parents by the elbow and moved them away from the doorway to the dining room, probably disappointing the nearest tables of guests who'd been following along with great interest.

I headed to the kitchen. Let Thalia handle it; I had food to get plated. The salad dishes were beginning to come back to the kitchen as the wait staff returned with the empties. Meanwhile, Dex Gleason, our line cook, occasional server, and general man of all work was dishing up the soup course. We were behind on the mains because I'd been busy preventing the bride's parents from killing each other, which meant I'd have to step it up if we were going to get people's entrees served.

The next thirty minutes were a blur. Nate came in, but I didn't have time to give him any details. We were too busy getting the plates ready to go. We had the counts for the individual dishes. Thank God the bride and groom had decided to have just two choices—beef or salmon—and the majority of the guests had taken the beef. Dex, Nate, and I got all the plates filled, along with the baskets of rolls from Bianca Jordan's bakery and butter crocks borrowed from Robicheaux's Café. As the last waiter disappeared out the swinging kitchen door, the three of us collapsed against the counter.

"I hate plated dinners," I said after a minute.

"But we don't have to stand there and serve," Nate pointed out. "We're off duty until the cake gets cut. Now tell me what happened with the dueling parents."

I filled Nate in, but I didn't have any conclusion. Thalia had removed the combatants from view, and I had no idea how she'd managed everything. I was just glad she'd arrived and taken care of it all.

"I didn't see anyone out there when I came through," Nate said. "Maybe she found an extra plate so the FOB could share."

"I did not," Thalia said as she swept into the kitchen. "That poor girl just wanted to leave, and I was a hundred percent on her side. But that dimwitted FOB had to keep arguing with his ex-wife. I think that's what this was all about. The wife hadn't given him a 'plus-one' invitation, maybe to spite him. And he decided to show up with a date to spite her. Neither of them was thinking of their daughter or the poor date who had no idea what she was getting into when she agreed to come to the reception."

"So what happened?" I asked.

"The girl, Sandra, walked out. I helped her get a ride to town. The FOB was on the verge of leaving, but his former brother-in-law talked him into staying. You could say the MOB won the battle, but she got all tearful and ruined her makeup before the pictures, so I don't know how much of a victory it was." Thalia blew out a long breath. "Weddings like this make me want to break my own rule about not drinking champagne at the reception."

"How's the cake?" I asked. Nate's sister, Coco, baked desserts for the catering company, but she didn't do wedding cakes. I hadn't had a chance to check out the one this bride had ordered.

"Spectacular." Thalia's smile warmed. "Marla has outdone herself this time. I'm going to want some shots to put in my sample book."

Marla Purdue was the wedding cake lady. I hadn't met her yet although Nate had talked to her on the phone a couple of times.

"Speaking of the cake, I'd better get out there to make sure everything's ready." Thalia glanced up as the kitchen door swung open and one of the waiters came in with a tray of dirty dinner dishes. "Looks like they're finishing up."

"Okay, tell one of the waiters to give us the high sign when they're ready to cut the cake."

"Oh, I'll send Beverly. The waiters are going to have their hands full." Beverly Freedman was Thalia's assistant, and only somewhat less terrifyingly organized.

After the bride and groom cut their slice of cake and did the whole feeding each other bit, Nate and I would cut the cake for the rest of the guests, which usually didn't take long. Once that was done, so were we, except for getting the dirty dishes to the kitchen and loading up our pots and pans. Fortunately, the event center had its own cleaning staff, so we'd leave everything to them.

"Right." Thalia went out to work her wedding planner magic while I started loading more dishes in the industrial-sized dishwasher.

Dex blew out a long breath. "We made it through another one."

Nate nodded. "We did." And then he thought better of it and rapped his knuckles on the wooden prep table.

We made it home a couple of hours later, having sliced cake, loaded and unloaded the dishwasher, and delivered our own stuff to the catering kitchen. We were both too tired to cook—that was a given after big catering gigs like this one. But we'd learned to keep a few casseroles and a pot of soup or two in the freezer so that we didn't end up ordering pizza every time. Now I grabbed some lasagna and pushed it into the oven. "What did you think? Did everything work out like it was supposed to?"

Nate shrugged. "Everything on our end worked fine. But we didn't have to deal with all the family crap."

"Thank God for Thalia," I said fervently. When we

catered parties and dinners, we were the ones who had to deal with the people who were throwing the party, which was sometimes a pain. Having someone run interference between us and the people who were eating our food was a relief, particularly with an event as fraught as a wedding.

"Yeah. I think she was satisfied with what we did. Here's hoping she keeps us on the list." Nate pulled a bag of lettuce out of the refrigerator and dumped it into a bowl.

I paused as I took the plates down from the cupboard. "You like being a wedding caterer?"

"Sure. Not full time—there aren't enough weddings around here to make up for all the regular business we do. But it's fun occasionally. And it's lucrative."

I couldn't argue with that, but I still didn't enjoy it as much as Nate did. When we did birthday parties, we gave the people throwing the party a choice of entrees, and they went with the one they liked best. Or they told us what they wanted, and we did our best to whip up something that they'd like. But with weddings, you were dealing with people who were already under a ton of pressure, planning something they'd been told would be either the supreme event of their lives or a freaking disaster. These were not people in any shape to make rational decisions.

Nate had already encountered a bride who'd dissolved in hysterics when she had to decide whether to have a plated dinner or a buffet. And he'd had to deal with a couple of very tense showdowns between parents and their bridal couple children, and one between the bridal couple themselves.

I always sympathized with the people involved

because they were having a tough time. But no matter what Nate said, I didn't consider it fun. There was too much stress involved, even on the day of the wedding. Maybe especially on the day of the wedding. It made me want to withdraw into my jam-making kitchen and leave the wedding catering strictly to him.

Of course, part of my negative attitude might have been a result of our own wedding stress. Well, not *ours*. Nate's mom and my uncle were getting married on New Year's Eve, and we were supposedly doing the catering for that one, too. I say *supposedly* because Madge hadn't yet told Nate what she had in mind for the food. Also, so far as I knew, she hadn't yet finalized her guest list. We were about six weeks out from the wedding at this point, and I still had only the haziest of ideas about what was going to happen.

Each day the stress meter rose a little more for all of us—Nate, me, Nate's sister Coco, and Nate's brother Bobby. Bobby had additional stress to contend with since his wife, Marigold, was around seven months pregnant. And none of us could decide how to get things moving because none of us wanted to upset Madge. And pointing out how close we were edging to disaster would definitely be upsetting for her.

All I knew for sure was that the wedding was taking place in the old barn on our farm. Uncle Mike had gotten it cleaned up and renovated so that it could be used for dining and dancing. Among other things this meant insulation and an HVAC system since no one would want to attend a wedding wearing parkas and snow boots, no matter how much they cared about the bride and groom.

"Any news about The Wedding?" I asked. I didn't

need to specify which wedding I was talking about. We were only intimately involved with one, and we always referred to it in capital letters.

Nate shook his head. "I even suggested Mom might want to talk to Thalia and get some advice. She shut that right down."

Probably a good idea, given that Thalia's services were booked months in advance. I doubted she'd be able to clear space for Madge on her schedule even if she'd wanted to.

"Maybe they'll just elope," I said hopefully. "Then we can have a big party when they get back."

Nate tossed the lettuce with a bare-bones vinaigrette. "Not likely. Mom's committed herself to this thing, even if she doesn't want to be in charge of it." Madge had started out wanting a small wedding for family and friends, until she'd realized just how many people that entailed, which translated into a big wedding no matter how you defined it. She and Uncle Mike were both well-known and well-liked in Shavano and environs.

"Do you think she doesn't want to, or is she just nervous about getting started?"

Nate shrugged. "Doesn't matter. The result's the same. We're dead in the water until she makes some decisions."

That sounded grim. On the other hand, we could come up with a menu on short notice since I doubted Madge was going to want anything exotic. "Are you and Dex okay to put together the stuff for next week's parties without me?"

"Sure. I can handle the Wednesday night thing with Dex if you can do the one on Saturday night."

Winter used to be my slow season since I do a lot of my jam sales at the local farmers market. But since my mail order business has taken off, I'm spending a lot more time making jam in the winter than I used to. Plus I'm now selling in three stores in the area—the Made in Colorado shop, Bianca Jordan's bakery, and Sylvano's grocery in Geary. All of which is to say I don't have as much time to devote to Nate's catering business as I used to.

"Sure, I can do Saturday. What is it?"

"Anniversary party. Buffet. Lots of apps."

"How many people?"

Nate gave me a dry smile. "For a while, the count kept changing, but I've finally got them to nail it down. We'll have food for sixty, and if more show up, we'll still have food for sixty."

"Life in the catering business." The oven timer sounded, and I pulled out the lasagna. Nate grabbed a bottle of wine and a couple of glasses from the cupboard. "Come on, gorgeous," he said, "you look like someone who needs some alcohol."

Maybe I should explain about Nate and me. We've been together a little over a year, and we live together in my cabin at the farm. We're a definite couple, but we've never really talked about marriage. That never bothered anybody in the past, then, boom, his brother Bobby got married to his fellow cook, Marigold Watson. Not only that, but Marigold was pregnant, due to deliver sometime after the first of the year. And around the same time, we were absorbing that little bombshell, Madge and Uncle Mike announced they were getting married, too.

It's not like there's a lot of pressure on Nate and me, but there's some. We're a couple, and we're surrounded by people who are getting married. There's a sort of obvious question hanging over us: what about us? Are we going to join the parade or are we going to go on as we are?

Frankly, I'd be happy with the *go on as we are* option, but I wasn't not sure about Nate. We hadn't talked about it, and sometimes it felt like we were deliberately not talking about it. But one of these days we'd probably have to.

Just not today. "Let's eat," I said.

Chapter 2

The next day I spent making jam, which is how I spend most of my time. I had to make a few dozen jars of my basic flavors for the stores where I sell—peach, raspberry, strawberry, and pepper peach. I also had to do a few more jars of my mail mail-order jam of the month, which was cranberry chutney. I'd wanted to do a Thanksgiving special, so cranberry was promising. But it turned out people weren't as much into chutney as they were into regular jam. I'd sold fewer jars than usual, but still enough to make a small profit. I'd take the remaining jars to Sylvano's, where they sold a lot of holiday foods.

What I was mainly interested in, though, was figuring out what jam I'd make to give out as favors for Madge and Uncle Mike's wedding. And my interest was beginning to become panic.

If they'd decided to get married in summer, I'd have been fine. I can usually come up with something exciting to do with fresh fruit and herbs. But it was November, and I was working with frozen fruit for the most part. It's good frozen fruit, mind you, grown on our farm and frozen by me and my assistant. But it's still frozen, which means it will never taste quite as good as fresh.

And I wanted something special, and something that said *wedding*. It would be a limited-edition jam with only enough jars to serve as wedding favors, and miniature jars at that. But what was supposed to go into a wedding jam, anyway? Orange blossoms and rice?

My first thought had been champagne, and champagne jelly is straightforward. I bought a bottle of California sparkling wine and made a couple of jars from a simple recipe involving wine, sugar, and pectin. It tasted…all right. Fine, really. But truthfully, there wasn't much to it. Champagne doesn't have a distinct taste, so far as I can tell. It's all about the bubbles and the occasion. And you cannot make a bubbly jam, no matter how hard you try.

I looked into other recipes, some for champagne mixed with fruit like peaches. And I could see doing something like that during the summer, maybe for one of my jams of the month. But it just didn't seem right for a wedding, particularly one like this where I wanted everybody to know how happy I was about the whole thing.

Which sent me back to the beginning again. What was supposed to go into a wedding-favor jam, anyway?

I'd been tossing ideas around with Dolce and Bridget, my two assistants. Dolce is a high school student who lives down the road from us. She's a gifted cook in her own right and has taken over a lot of my more routine jam production. Bridget is in charge of my mail orders, but she's turned into one of our most reliable jam tasters, someone who can tell me whether something will work with our typical buyers after a couple of spoonfuls. They both knew about my ongoing frustration with the wedding jam, but neither of them had been able to come up with much themselves. That day I leaned against the kitchen counter, watching jars process in the kettle while I waited for fickle inspiration to strike.

"Does it have to be a wedding thing?" Bridget was

slapping mailing labels on the newest bunch of packages. "The wedding's on New Year's Eve, after all. Couldn't it just be jam that's appropriate for the holiday season?"

"New Year's Eve just gets me back to champagne," I said glumly.

"What about your rose petal jam?" Dolce asked. "That's lovely, and it goes with a wedding."

I nodded. "It would, but I don't have enough of it on hand. I never do—I just make a dozen jars or so. I usually give it out for Christmas presents." And once upon a time I'd given Nate a jar for a dessert he was making that won an award. It had been the start of our relationship, more or less. My cheeks warmed briefly at the memory.

"I wonder if you could buy rose petals from Bette's Floral downtown," Bridget mused.

"The ones from our rose bushes are sort of 'food grade,'" I said. "They've never been sprayed with anything like insecticide or fertilizer. I don't know if Bette's could promise that." Plus the amount of rose petals I'd need might exceed what I was willing or able to pay, even for something as special as Madge and Uncle Mike's wedding.

Dolce started removing the jars of peach jam from the processor with the jar lifter as the timer sounded. "What else goes with celebrating? Could you do something with confetti? Like little bits of something colorful floating in a clear jelly?"

I paused to think about that—it had potential. But I wasn't sure what kind of thing resembled confetti that I'd be willing to actually put in jam. Marshmallows and sprinkles, the things that quickly came to my mind, were absolutely out of the question. The thought of marshmallow jam almost activated my gag reflex.

"Let me check online." Bridget began clicking at her keyboard, frowning. "There are some recipes that say they're for confetti jam. But it's chili jam under another name. Like the confetti is little bits of pepper floating in the jam."

"No good." I sighed. "I'm already heavily into chilis for summer jam. It would just be like I was handing out my regular jam in much smaller jars."

Dolce went on pulling jars out of the hot water, and Bridget returned to her mailing labels. They'd tried to help. It wasn't their fault none of us could come up with anything right.

But Dolce's question, *what else goes with celebrating,* still tripped around my brain. What else? Confetti? Champagne? Wine, women, and song, or in my case, wine, hot chefs, and song?

I paused. I couldn't do anything with the hot chef and song part of things, at least in terms of jam, but wine was an interesting possibility. Champagne didn't work because it didn't have a distinctive flavor. So, what did have a distinctive flavor?

I used chardonnay and sherry in some summer jams, mixed in with fruits and herbs and sometimes nuts. They had distinctive tastes, but they blended well, and that was the point when they were being mixed with fruit. The fruit was the star; the chardonnay was the supporting player. Red wine, on the other hand, didn't mix in quite as well. It tended to stand on its own, its distinctive flavor setting it apart.

I had a sudden image of a jar filled with brilliant crimson jelly. Maybe with a forest green ribbon wrapped around it and a label done in a nice script font. *Best wishes, Madge and Mike.* It would be gorgeous.

But what would it taste like? Red wine jelly? On one hand, my heart was racing as I considered the visuals. On the other hand, if it tasted like crap, the visuals wouldn't matter, as I knew only too well.

"What's up?" Dolce asked. By now she knew the signs when I'd latched onto an idea.

"Red wine," I said. "Jelly."

Dolce nodded slowly. "Pretty. What'll you put in it?"

"Not much. Maybe a cinnamon stick or cardamom. I'll have to dig through some recipes and see what other people are doing."

"I volunteer for tasting," Bridget called from her computer. "And for leftovers."

I frowned. "Leftover jam?" I never had any to speak of.

"Leftover wine." Bridget grinned. "I figure you'll need to try a bunch of varieties before you settle on the best one."

That hadn't occurred to me, but I'd need to try some different wines to see which one I liked best. Cabernet, merlot, pinot noir, even syrah, all possible red wine varieties. And yes, there would be leftovers. Definitely.

I grinned, anticipating the next few days. I could see a way forward and a possible solution to my problem. A trip to the liquor store was in order.

When Nate got home that afternoon, I was unloading my purchases—an array of moderately priced red wines, all needing to be tested. I'd need to sip a little of each bottle before I committed to making it into wine. If it tasted nasty, I wouldn't want to waste time on it.

He raised both brows as he studied the lineup. "Were we out of wine?"

"Nope. Experiment time."

As I explained about the wine jelly, his grin widened. "I volunteer to be a taster."

"Bridget beat you to it, but you can certainly partake of any bottle I don't finish." I pushed the bottles into one side of the wine rack. "How's the corporate thing coming?"

"The Wednesday one? Okay. It's just apps for a cocktail party, only twenty people or so. And it'll be over by seven-thirty. The Saturday one's bigger."

"Do you need any more help with prep?" I was hoping he'd say *no* because I wanted to devote the rest of the week to making red wine jelly. But if he needed me, I'd do what I could to help.

"Dex and I have the prep under control. We're using some of the same apps for both events. I do have something I need your help on, though."

Well, crap. "What's that?"

"I've got a bride who wants a tasting next Tuesday. Thalia usually does those with me, but she's got another commitment. Can you fill in?"

I blinked at him. Nate had never asked me to do a tasting before, and I wasn't sure what I'd be committing myself to. "Sure, I guess. What does it involve? I'm not as adept at sales as Thalia." Except with jam, of course.

"I cook up small samples of all the courses they're interested in. They taste. We answer questions. It's straightforward."

"Do we charge them for the tasting?" It seemed like we should, given that we'd be paying for the food whether they liked it or not.

"Depends. In this case, they've signed a contract, so they've put down a deposit. That usually entitles them to a tasting for two—the bride and groom or the bride and her mother or the bride and whoever she feels like bringing along. I've never done one of these where the bride wasn't involved, but it's bride plus one. Any more people beyond that, and we'll charge them for the extras."

"Has this bride already chosen what she wants?"

Nate frowned. "That's where things get a little weird. I'm not sure how much influence she has on the choice. Her plus one is her father, and according to Thalia, he's the one who sent her the menu choices they're considering. So this is the bride's chance to taste what her father thinks she should be serving at the wedding."

I frowned back. In my very limited experience, the bride's father's participation in the wedding planning was usually confined to writing checks. It struck me as a little odd to have a father who was so deeply involved, but maybe he was a restaurant professional or something. "Who is he, do you know?"

Nate shrugged. "Never heard of him before this. Thalia says he's loaded, but she wasn't too specific about where the money came from."

"Is he local?"

"From Geary. He's got a house over there, anyway. But that doesn't mean he's from the area."

Geary was a few miles from Shavano and several degrees of income richer. The historic downtown was surrounded by high-end developments and major mansions in the hills. Shavano had its own toney suburbs, but we still weren't as high end as Geary. But not all the people who had homes in Geary lived there full time. A large percentage were from outside the area and came to the mountains during ski season or fly-fishing season or escape-your-creditors season. I hoped the FOB didn't fall into the latter category.

"So what's the menu they're considering?" I hoped it was a buffet, but they sounded more like the plated dinner type.

"Served apps while the pictures are taken. Plated dinner for, I think, seventy-five, but that could change. Salad, probably pears with walnuts and balsamic vinaigrette, but they're also considering goat cheese with apples and arugula. They've narrowed the entrees down to beef tenderloin with burgundy mushroom sauce, poached salmon with dill sauce, and a vegetarian risotto. Sides of duchess potatoes and asparagus. Bianca's bread. Cake. Pretty simple overall."

"Special apps?"

"Crostini, quiche tartlets, cheese balls with pesto and black sesame seeds, caprese kabobs, and the ever-popular Asian meatballs."

Most of which could be made ahead and rewarmed at the event, which would make our lives much, much easier. "When is all this happening?"

"Another weird thing—this is a last-minute deal. Wedding's the first part of January. Thalia said they're paying her a king's ransom to put together a major wedding on the fly. She just got the contract a couple of weeks ago. That may be how we got the deal for the catering. My guess is all the big catering outfits are fully booked and not interested in picking up a last-minute wedding. Since it's only seventy-five, we can handle it, since it's a relatively simple menu. And like I said, the contract's signed, so we get to keep the very generous deposit even if they back out."

"Did Thalia give you any idea why they waited until now to start planning? I mean seventy-five guests is still a fairly big group."

Nate raised one brow. "You mean besides the most likely reason?"

"Pregnant bride? Surely, that's not such a big deal anymore." Or it wasn't as far as I was concerned. Maybe the bride's parents were old school.

Nate shrugged. "Got me. All I know is we've got a couple of months to get this ready to go. Once they do the tasting and approve the menu, we can start figuring out the schedule. And I'll get the orders in once they confirm the number of guests."

Despite the rushed nature of the wedding, I figured it would work out well for us in the end. Having a large wedding with a large final payout coming in at the first of the year would give us a nice cushion after the holiday party season died down.

"So what will I be doing at this tasting? Serving?"

"Yeah, part of the time. I'll have to be out there giving my explanations for what they're eating. You know, 'Lightly poached salmon in a delicate sauce of dill and sour cream.' You bring the stuff out and stand there looking sophisticated until they're ready for the next dish."

Nate sighed as he opened the refrigerator, checking to see what we had to munch on. Right now, a lot of the space was taken up with my previous wedding jam experiments. "To tell you the truth, I just like having somebody there besides me. I mean, we're a small company as caterers go, but I like to give them the illusion that we've got lots of resources."

"Okay, I'll wear my spiffiest waiter outfit. Strictly

black pants and a tuxedo shirt. Would you like a bow tie with that?"

Nate grinned. "You don't need to go that far. Dark pants with a light shirt and one of our Robicheaux Catering aprons."

"You're sure?" I asked. "I want to look presentable. Hell, I want to look cool."

"You always look cool to me." Nate pulled out a bottle of sauvignon blanc, along with a chunk of cheese.

I leaned over to kiss his ear, which led to a certain number of liberties being taken, which I thoroughly enjoyed.

"Okay," Nate said finally, "you're hired. You're officially my wedding assistant."

"Sounds good to me." Actually, it sounded a little hectic. But weddings were always interesting and could sometimes be fun.

Or anyway, that's what I thought at the time.

Chapter 3

Since Thalia wasn't available for the wedding menu tasting, neither was her office with its spiffy conference room where Nate usually did the tastings. Instead, we decided to present the samples for the January wedding at the café. The whole thing would have been a lot more elegant if we could have used Thalia's conference room, which had been custom decorated to soothe the most hysterical brides and their significant others. But Robicheaux's Café is a Shavano institution, and it's both homey and comfortable. I only worried that the elegance of Nate's food might clash a little with the upscale diner ambiance of his family's restaurant.

Considering that this was a sort of rush job, lubricated by lots of cash, Nate had put together a more than respectable set of menu possibilities for the wedding. He'd kept it simple to make sure he could find the ingredients on short notice, but the food was still very special. And it showed off Nate's skills both as a chef and as someone who could come up with an elegant wedding dinner more or less on the fly. Even though we were working on a short deadline, the tasting was part of the package.

The bride, or more likely the FOB, had chosen these menu items from a list of possibilities Nate had supplied. Theoretically, this tasting should just nail down their final choices, although I supposed it was always possible that they might decide they hated beef tenderloin.

The last of the café's customers had cleared out by two, and Tres, the café's ever-reliable janitor, had done a quick sweep of the dining room without mopping since the smell of cleaner wasn't likely to enhance Nate's gourmet dishes. Madge breezed in a few minutes later, a stack of menus in her hand.

"All ready for the tasting?" she said, then gave me the once over. "My, don't you look professional."

She said it without an ounce of sarcasm, and I took it as a compliment. I'd gone with the black pants and tuxedo shirt, although I'd taken Nate's advice and ditched the bow tie. The red Robicheaux Catering apron was appropriately spiffy. "I think we're good to go."

"Who's the couple? Nate didn't mention the name when he told me what you were doing. Are they local?"

I shook my head. "They've got a house in Geary, or anyway the FOB does. His name is Pollack. Emerson Pollack."

"FOB?"

"Sorry, that's wedding speak. Father of the bride."

"Oh." Madge shrugged. "Name doesn't ring a bell. What time does the couple get here?"

"It's not the couple, just the bride and her father. They're supposed to be here at three. Nate's getting everything finished up."

"The father?" Madge frowned. "That's unusual, doesn't it? When I married Robert, my dad just told me to make sure we had some chili at the reception. Honestly, I think Robert's chili was the reason Daddy approved of the wedding in the first place." She gave me a brilliant smile, but her eyes were a little sad. I wondered if she was having flashbacks to her first wedding now that she was getting ready for number two.

"I thought it was a little weird, too. But I gather Pollack's wealthy. Maybe he just wants to make sure he gets his money's worth, even if it is a kind of last-minute wedding."

Madge grimaced. "Hope he's not like that. Those kinds of people can be a real pain when it comes to a menu. Remember the guy who wanted Nate to do hotdogs and potato chips for his anniversary because hamburgers cost too much? According to Lena Goodman, he's a multimillionaire but he's obsessed with pennies."

I remembered him only too well, but fortunately for us, he'd been an exception to our usual type of customer. "We'll see, I guess. Thalia didn't mention having any problems with the wedding planning so far, besides the short time frame."

Nate leaned through the swinging door to the kitchen. "I'm going to move everything over from the catering kitchen. Any problem if I use the warming oven?"

"None at all," Madge said. "I'll give you a hand, and then I'll disappear so you can work your magic." Madge had turned Robicheaux Catering over to Nate within the first six months of its existence, and she kept her distance unless asked to participate.

Nate grinned. "I don't know how magical I'll be. But at least I've got Rox to back me up."

Madge kissed his cheek and gave my shoulder a squeeze. "Break a leg, you two. Or is that what I'm supposed to say? It sounds a little gruesome."

"Nothing gruesome about a wedding," I said cheerfully. I should have knocked wood after that, but I didn't.

I heard a knock on the front door promptly at three, and I stepped quickly to answer it since Nate was still in the kitchen. "Good afternoon, Mr. Pollack."

I assumed that's who it was since the couple standing in the doorway didn't resemble any of our usual customers. The girl, who had to be the bride, was tiny, with shoulder-length dark hair and fashionable bangs so long they almost interfered with her eyelashes.

The man looked like a toad.

I don't usually use nasty descriptors with perfect strangers, but Emerson Pollack was one very toadlike individual. He was only a bit taller than his daughter, and he seemed to have no neck although given the size of his muffler, his neck may just have been concealed by his collar and his scarf. He also wore a woolen Tyrolean hat that covered a large portion of his head. What I noticed most of all were his bulbous gray eyes and his thin-lipped mouth, currently turned down in a grimace that appeared semi-permanent.

"Robicheaux?" he croaked.

"Right here. Welcome to Robicheaux's, Mr. Pollack." Nate stepped forward and extended his hand to Mr. Toad. After a moment, the FOB took it in a rather limp handshake.

"Please come in. We've got a table set up over here." Nate had chosen one of the window tables, which was in a sort of alcove at the side, away from the counters. It had a banquette across the back with a couple of chairs at the front. Nate started to pull out a chair for the bride, but she scooted onto the banquette. Her father took the spot beside her. After a moment's hesitation, Nate took a chair.

I took a quick survey of the bride. She was wearing a gorgeous cranberry woolen dress with gold earrings and a gold bangle bracelet. Her engagement ring caught a quick flash of sunlight that almost blinded me. Definitely not poverty-stricken.

And she didn't look pregnant to me, but what did I know?

"Are there any questions about the menu before we get started?" Nate asked.

The bride gave him a bright smile. "I think…"

The FOB shook his head as he placed his coat, muffler, and hat on the banquette beside him. "Let's get going."

I glanced at the bride, but she'd shifted her attention to the printed menu Nate had provided. Clearly her father was in charge of this show.

Nate nodded. "All right, then. Roxanne, could you bring in the appetizers?"

I brought out a tray with a selection of the appetizers they'd said they were interested in. Nate had warmed the ones that needed to be heated and brought the others to room temperature, so we wouldn't be serving ice cold food. He'd been careful to arrange everything so that the presentation was appealing.

Mr. Toad apparently couldn't have cared less.

Nate picked up the plate with the two mini cheese balls, one rolled in black sesame seeds and the other in pesto. "These are the cheese balls. They're a mixture of goat cheese from a creamery in Antero, Gruyère, and Neufchatel, along with chopped pine nuts for the one rolled in pesto. We'll serve them with water crackers."

"What's the black stuff?" Mr. Toad managed to narrow his bulbous eyes.

"Black sesame seeds," Nate explained. "The green is basil pesto."

Mr. Toad wrinkled his nose like he smelled something foul. "Looks like bugs. Fruit flies."

Clearly taken aback, Nate paused, then said, "We can use something other than black sesame if you prefer. Chopped pecans would make them more like traditional cheese balls."

The bride rolled a sesame cheese ball onto her plate, along with a cracker. She spread the cheese carefully, as if she expected her father to inspect the results. "It's delicious," she said after a moment.

Her father glared at her, but she stared off into space as she nibbled on another cracker with cheese. Probably a good idea.

"Get rid of the black stuff," Mr. Toad said. "Rest of it's okay with me if it's okay with her."

"Yes, sir." Nate made a quick note, although I doubted either of us would forget Mr. Toad's objections.

Mr. Toad wasn't crazy about the crostini with chopped tomatoes and basil because he said the bread would get soggy even though it had been toasted with olive oil. He sneered at the caprese kabobs, describing them as "Just cheese and tomatoes." The quiches merited no more than a raised eyebrow, although they featured some of Coco's magical pastry. The only thing that didn't rate a snarl was the Asian meatballs, but he questioned Nate carefully about what went into them.

"No spice," he said flatly. "No hot stuff."

"They're more savory than spicy," Nate said. He passed the plate toward Mr. Toad, but he waved it off, although his daughter took nibbles of everything.

In fact, Mr. Toad tasted nothing. He treated the food

with a mixture of contempt and hostility, as if it was nothing he'd be willing to taste in front of the help, namely, Nate and me. I sensed this tasting was mostly a power play, a demonstration of Mr. Toad's authority without the bother of eating.

The bride, on the other hand, tasted everything. And liked everything. She didn't say much, but she was relentlessly positive, as if she was trying to counterbalance her father. She occasionally gave Nate that bright smile, but she didn't look at her father more than once or twice. Maybe she was trying not to be distracted by his opinions.

Nate was able to remain polite, no matter how much Mr. Toad provoked him. But he wasn't having fun by any means.

Finally, Mr. Toad waved the apps away, and I went to the kitchen to bring out the salads. They were both reliables—mixed greens with sliced Bosc pears and dried cranberries, and walnuts and arugula topped with tart apple slices and bleu cheese. The dressing for both was a balsamic vinaigrette, the fruity taste of the vinegar working well against both the pears and apples.

By now, I was pretty sure Mr. Toad was going to hate both of them, but he seemed indifferent. Apparently, he considered salads beneath his notice, and once again he declined to taste anything. The bride, bless her, glanced shyly at both Nate and me and pronounced them both luscious. "But I like the pears a little better." She turned to her father, then Nate. "Let's go with the pear salad."

Her father sighed but said nothing. Nate made a quick note, then gave me a very tight-lipped smile. "We'll try the entrees now."

Beef tenderloin isn't as easy to cook as you might think. It's very lean, which means it doesn't have a lot of flavor on its own. There's a reason butchers wrap filet mignon, which is cut from the tenderloin, in bacon because it adds a little pop of fat and flavor. Nate's solution to this perennial problem was to use careful seasoning on the meat and to accompany it with a gorgeous burgundy mushroom sauce. For the sample, he'd prepared two beautiful slices of the beef, with pools of sauce beside them on the plates. The salmon was easier, just grilled filet with a dill sauce made from sour cream, dill, and a touch of mayonnaise. He'd plated two small cuts with dollops of green-flecked sauce. Both entrees looked gorgeous and tasted better, as I knew from experience.

The mushroom risotto was the vegetarian option, which didn't mean it wasn't delicious in its own right. Nate used a mixture of cremini and shitake mushrooms, with some dried porcini for a little kick, plus the soaking liquid that was part of the liquid for the risotto.

Small servings of the side dishes were presented alongside the entrees, the duchess potatoes piped in rosettes and browned briefly under the salamander broiler along with a small pile of asparagus spears luxuriating in lemon butter. The bride clasped her hands in delight when she saw the plates, and she quite deliberately ignored her father's stony face.

Nate took a breath and went into marketing mode. He described the tenderloin and sauce and the salmon and sauce, along with the risotto, then leaned back to let the two take a taste of each. The bride cut off a small sliver of beef and dipped it in sauce, allowing herself to smile briefly as she tasted. "Delicious," she murmured.

"So tasty." Mr. Toad kept his hands at his sides, deliberately not tasting.

The bride tasted the salmon and risotto, too, smiling happily. Mr. Toad stayed stony. Then he nodded at the tenderloin.

"In Texas they say only bad beef gets smothered in sauce," he said. "Good meat doesn't need it." I didn't know if he was from Texas or not, but he delivered that judgment as if it was carved in stone somewhere.

I swear I saw the moment when Nate finally thought *the hell with it*. Mr. Toad was a jerk, and he was going to stay a jerk. Nate had done his best, but he'd reached his limit. If we lost the order, we still got to keep the deposit—we had a contract. I only hoped the deposit covered the cost of the tasting, given the price of tenderloin and salmon.

"This is prime beef tenderloin." Nate's voice was flat. "The best meat available. The sauce doesn't smother the meat; it's served alongside so that you can choose to taste it or leave it. And the sauce is designed to enhance the meat, to give it even more flavor. It doesn't smother anything. It doesn't need to. This dish has earned us high praise whenever we've served it. I can assure you nothing about it is anything other than first-rate."

Mr. Toad narrowed his bulbous eyes again. Apparently, Nate was supposed to grovel for his approval, not challenge his judgment. After a moment, he straightened. "The contract says we have final approval. We don't have to take this menu if we don't like it."

Nate nodded. "You don't. However, this contract covers only one menu and one tasting. If you decide on another menu, you'll be charged for a second tasting, based on the food you choose. Or you can find another caterer if you prefer. However, the deposit is nonrefundable."

That was a clear challenge. All of us knew the chances of Mr. Toad and his daughter finding another caterer at this point were close to non-existent if he expected to have the wedding when it was scheduled.

Mr. Toad somehow appeared even more sour than he had before. I was certain he was going to cancel, even though it would leave his daughter's wedding without a caterer. Then his daughter leaned forward, resting her hand on his arm.

"Taste it, Daddy," the bride murmured. "It's really good. Please. Just try it." She gave him a pleading look.

Mr. Toad whipped around. I guessed he'd forgotten his daughter was there. Nate looked almost as surprised as he did.

The bride cut another sliver of salmon and dipped it into the cream sauce. Her lips edged up in another tentative smile. "This is so good, too. I like it a lot. And the risotto will be perfect for the vegetarians." She put her fork down and turned to her father. "This menu is just what I want. It's elegant, and it tastes wonderful. Trent will love it, too."

I guessed Trent was the groom, but I wasn't sure. For all I knew, it could have been the bride's poodle.

Mr. Toad remained frozen, staring at his daughter.

She looked toward Nate. "Tell us about the side dishes," she urged.

Nate launched into a slightly more friendly description of the sides, giving her a quick rundown of the ingredients in duchess potatoes and a little background on our source for the asparagus. He didn't look at Mr. Toad, but I did.

It was hard to tell if he was angry or just being his normal self, that is, terminally annoying. He regarded his daughter as if she were some kind of specimen he needed to analyze, but he didn't interrupt or correct her. If he thought she was being too familiar with the help, he didn't say so.

When the bride had taken a couple of bites of the sides, she put her hand on her father's arm again. "I like it all, Daddy," she said. "It's very good."

For a moment, I thought he'd tell her he didn't give a damn what she liked, but then he drew himself up, with the sigh of a long-suffering parent. "All right. I suppose your judgment is the one that matters. We'll accept the menu, just lose the black stuff on the cheese, and add something to those kabobs to make them special."

Nate gave him a tight smile. "I'm glad you enjoyed it. If you could just sign and initial the final contract."

This led to another extended period of silence while Mr. Toad reviewed the contract word by word. Meanwhile, the bride sampled more of the caprese kabobs and the quiche with quiet gusto. She also finished off one of the duchess potato rosettes. I'd been going to remove the dishes to the kitchen, but I decided she should have a chance to eat as much as she wanted, given that her father's portion had gone untouched.

I hate to see good food wasted myself.

After Mr. Toad signed the contract, he wound himself into his coat, muffler, and hat without saying anything. The bride smiled apologetically at me and at Nate, and I had a flash of sympathy. What must it be like to live with Mr. Toad? Did he ever approve of anything? I wondered how the bridegroom had gotten his okay. I found it hard to believe that Mr. Toad would consider anyone good enough for his little girl. On the other hand, he wasn't particularly affectionate with his daughter either. I couldn't imagine him being affectionate with anyone, to tell the truth.

I watched the two of them walk to a limousine parked near the front of the Robicheaux parking lot. A man in a suit had been lounging against the side of the car, but he came to attention as soon as Mr. Toad and daughter walked out of the restaurant. He opened the car door and stood waiting until they were both inside. Then he closed the door behind them and climbed into the driver's seat. A moment later, they were headed toward Geary.

Considering how much money they were paying us, I should have been a lot happier than I was. But, weirdly enough, I found myself wishing Mr. Toad had accepted Nate's veiled challenge and fired us. I couldn't help thinking this wedding was going to be a major drain on our lives and our enthusiasm, such as it was.

Chapter 4

"What a creep," I said as we watched the limousine disappear.

"That's putting it mildly," Nate muttered. "This is going to be our first true Wedding from Hell. I can't believe Thalia didn't warn me."

"Maybe he's been okay with her," I said.

But I didn't really believe it. I was pretty sure Mr. Toad was a jerk with everybody, just because he could be. And because he needed to feel like he was in control. In fact, he might well have been worse with Thalia just because she was a woman and therefore inferior. Thalia's revenge would be the very healthy fee she'd charge him for the short-notice wedding.

"Will we have to do anything more with him? I mean, of course we will, but when?"

"Not until we get a lot closer to the wedding," Nate said as he slid the contract into a folder and dropped it into his briefcase. "They'll need to give us a final number of plates before we can order the food. That's the biggest thing we'll be waiting for. With any luck, we can avoid any more contact with Pollack for another few weeks. And I'll make sure he pays his deposits on time if he wants food for his daughter's reception."

I gave him my driest smile. "Still think weddings are fun?"

"Sure. Just not this one." He started stacking the

empty plates the bride had left behind, then paused, shaking his head. "Bugs. Jesus Christ. He thought the black sesame seeds looked like bugs. Maybe he even thought they *were* bugs."

"You think so?" I said slowly. "My guess is he just pretended he thought they were bugs to make trouble. He struck me as the type who likes to stir things up just to see what happens. The thing with the bugs was just his opening shot to see if he could get you on the defensive. I think he'd have been even more unpleasant if he'd succeeded."

"Well, he didn't." Nate paused. "Not exactly. As far as I was concerned, we had nothing to be defensive about. The food was first-rate, and it was what they chose. Mostly, he pissed me off. But I gritted my teeth and let it go until that crack about the tenderloin."

"You did a great job." I leaned up and kissed his cheek. "You were a lot more reasonable than I would have been. I wanted to conk him with something."

Nate gave me a small smile. "Probably not a good idea, given the number of lethal objects around a kitchen."

"The bride was…sweet." Actually, she was intimidated by her father, at least at first. But she'd gotten her way, even though she'd had to be deferential when, in her place, I would have been snarling at him.

Nate paused again. "*Sweet* isn't the way I'd put it. I thought she was sort of manipulative. Pretending to be submissive so she could get what she wanted."

"Well, yeah. But that's probably the only way to get him to agree to her choices. It's learned behavior."

"Maybe. But I wouldn't trust her very far. All those smiles seemed too practiced."

Actually, I'd thought she was a little pathetic, but I wasn't about to criticize a woman for doing whatever she had to do to function in her family. "Learned behavior, like I said. She's got an impossible father, so maybe she does whatever she has to do to get along with him. And she got him to back down in the end. I figure she knows what works with him by now, and she knows how to use it when she has to."

Nate hoisted a tray full of dishes to his shoulder, a callback to his busing days when he was a teenager. "Whatever she did, it worked. I guess I should be thankful. At least I'm not the groom." He started toward the kitchen, and I followed him. "Marrying into that family would be a nightmare, no matter how much money the old man's got. I'm only glad we're being paid a king's ransom for this. I sure as hell wouldn't do it for less."

I was doubly glad since I wouldn't have any more contact with Mr. Pollack until the actual wedding. Or anyway, I assumed I wouldn't. But assumptions could always be wrong.

****

The next day I was in the jam kitchen with Dolce and Bridget. Dolce was on the verge of Thanksgiving vacation, which would mean she could spend a lot more time in the jam kitchen if she wanted to. In her place, I'd have wanted to spend that time hanging out with my friends, but Dolce was more devoted to work than other kids her age. She was earning money for college, as well as picking up a few culinary skills that might come in handy in future jobs.

"What are we doing today?" she asked.

"I'll put you in charge of making a dozen jars of

strawberry preserves. I'm going to work on the red wine jam and see how it comes out." I'd already decided to go with a medium-priced cabernet sauvignon I'd picked up at the liquor store. It was strong enough to provide some definite flavor without totally overwhelming whatever spices I decided to throw in.

Dolce went to work on the frozen strawberries, but she also kept a curious eye on what I was doing. "What are you going to put into it besides wine?"

I leaned against the counter, checking my supplies. "Sugar, of course, but not so much that it tastes like grape jelly. And low-sugar pectin. And some spices. I'm still trying to decide just which ones, based on the recipes I've read."

"You're using pectin?"

I nodded. "There's no fruit in the jam to provide natural pectin, plus I can't boil the mixture for very long because I don't want to destroy the wine flavor. The low-sugar stuff works well if you don't go overboard." I started considering the spices again, trying to decide just what I wanted to use.

Dolce was on the same wavelength. "What spices will work?"

"I don't know yet. Maybe something like the spices you put into mulled wine."

"Cloves?" Bridget called from across the room. "My mom always put orange slices with cloves into ours."

I shook my head. "Cloves are too strong. You might not be able to taste the wine, and that's the whole point."

"Cinnamon," Dolce said decisively.

"Right. At least one cinnamon stick."

"What else do you need?" Bridget asked.

I paused, considering. "I'd like something a little

spicy, something that might give it some kick at the end."

"Chilies?" Dolce seemed doubtful, as well she should. I put chilies in a lot of different jams, but not this.

"Too strong, again. I don't want something that will interfere with the taste. Just something that will give it some character." I'd been tossing ideas around, but I hadn't come up with anything yet.

"Why not just use pepper?" Bridget said. "It's spicy and it's cheap. Of course, you probably don't want black flakes in your jam."

"Definitely not, but pepper's a good idea. Maybe peppercorns. They'd spice things up without throwing the balance off."

"Are you going to strain it?" Dolce asked. "Like with a jelly cloth? Mom said that's how she used to make crabapple jelly."

"I don't think I'll need to go that far. I can just pour the mixture through a sieve before I do the final boil." If I kept all the spices whole, I should be able to strain them out easily and leave the wine jam clear and gorgeous without the bother of a jelly cloth. Fingers crossed.

Dolce and Bridget returned to what they'd been doing, but I could feel them watching me as I set to work. I needed to soak the spices in the wine for a while, but I'd need to warm everything up first. I poured the wine into a saucepan along with my cinnamon stick and peppercorns, then I heated everything up for thirty seconds or so. I didn't want to risk burning off the alcohol, but heating the mixture would get the aromatics going. I set it aside then to let it steep for fifteen or twenty minutes, enough time for the spices to infuse the wine.

Twenty minutes later, after I'd managed to get a bag of frozen peaches chopped up for some pepper peach preserves, I strained the wine mixture into a bowl. I wasn't sure what, if anything, I could do with the cinnamon stick and the peppercorns, but I hate throwing out food that's still got some possibilities, so I put it all in a jar in the refrigerator.

I heated the infused wine in the same saucepan on the stove, stirring in the pectin and the sugar. And then I started stirring like hell with a whisk. I needed to heat the mixture to a high temperature to make sure the sugar and pectin dissolved, but I couldn't leave it at that high temperature for very long or I'd destroy the wine flavor. The whisking would get the solids to dissolve and keep the mixture from setting up before I was ready for it.

Jam making involves a certain amount of nerve. You always heat the jam mixture over high heat, which means it starts bubbling up toward the top of the pan quickly. Keep in mind, jam involves molten hot liquid sugar that can inflict nasty burns on the unwary. I've had a few in my day. And if it boils over onto the burner, it can stink up the kitchen and be hell to scrape off the stove. But you can't let that bubbling pan intimidate you. You need that heat to get the jam processes to work, evaporating the excess moisture. You have to keep stirring until the level of the jam drops below the top of the pan without turning down the heat. I had the timer going so I'd have precisely the amount of time on high heat that I needed but no more, and I whisked that jam for all I was worth, hoping desperately that I'd hit the two-minute mark before the jam got so hot that I couldn't stir it down.

As it happened, the timer went off just when I was ready to slide the pot off the heat to get the boiling liquid level to drop. I got the pan onto a nearby cold burner without burning myself or scorching the jam, always a good sign.

Dolce gave a quick stir to her own pot of strawberry jam on the other side of my commercial-sized stove. Strawberries weren't as persnickety as my pot of boiling sweet wine. "Are you going to put it in the jars now?" she asked.

I nodded. "Yeah, I'll let it cool in the jars so it doesn't set up in the pan." The cooling jam would solidify quickly because of the pectin, and getting solidified jam into jars is something that inspires creative profanity. I skimmed the foam off the top of the jam, which isn't strictly necessary for flavor but makes the jam prettier. Then I grabbed a ladle and wide-neck funnel so I could pour the jam into the jars I'd had boiling in the processing kettle. I wouldn't bother with processing this batch since it might not be the final recipe I'd use for the wedding jelly. My tasting jar could just sit in the refrigerator for now, and if I had extra, I'd freeze it.

Bridget appeared at the counter, peering at the jars as I filled them with jam lava. "That's a gorgeous color."

"Wine red," I said. "For once the color absolutely fits that name."

Dolce had set up her own line of jars for her strawberry preserves, but she paused to study the two jars I was filling. "They'll look gorgeous with light shining through them."

"Yeah." I wasn't sure how I could set that up at The Wedding, but it might be worth a try.

"Any leftovers we can sample?" Bridget asked, eying the bowls and whisks to see if any jam was clinging where she could taste.

"Better wait. It's all still pretty hot."

A few minutes later, Dolce took a tasting spoon and

pulled it through the foamy jam I'd spooned off into a measuring cup. It had already begun to solidify from the pectin. I watched her a little nervously, waiting to see how she'd react.

"It's good," she said after a moment. "I'm not sure what it tastes like. It's different."

I wasn't sure how much of an endorsement that was. *It's different* often means *it's awful.* "Is it terrible? Just tell me."

Dolce shook her head. "I've never tasted red wine, so I don't know how it's supposed to taste. But this tastes nice. Fruity and sort of spicy."

Bridget grabbed a spoon and scraped up a taste of her own. She grinned at me. "Tastes like mulled wine. It's sort of sweet, but not too sweet. The grapes are there. And the cinnamon makes it taste like the hot wine you get at Christmas."

I decided I needed to see how close we were to reality. I scraped up a little of the jellied foam myself. Bridget was spot on. It tasted like mulled wine, all luscious and fruity. Maybe a little on the sweet side, but I could deal with that.

And it was simple to make. That was a huge point in the jam's favor, given the amount of work we were likely to be snowed beneath as we got closer to The Wedding. Particularly now that we had the Pollack wedding later in January. I didn't want to have to spend a lot of time cooking up jars of jam for the favors, but I wanted it to taste and look great.

As far as I could tell, this recipe fulfilled both those requirements.

I put the jar on the table after dinner that night to get a reaction from Nate. Once upon a time I could also have also gotten a reaction from Uncle Mike, but he seldom ate with us anymore, probably because he was with Madge.

Nate picked up the jar and held it to the light. "Color's great."

I nodded. "It's a looker. But the taste is the part that matters."

Nate grabbed a cracker and spread a little of the jam on it. "Nice texture, too."

He was right about that. The jam was crystal clear and spread smoothly. The pectin hadn't made it too rubbery. I found I was holding my breath as Nate took a bite.

He chewed slowly, staring off into the distance as if he was weighing everything. Nate's my best taster because he knows not to spare my feelings. If the jam sucked, he'd say so.

"I like it," he said finally. "I think you need to fine tune the sugar a little. You don't want it too sweet—the wine taste needs to come through. But it already tastes a lot like mulled wine, in a good way."

"That's what Bridget said."

"What did Dolce say?" Dolce was still a teenager, but she was developing a great palate.

"She liked it, but she'd never tasted red wine, so she wasn't sure what she was tasting."

Nate narrowed his eyes. "She's never tasted wine? How old is she anyway?"

"Seventeen. And I don't think Carmen and Donnie drink wine. All I've ever seen Donnie drink is beer."

"Geez, a culinary innocent." Nate grinned. "I bet she'll have champagne at The Wedding. My guess is nobody will get away from The Wedding without having a taste of champagne. For the toasts, if nothing else. It's New Year's Eve, after all."

I sighed. "We've got the favors now. We've got the venue, if you can call the barn a venue. We even have the date. What we don't have is a menu and a guest list. And a cake. So far as I know, there's no cake yet."

"Yeah, so far as I know they haven't made up their minds about most of the details. At this rate there may not be a cake since no wedding cake specialist can put something together quickly. Actually, that would suit Coco just fine since she doesn't want to bake one. She can throw some kind of dessert together that would be a good substitute. But Mom has to make the decision."

I grabbed one of the bottles of red wine that was left over after my jam-making session. "You want a glass of the real thing? We can commiserate over wedding planning."

Nate nodded. "Sure. At least Mom understands that the longer she waits, the simpler the menu gets, given how much lead time we'd need for special orders. We may end up with hot dogs and chips."

"No, we will not," I said decisively. "We may end up with spaghetti and Bolognese sauce, but it will be first rate spaghetti and Bolognese sauce. This is going to be a lovely wedding if I have to kill somebody to make it happen."

Nate grinned at me. "Murder doesn't usually go with a wedding, gorgeous. But I guess there's always a first time."

Again, I should have knocked wood after that observation. But who knew it would be necessary?

Chapter 5

Thursday was always a little slow for me because it was a day when I was on my own. Bridget worked the lunch shift at High Country and Dolce had some kind of after-school activity. I usually spent the day making jam, but I was caught up for once. I decided I'd work a little more on the wine jelly, trying to get the sweetness right. But truth be told, I wasn't all that excited about fiddling with the sugar content all afternoon. Still, other than that, I didn't have much on my plate.

Or I didn't until Nate called me a little after lunch. "Could you do me a favor?"

"Sure. What do you need?"

"I left a contract I need to give Thalia on my desk. Could you take it over to her office? It's the contract for the Molina wedding."

Nate and I shared an office that was also our guest room, but he used it more than I did since I spent most of my time in the kitchen. "I can do that. I'll be glad to." Particularly since it gave me the perfect excuse to get out of the house and do something interesting.

I found the contract easily enough, along with a manila folder to put it in. And then I headed into town. We were at that transitional period before Thanksgiving when the Halloween decorations come down, but no one's quite sure what to put up next since it isn't that close to Christmas yet. A lot of the local merchants had just gone with generic fall—lots of autumn leaves and pumpkins, along with a turkey or two.

Thalia's office was in an upscale strip mall close to the entertainment district on Second Street. At first glance, it might have been mistaken for a real estate company, but the photos in the windows showed wedding décor rather than houses for sale. Inside, everything was muted pastels, with a warm yellow on the walls that reminded me a lot of butter cream frosting. Thalia had been in business for over twenty years, and she knew her stuff.

Her receptionist gazed up at me with a slightly suspicious air. In my jeans and sweatshirt, I didn't resemble their usual client. Then her expression cleared. "Roxy?"

I nodded, giving her a closer look. "Danielle?"

She grinned delightedly. "Good Lord, how long has it been?"

"Since high school." Danielle and I had been on the same volleyball team, and we'd gone to state finals. But I didn't necessarily want to reflect on how many years ago it had been since we were the Mighty Panthers. "How are you doing? How's your mom? When did you go to work for Thalia?"

"Everybody's fine. I decided to go back to work after Sasha was born. That's been a couple of years now." I vaguely remembered Danielle was married, although I wasn't sure I knew who her spouse was.

"Working in this office must be an interesting job." To say the least, given the dramas we'd seen so far.

Danielle beamed at me. "Oh, it is, believe me. I just love it."

I would have loved to have asked her about the

Pollacks and a few other customers, but I knew that would be unprofessional. "Is Thalia here? I have a contract for her from Nate Robicheaux."

Danielle's grin took on a knowing air. "I heard you two were together. He's super cute."

I grinned back. "Yeah, I like to think so. His catering company is doing some wedding work with Thalia."

Danielle sighed. "Actually, Thalia's out of the office, but I could give Beverly a call. She could run the contract over to her if you want."

"Is she somewhere in town? I could take it to her myself—I've got time." In fact, I had lots of time and a certain amount of curiosity concerning wedding preparations since I'd be involved in whatever Madge and Uncle Mike needed done.

"She's meeting with the wedding cake lady, Marla Purdue. You know where her place is?"

I shook my head. "She's new, isn't she?"

"Relatively. She used to have a business in Frisco. Then she came over here a year or so ago. Her stuff is terrific. Her shop is on Spruce, near that modern monstrosity." Danielle was born and raised in Shavano, like me. People who used ultra-modern architecture in our historic downtown didn't rate high in our estimation.

"Okay, I've been curious about Marla's shop. Maybe I'll use Thalia as my excuse." Although the chance that she could do something for Uncle Mike and Madge was almost nonexistent, I figured it was still worth a shot.

"Go for it. If she's not there, you can always come here and drop it off."

Danielle and I exchanged a few more pleasantries, and I left the shop feeling very upbeat. It's always nice to renew acquaintances you've forgotten about.

I knew just which modern monstrosity Danielle was referring to when she gave me directions to the wedding cake lady's shop. It had been built by some real estate types from Fort Collins who'd decided Shavano needed an up-to-date office building and event center. It was sort of Southwest Modern, all fieldstone and glass and metal. It stood out like a sore thumb on a block of hundred-year-old storefronts, and it had never been fully occupied since it had opened. It was now undergoing some renovation to make the spaces more appealing to the locals, but so far there weren't many customers. There was a reasonably nice event space on the lower level, though, with a modern kitchen and lots of room for dancing or beer pong, whatever the group was in the mood for. Robicheaux Catering had done a couple of cocktail parties there, and it had been surprisingly pleasant.

I surveyed the strip mall across the street and immediately found Marla's Cakes. It was an unassuming storefront with an array of photographs in the front window. I glanced at them, and then stopped.

The cakes in the photos were spectacular. Except that wasn't the word I wanted. They weren't showy or in-your-face. They were just beautiful. Flowers cascaded down the sides or along the tiers of several, and it was impossible to tell whether they were made from paste or were real. One had sculpted ornaments in shades of white and silver on top of the white icing. Lovely, wintry colors that made me think of the snow queen. I swore I could hear Tchaikovsky's "Sugar Plum Fairy" tinkling in the background. A couple had cake toppers, and one appeared vintage, as if it had been handed down in the family from bride to bride.

I was mesmerized. Marla Purdue clearly knew her stuff. I hadn't heard much about her, but that was probably because we hadn't been involved in weddings before this past summer. My friend Bianca Jordan bakes the best bread and breakfast pastries in town, and Nate's sister Coco was a whiz on sophisticated desserts like tarts and galettes. But neither did cakes, and aside from the Cake Lady and City Market, neither did anybody else. Marla would probably have the upscale cake trade to herself, at least around Shavano. Still, I intended to ask Bianca about her, just to find out what the locals were thinking. She was likely to be a success since nobody else in town came close to this type of artistry.

I opened the door and stepped into the shop. It was larger than I'd realized, with a line of café tables stretching along the side. I could smell coffee and see a small array of pastries in the display case, so Marla must do a few less exalted forms of baking along with her fairy-tale cakes. But I guessed the tables were mostly for prospective bridal couples so that they could taste Marla's specialties and decide what they wanted.

A woman behind the counter gave me a quick smile. "Can I help you?"

"I need to see Thalia Rosenberg," I said. "Is she still here?"

The sales lady gestured toward the tables at the side, and I caught sight of Thalia and Beverly at the last table in the row, talking to a pleasant-looking blonde who might well be Marla Purdue. Thalia glanced up as I started in her direction. "Roxanne. Were you looking for me?"

"I am," I said. "I brought you a contract Nate said

you needed."

"Oh, that must be for the Molinas. He said he'd send me a copy." Thalia pushed to her feet as I handed her the manila folder, then passed the folder off to Beverly, her assistant.

The pleasant-looking blonde was staring up at me with a stunned expression. I get that a lot. I've been a little over six feet tall since I was in high school, and I'm a solid girl. I used to have masses of black hair, too, but I'd had to have it cut off after a concussion, and it was still growing back. I resemble, in many ways, a Greek-American Amazon. Still, it wasn't polite to stare.

"Hi," I said, extending my hand. "I don't think we've been introduced. I'm Roxanne Constantine."

The woman who was probably Marla gave my hand a sort of limp shake. "Marla Purdue," she said. "Pleased to meet you."

Actually, what she said was *pleaseta meetcha*, which made me think she wasn't from around these parts.

"Roxanne owns Luscious Delights, the jam company," Thalia supplied. "She helps Nate Robicheaux with Robicheaux Catering."

The blonde nodded, giving me a very slight smile. "I've heard of Nate."

"You have a lovely shop," I said. "The cakes are spectacular."

"Thanks." Her very slight smile didn't waver, and she glanced away from me toward the street. For no clear reason, I felt a little annoyed. Her reaction seemed rude. Then again, I was the one interrupting their meeting.

"Well, nice meeting you," I said. "I guess I'd better get back."

"Tell Nate thanks," Thalia said. "I'll give him a call later."

I turned toward the front door just as it opened, and a couple stepped inside. I recognized them immediately—Mr. Toad, Emerson Pollack, and his daughter. He wore the same outfit he'd had on before—overcoat, muffler, gloves, and green wool Tyrolean hat—with the same general effect. He resembled an amphibian. His daughter wore a lovely gray wool coat with a fur collar that might have been mink. She glanced at me and then gave me a sort of tentative smile, the kind of smile you give someone you sort of recognize but not really. Mr. Toad stared straight through me. Obviously, servers made no impression on him.

I nodded noncommittally at the daughter, stepping aside to let them pass. Thalia moved toward them, wearing an expression that might pass for a smile if your smile standards were modest. Maybe Nate and I weren't the only ones who found Mr. Toad a little tough to take.

"Good afternoon, Mr. Pollack," Thalia said. "Let me introduce you to your baker. This is Marla Purdue. Marla, this is Mr. Emerson Pollack and his daughter, Jennifer."

Marla rose from her table, her faint smile still in place. Maybe that was just her reflex expression. If so, I shouldn't have taken it personally. She extended her hand toward Mr. Toad. He studied her hand for a moment before taking it in a limp grasp, just as he had with Nate. And just as with Nate, it struck me as a nasty little power play. Marla's smile curdled a bit, but she let it go. Maybe she was more accustomed to jerks in her line of work than I was.

Thalia motioned to Beverly, who was watching the

interplay between Mr. Toad and Marla, frowning. I wasn't the only one who'd noticed Mr. Toad's gambit and Marla's reaction. "Beverly," Thalia said, "we need the paperwork."

Beverly looked up and then flushed. "Of course." She dug through her briefcase. "Sorry."

No one was paying any attention to me, so I decided to stick around a little longer, just to see if Emerson Pollack was as unpleasant to Marla as he had been to Nate.

"I have samples of the cakes and fillings we discussed," Marla said. "Just to be clear, these are the only cakes I could make on such short notice. I hope one of them will be satisfactory."

Mr. Toad gave her one of his bulbous-eyed stares as if he was weighing her words for hidden insults. "We'll see," he said.

Of course he wouldn't make things easy for anyone. Even though Marla would undoubtedly be working a great deal faster than her usual work process and rearranging her existing schedule to make this wedding cake come in on time, Emerson Pollack wasn't going to be impressed. He probably thought that the amount he was paying for the cake more than made up for any extra work Marla would put in.

And he was right. Marla could have refused the order, just as Nate could have. And she could still back out, just as Nate had threatened to do. Still, I had a feeling Emerson Pollack enjoyed putting people on the spot. Maybe he'd pushed timorous Jennifer into this last-minute wedding just so that he could have the opportunity to throw his weight around a little.

I would have liked to have stuck around to watch the

tasting, but no way could I justify it. After a moment, I stepped out the door with one quick backward glance. As she had when she'd met with us, Jennifer was concentrating on her servings of cake, taking a small bite. And as he had with us, Mr. Toad sat in his chair, arms folded across his chest, ignoring the slices of cake on the plate in front of him.

It was going to be a long afternoon for Marla and Thalia. Maybe even for Beverly.

I stopped by the café on my way to the farm. Nate and Dexter were working on the food for an anniversary party we were doing tomorrow. The kitchen smelled like heaven, which is always a good sign.

"Hey, Rox," Nate called. "Did you get the contract to Thalia?"

"Just did. She was over with the wedding cake lady, so I got to see her place."

"Nice?"

"Very. But probably not a possibility for The Wedding. She needs more lead time than we could provide."

Nate shrugged. "Yeah, I figured as much. Coco's talking cupcakes, which would work for me."

"I thought she didn't like making cakes."

"She doesn't, but she said she places cupcakes in a different category."

"Will they work for your mom?"

"Who knows? At this point, I think she'll have to take whatever we can do for her. Unless she wants a sheet cake from the grocery store." Nate dropped the potatoes he'd been cutting up into a pan of water.

"Oh, I almost forgot. I also saw out favorite client, Mr. Toad."

"Pollack?" Nate raised an eyebrow. "What was he doing there?"

"Getting a cake for his daughter's wedding. She was there, too. Her name's Jennifer, by the way."

Nate sighed. "Of course he was. When money's no object, you can get the town's best wedding cake designer to do your bidding at the last minute. God only knows how much she's charging him. Did I tell you he's hired us for the engagement party?"

"No. Isn't that kind of weird? Don't they usually have engagement parties several months before the wedding? When is this happening?"

"Pollack's the one who set it up. Maybe it's a short engagement. It's happening next week, Thursday night. Thalia's supposed to get me the guest numbers."

I frowned. Given the tension between Nate and Mr. Toad, I thought just getting the wedding dinner done would be enough. Now we were stuck doing another meal with him. "Did Thalia talk you into it?"

"Sort of. Plus I'm charging them enough to take care of any trouble Pollack tries to make. It's way too late for them to make arrangements with another caterer. It's us or delivery pizza."

"Do we have to do another tasting?" The thought made my stomach clench tight. Yeah, it would be a lot of money, but there were some things money couldn't make up for.

Nate shook his head. "I sent them a couple of sample menus and they took rustic beef stew, which simplifies life considerably. I can put it together the day before, grab a couple of baguettes from Bianca and do some kind of salad, and we're good to go."

"Good. I don't want to have to put in any extra hours

for Mr. Toad. Where's it going to be held?" I was guessing it wouldn't be at Pollack's place, although I admitted to a little curiosity about what that place was like.

"At that event center on Spruce. You know, the modern place."

"The modern monstrosity." Strange that I'd been thinking about the place only that morning.

Nate's lips quirked up. "I guess that's as good a description as any. Got a good kitchen, though. They're doing the wedding there, too. They're using the big event space on the lower floor for the engagement party and the reception, and the smaller room upstairs for the ceremony."

I grimaced. "Does that mean we have to take the food up a flight of stairs?"

"Nope, the kitchen and the larger event space are on the same floor. We just have to have it on trays so the servers can get it out to the tables. Dex and I can handle it. Shouldn't be too hard."

As long as the two of them were in charge of getting the food ready to go, the event center should work out fine. "You're right—it has a great kitchen. And I'll bet Mr. Toad got a special rate, given all the problems they've had getting tenants."

"For all I know, he's one of the owners." Nate gave me a sour smile.

"I never did find out what his business is. Is he into real estate?"

"No idea. But his checks have cleared, which is all that matters at this point."

It wasn't all that mattered, but it went a long way. I gave Nate a goodbye kiss (always the best part of a quick visit) and went to my truck.

The question of Mr. Toad's occupation bounced around at the back of my mind as I climbed inside. It shouldn't have mattered since he was paying us a goodly amount for our services. And as Nate pointed out, his payments cleared with no problem. That should have been the end of it.

But it wasn't. Shavano is still a relatively small city. I don't know everybody who lives there, but I know a lot of them. And the restaurant community is also small, which means we gossip like crazy. Somebody had to know something about Pollack. He couldn't have been hanging around the area, spreading cash wherever he went, without arousing somebody's curiosity. I considered my most promising sources of information. My best friend, Susa Sondergaard, knew a lot of the movers and shakers in the area because she ran the town's best computer support company. Even if Pollack hadn't hired her, she might know about him.

My other best source was undoubtedly Bianca Jordan, baker extraordinaire and the town's most efficient gossip. If Emerson Pollack had had dealings with anybody in the food business in Shavano or, probably, Geary, Bianca might know about it. Nate had said we needed baguettes from Bianca. I might as well take the opportunity to put in an order.

And if our conversation stumbled around Emerson Pollack—and maybe even Marla Purdue—so much the better. After all, knowledge was power.

Chapter 6

Bianca's shop was downtown near the restaurant district. Since it was afternoon, the crowds on the street were only moderate, made up chiefly of office workers on coffee break. Nothing went better with coffee than one of Bianca's muffins unless it was one of her cookies. The café tables arranged along the windows at the front of the shop were mostly full, and her display cases were mostly empty, which is definitely what you want in a bakery toward the end of the day.

Somebody new was behind the counter, a youngish woman who appeared eager to help me with something. Her name tag said, *Sharon.* That was a change from Bianca's typical bored teenage helpers who usually gave the impression they had much better things to do than sell you anything.

"Good afternoon," Sharon said. "Can I interest you in some fresh-baked muffins?"

This was also a bit of a change since Bianca usually does muffins in the morning and cookies in the afternoon. "I'm just here to talk to Bianca. Is she in her workroom?"

"Oh." Sharon looked a little doubtful. "I'll ask her if it's all right. Who should I tell her is here?"

Another change. This one not as welcome since I usually walked straight into Bianca's workroom without having to wait around. "Tell her it's Roxy. That's my jam on the counter." I nodded toward the display of Luscious Delights.

"Oh." This time Sharon dimpled. "I'm sure it's delicious. I'll be right back." She returned very quickly, her cheeks a slightly deeper pink. "I'm sorry for the delay. She says for you to go right in."

"Thanks." I was betting that wasn't all Bianca had said, but Sharon was new, so I was inclined to cut her a break.

Bianca was cleaning up her table when I walked into her workspace. "Hey, kid, what's up? Sorry about the new girl. She doesn't know who's a friend yet."

"That's okay. Better to be careful. Nate needs a half-dozen baguettes for an engagement party on the twenty-first. I thought I'd get the order in, so you don't sell out."

"Always appreciated. Who's the bride?"

That was, of course, the perfect lead-in. "Her name's Jennifer Pollack. Her father's some rich guy from Geary—Emerson Pollack."

Bianca frowned as she thought. "Don't know him. Is he new around here?"

"Maybe." I paused to decide how much further to go with this. "He's a little like a frog. Short and squat with eyes that sort of bulge out."

Bianca snorted a laugh. "Well, that's memorable, but it still doesn't ring a bell. You say he's from Geary, but his daughter's getting married in Shavano?"

I nodded. "The groom might be from here. I'm not sure. It's a last-minute thing. They're paying top dollar for everything because we all have to scramble to get it done in time."

"And they're using Thalia?" Bianca looked incredulous, and I could see her point. Thalia wasn't the scrambling type. And she was usually booked months in advance.

"Yeah, like I said, the guy's rich. Best of everything for his little girl."

Bianca gave me a half smile. "Well, Nate's the best caterer in town. I'm surprised he had time to do it."

"The date was open, plus, like I said, money's no object for Pollack. He got Marla's Cakes, too."

Bianca raised her eyebrows. "That's another shock. She's usually booked up so far in advance you have to start thinking about it a year before the date. Which works for weddings."

"You know her?"

Bianca shrugged. "I've met her. I wouldn't say I know her. You know her?"

"I can't say I've even met her, really. Thalia introduced us, but she'd pretty much forgotten I existed two minutes later."

"Wedding bakers." Bianca grimaced. "I mean all bakers are sort of snotty about what they do, including me. No offense, but it's harder to bake a loaf of good bread than to stir up a pot of chili."

"Okay, I'll buy that." Bakers were notorious snobs about the kind of cooking they did, and I couldn't argue with them. A good baker needs a lot more practice and a lot more precision than a short order cook, for instance.

"But wedding cake bakers are the worst," Bianca said flatly. "They spend more time designing stuff than the rest of us, and they've got all that architecture to deal with."

"Architecture?"

"You know—making sure all the parts fit together, that it won't fall apart when you move it, that kind of thing."

"Oh, right." I'd seen some wedding cakes that looked like architecture, all arches and offset rectangles. "I saw some pictures of her cakes. They were spectacular."

"Oh, she's talented. I won't argue with that. She knows her stuff. She's just kind of standoffish. But like I said, that's the way wedding bakers are. On their own special plane, with the rest of us several degrees below them."

"Why did she come here, do you know? I mean, she used to be in Frisco, and that's more of a crossroads kind of place than Shavano. Over there, she could get orders from Frisco, along with Breckinridge and Keystone and Silverthorne and maybe Vail. Here she's just got Shavano and Geary and some of the smaller towns, so far as I can tell."

Bianca sighed. "Ask your buddy, Ms. Rosenberg. I hear she's the one who persuaded Marla to come to Shavano. And Thalia may generate enough business to keep Marla hopping."

That was an interesting development. I hadn't been aware that Thalia was involved with bringing Marla to Shavano, but she did seem to treat the baker like a rock star. Maybe more was going on in Shavano in terms of wedding business than I'd realized. Plus Thalia drew customers from all over the mountains. She was the most successful event planner in the area.

"You got any new jam for the holidays?" Bianca asked. "I'm almost out of raspberry."

"I did some red wine jam a few days ago, but it's for wedding favors. Assuming Madge and Uncle Mike like it."

"Red wine?" Bianca stared off in space, considering. "You going to make any extra?"

"Hadn't thought about it. I guess I could. It tastes sort of like mulled wine, and it's gorgeous. You think people would like it on bread?"

"What color is it?"

"Deep red. It's really pretty when the light catches it."

Bianca shrugged. "People will buy it for Christmas most likely. Put a green ribbon around it, and it'll sell."

"I might have to raise the price a little. Wine costs more than fruit." Particularly since I got the fruit from my own farm.

"Christmas, like I said. People will pay a little extra." Bianca grinned. "We can work up a gift box with wine jam and stollen. Or challah, if I decide to put in the work braiding the stuff."

"You're on," I said. "I'll bring you a sample next time I come to town."

"Do that." Bianca paused. "Everything going okay with Madge and Mike and The Wedding?"

"Far as I know." I tried to sound breezier than I felt. No sense in spreading doubt. "New Year's Eve. Invitations going out soon." Or they'd better be. Something else I needed to check on with Uncle Mike.

On the way home, I decided it was, in fact, past time to have a conversation with my uncle. I could let him taste the jam to see if he liked it, and I could find out where things stood with the wedding preparations.

I grabbed a jar of the wine jam and headed up toward the main house. Once upon a time I could have waited for Uncle Mike to come down to my cabin for dinner or sometimes for breakfast, but he rarely did that anymore.

He spent most of his time with Madge, and when they weren't together, he was usually working somewhere on the farm. But work had slowed down considerably as we entered November. We'd already had one snowfall, and the forecast called for more this weekend. My chances of finding Uncle Mike at home were a lot better now than they'd been a couple of weeks ago.

As I walked in the front door of the main house, I found myself wondering just where Uncle Mike and Madge were going to live. Madge had a lovely Craftsman cottage in town that she'd once shared with her husband and kids. Now she was a widow with grown children, on her own. For a while, Nate had lived in the apartment over her garage, and when he'd moved in with me, Marigold had taken it over. But now Marigold had married Bobby and settled in his small ranch-style house on the edge of town. Madge had no one living at the house with her except Uncle Mike when he stayed over.

If Madge moved to the farm, she'd have Nate and me just down the hill. I wondered if that was a plus. Maybe she was just as happy to be on her own again. Except she wasn't on her own. She had Uncle Mike.

I was so caught up in my own cogitations that I almost missed the light in Uncle Mike's study as I walked up the hall. I backtracked to peek in. "Uncle Mike?"

He sat up straight in his desk chair, peering at me over his half glasses. "Hi, sweetheart. What's up?"

"You have a minute? I've got some jam for you to try." He had a pile of papers on his desk and looked so busy I felt a little guilty for interrupting him.

He sighed, pulling off his glasses to rub his eyes. "Sure. I need to take a break anyway. Let's do it in the kitchen."

I found a box of saltines in the pantry and put a few on a plate. "This is what I'm thinking of for your wedding favors," I said. "If you and Madge like it, that is."

He looked a little confused. "Wedding favors?"

"The take-home gifts you give your guests at the reception. I thought little jars of jam might be nice."

Uncle Mike narrowed his eyes, studying the jar of deep red jam. "What kind is it?"

"It's red wine jam, although it's more like jelly. I made it with cabernet, but I could do something else if you'd prefer. I mean, something like pinot noir might be a little milder." Now that the time had come for tasting, I found I was nervous.

Uncle Mike gave me a smile that was somewhat more relaxed. "Let me taste it before you start changing it."

I spread a decent-sized plop of jam on one of the saltines then handed it to him. He bit off a quarter of the cracker and chewed contemplatively. "Hmm," he said after a few minutes.

My heart sank. "Too strong?"

"No, it's good. It's just...different. Don't think I've ever tasted wine-flavored jam before."

"Too different?" *Come on, Uncle Mike, put me out of my misery.*

"I like it, honey. It tastes like sweet wine and the color's gorgeous. You'll need to let Madge taste it, though."

"I know. I need to find some time when she's around." I hadn't seen Madge since the tasting with Pollack. Business at the restaurant always picked up at the holidays with office parties and celebrating shoppers.

"Yeah," Uncle Mike said. "She can be hard to pin down."

Something about his tone of voice sounded off. I took a breath and decided to wade into the swamp. "Is everything all right with you two?"

"With us?" He raised his eyebrows. "Sure. Of course. Why wouldn't it be?"

Talk about being over-emphatic. "I don't know. But things have bogged down a little with the wedding planning. Have you sent out the invitations yet? I mean, everybody knows the wedding's on New Year's Eve, but they're waiting to be officially invited." That was the polite way of saying what I'd been hearing. A whole lot of people wanted to come to the wedding, and there'd be lots of hurt feelings if some got invitations while others didn't.

Uncle Mike sighed. "We got the invitations, and Madge said she'd take care of it. I haven't asked her about them lately, though."

"You haven't? Why not?"

He looked down at his hands. "I don't want to stress her out."

That sounded like he wasn't saying what was really on his mind. I put my hand on his shoulder. "What's going on, Uncle Mike? Are you two having problems?"

He gazed up at me then, and I realized how tired he was. He reminded me of how we all looked during harvest season. "We don't talk about the wedding much," he said. "I offered to do some of the preparations, like the invitations and such. But Madge said she wanted to do it. I don't want to pressure her. She's got enough on her plate."

There were a lot of things I could say to that, mostly centered around the idea that he needed to know what was going on, and they needed to make sure they were getting everything done in time. But something more serious was at the heart of this. "Are you worried Madge isn't all in on the wedding?"

Uncle Mike glanced away again. "Not exactly. I mean, Madge isn't the type to back down on something once she's given her word."

"But?"

"But. Now I wish I'd said we'd get married next summer, given her a lot of time to make sure she was doing what she wanted to do." He ran a hand through his short gray hair, mussing it on top. "I mean, I think she wants to go through with it, but so much is going on…" His voice trailed off. "She might be trying to put everything off as long as she can."

Well, hell. "She's just tired out, Uncle Mike, like you are. I'll talk to her. I've got a little extra time right now, and I'd be glad to take over some of the work y'all need done."

Actually, I didn't have as much time as I'd had earlier, but I'd *make* time, dammit. This was my uncle, my sole remaining relative on my dad's side. If The Wedding would make him happy, I'd move heaven and earth to make it happen.

Uncle Mike wasn't as relieved as I would have liked. "I don't want you to put any pressure on her, Roxanne. I don't want her to think we're saying she has to get things done. That's liable to make things worse."

I bit my tongue because that was precisely what I did want to say to Madge. She needed to get some things done, or she needed to delegate to some of her willing helpers, including me and Coco and, probably, Nate if he had a spare millisecond. Normally, I might have included Marigold and Bobby in that list, but Marigold was so hugely pregnant at this point that it was a major accomplishment for her to keep working in the café's kitchen. "I won't put any pressure on her. I'll try to take some off. She doesn't need to do everything on her own. There are lots of people who'd love to help."

Uncle Mike sighed again. This was a sighing kind of afternoon. "All right, I'll trust you to do that. But if Madge says no, you'll leave her be. I don't want her feeling put upon."

I nodded. "I promise. If she doesn't want me around, I'll let her be." But I might enlist Nate or Coco to help make the case. Madge could blow me off, but her own kids were harder to ignore. "About the jam."

"What about it?"

"What's your opinion of it, honestly? If you don't like it, I won't take it any further. Just tell me honestly what you think."

Uncle Mike picked up the cracker again and studied the jam. Then he popped it into his mouth and chewed slowly. I thought about asking him what he thought again but kept my peace.

"I like it," he said finally. "It's a holiday kind of jam—not your usual, but still tasty. The color's nice, and I think people will feel like they've gotten something special if you give it out at the wedding."

I blew out a quick breath. "Thanks. I'll start searching for jars. And special labels." Just as soon as I knew exactly how many people they were inviting.

"Don't forget to let Madge have a taste." Uncle Mike shook his head. "Nothing gets approved for The

Wedding without her saying okay."

"Oh, I'll get Madge to taste it. Never fear." In fact, I intended to get Madge's okay tomorrow, along with a lot of other okays that might get The Wedding moving forward again.

That night I told Nate about the problems with The Wedding. He groaned, rubbing his hands across his face. "Oh, man, just what we need. Another crisis to deal with. But I guess I should have figured out there were problems since Mom hasn't approved the menu yet for the reception."

"Oh, Lord, I forgot all about that. Do you want me to say something about it when I bring the jelly for her to taste?"

Nate sighed. "No, I'll talk to her. Gently. Patiently. It's no big deal. Basically, whatever we serve, it's going to be an upscale version of stuff we serve at the café all the time. Or maybe not so upscale, depending on how much time we have to prepare it. And we'd already decided the whole thing will be served buffet style, so no plating problems. We're going to have to rope in some new staff, though, because all the people who normally work for us at events are coming as guests. And I don't know what kind of kitchen facilities Mike has at the barn."

I hadn't thought about that, but now I realized it could be a problem. Without a kitchen at the barn, we'd have to cook the meal elsewhere and then transport it to the barn somehow. And to make things even more complicated, Nate and I would be front and center for The Wedding, so we couldn't also be in the kitchen getting the entrees ready to go. "What about Dex? Can he handle the prep work? Or is he a guest, too?"

"He said he'd do the final prep in the kitchen, but yeah, he and his family are going to be guests. I think we'll just have to bring in some part-time people for the day."

"Assuming we can find somebody in the Shavano restaurant scene who isn't already coming to the reception."

Nate slid his arms around me and rested his forehead against mine. " 'Sufficient to the day is the evil thereof,' or words to that effect. We've got around two months. We'll figure it out."

I hoped so. Because otherwise we'd both be as stressed as Madge was rumored to be now by the time we got everything set up.

Chapter 7

It took me a while to get enough time to see Madge. I had jam to make, for one thing, and the final menu had come in for the Pollack engagement party. Nate and Dex would normally do most of it, but Dex came down with a bad cold, and Nate banished him from the kitchen. Thus I found myself a couple of days later in the catering kitchen chopping mushrooms for hors d'oeuvres while Nate stirred up the stew for the main course. It needed to sit in the refrigerator for a day or so to get peak flavor.

There were a lot of guests for this party, or anyway I thought so. Of course, I had no idea how many guests you usually had for an engagement celebration. We had orders for sixty-five, which put it up there with some of the larger parties we'd catered. Nate shrugged when I mentioned it. "Maybe Pollack has a large family, and this is their chance to get together. Maybe Jennifer invited all her sorority sisters. And who knows who the groom might invite."

I didn't say anything more, but it struck me that if I had a relative like Pollack, I'd do my best not to spend any time with him at all. Then again, except for Jennifer, the whole family might resemble amphibians, and maybe this was their chance to hang out where no one would stare.

Serendipity finally struck when Madge stepped into the catering kitchen around two in the afternoon.

"Dexter's still sick?" she asked when she saw me chopping away.

"Improving, as I understand it, but still not a hundred percent."

Madge nodded absently. "Mike said you had some jam for me to taste?" She didn't seem particularly excited about it, but I'd take what I could get.

"I've got it right here. Do you have a few minutes?" I'd brought the wine jam with me because I'd been hoping to get a chance to talk to Madge.

Madge hid a yawn behind her hand. "Come to the café. It's more comfortable there."

Tres was just finishing up his janitorial duties behind the counter at the café when we walked in. Madge sank into a chair near the front, extending her legs in front of her. She looked so tired I almost felt guilty about bothering her with the tasting. "Long day?"

"They're all long this time of year." She sighed. "And now there's Thanksgiving to think about."

The Robicheaux family usually had a huge Thanksgiving party at the café for all the local restaurant people, as well as friends, relatives, and basically anyone who could beg an invitation. Everybody cooked, and the spread was unbelievable. I hadn't thought they'd be doing it this year, given how many other things Madge had on her plate. I thought maybe we'd just have a small family get-together, but Madge had other ideas.

"Nate and I could do that," I said impulsively. I doubted Nate would thank me for volunteering him, but I didn't want Madge to take this on along with the other things she was working on.

"It's not that hard," Madge said. "We do the turkey and ham and let everybody else take care of the sides.

It's mostly getting the word out."

"Well, let us help with that. I could let a few people like Bianca and Harry know. They'd get the word out to all the people who usually come." Harry Potter was the bartender at Dirty Pete's, where most of the restaurant people in town hung out, and telling Bianca something was the equivalent of telling the town crier in a medieval village.

"All right, I'll let you do that. And maybe I can let Coco and Bobby keep track of who's bringing what. People call to let us know, and it's a way to make sure we don't end up with six pans of stuffing and no green vegetables." She gave me a tired smile, reminding me of what Madge looked like when she wasn't hopelessly stressed. Uncle Mike was right. She was a woman near the end of her rope.

She closed her eyes, rubbing her forehead. "I know I'm way behind on the wedding, Roxy. And I know you're all tiptoeing around me like I might blow up. But I'll get to it. So help me. I know what needs to be done."

I leaned forward and put my hand on hers. "Madge, I want to help. So does Nate. So does Coco. Let us do the invitations. We can address them while we watch TV or something."

Madge narrowed her eyes, and I was afraid she was going to tell me to butt out. Then she shrugged. "I guess you all can do that. We've got the invitation list down to a number that will actually fit in the barn, which took a while, believe me."

"What's the number currently?"

"Currently, it's around ninety, and we started with three hundred, so that's a major adjustment."

I managed not to choke, but it was a near thing.

Three hundred people would never have fit in the barn. Hell, there were very few event centers around town that would hold that many people, and none of them would be available on New Year's Eve. "Yes," I muttered, "that would have been a problem."

"If we could do things outside, we could have asked everyone, but at this time of year…" Madge shrugged again. At this time of year, the guests would be icicles by the end of the ceremony if we held it outside. "Ninety's still a lot, but it's more reasonable. And some of those people won't come, after all."

That might be true although given the number of people who loved Madge and Uncle Mike, my guess was most of the invitees would be there with bells on.

"So give me the current list and the invitations, and Nate and I will get to work. If we see anyone questionable, we could take off a few more names." I wasn't sure about that, but chances were the list could still use a little winnowing.

Madge shook her head. "Nate will try to eliminate all his cousins."

"I won't let him. Trust me."

Madge stared at me for a long moment, and I was afraid I'd overstepped. Then she sighed. "That sounds like a good idea about now. I'm so tired of trying to deal with everything. We need somebody who hasn't been involved in this as long as we have."

"Exactly," I said quickly. "Like I said, we can address invitations while we're watching TV. I'd rather do that than watch Broncos games." That was heresy in Colorado. Sue me. "Maybe I can get Bridget to help when she's done with the mail orders. Dolce, too."

Madge narrowed her eyes. "Okay, they're both on

the invitation list. If they've got the free time, I'd welcome it."

"I'm sure they'd be happy to." Particularly since they'd both be on the clock and getting paid for helping.

Madge reached across the table for her tablet. "I'm going to email the list to you right now before I think better of it. Mike has the boxes of invitations up at the house." She hit a succession of keys, then smiled at me. "Thanks, Roxy. I'm already feeling relieved."

I hoped Nate and I could justify that feeling—without eliminating all the Robicheaux cousins. "Do you still want to try the jam?"

"Oh, yes, of course. What kind of jam is it? Mike wouldn't tell me anything more than that it was a perfect holiday kind of jam."

I crossed my fingers that he was right. "It's red wine jam." I pulled the jar out of my tote bag. "I made it with cabernet, but like I told Uncle Mike, I could make it with something lighter if you think it's too heavy."

Madge held the jar up to the afternoon sunshine pouring through the café window. "I love the color. That deep red is just stunning."

I snagged a couple of packages of crackers from a basket on the counter. "Let me spread a little on a cracker."

Madge studied the jelly as I spread it across the saltine. "Nice texture. And the color still looks marvelous." She took the cracker from me and nibbled a corner.

Madge is a restaurant professional who spends a certain part of her time deciding on food for the café menu. I valued her judgment more than just about anyone except Nate's. And I was afraid she'd decide she didn't like the taste, which would send me to the drawing board searching for some other kind of jelly.

"That's…different," she said.

Why was that the first thing everyone said when they tasted my wine jam? Was it really that weird? "Too different?" I asked dutifully.

Madge narrowed her eyes. "I don't think so. But it's not really showing up at its best on a saltine." She pushed herself to her feet, carrying the jam jar toward the kitchen. I got up to follow her.

By the time I got to the kitchen, Madge was digging through the refrigerator, frowning. "I know I saw some not that long ago."

"Saw some what?"

"This." She pulled away from the refrigerator carrying a carton of cream cheese. "This is what would work best." She turned to Coco's part of the kitchen, then emerged with the end of a baguette. "Let me slice this up."

A couple of minutes later we were both holding slices of baguette spread with cream cheese and topped with a smear of wine jam. I took a tentative bite, then grinned. The combination of slightly sour creaminess and slightly spicy sweetness was terrific. "You're a genius."

Madge gave me a genuine smile as she licked her lips. "I just knew what needed to be done. We should serve this at the reception, get a big wheel of brie and pour this over the top. Then we'll have crostini to spread it on. And everyone will know what a great favor they've been given when they see the jam in action. Oh, this is going to be fun! Thank you so much." She gave me an enthusiastic hug, and I felt like a dragon slayer.

It was the happiest I'd seen her, and it automatically raised my spirits, too. Maybe this was all going to work out after all. I sailed home and relieved Uncle Mike of the boxes of invitations sitting in his office.

"Madge is letting *you* do it?" He seemed stunned.

"She is. And we are." *Piece of cake.* Or something like it.

That happiness in my heart lasted until I told Nate what I'd roped us into.

"Ninety guests?" He stared at me. "And they started with three hundred? I don't even know three hundred people, let alone three hundred people I'd want to invite to The Wedding."

"Well, exactly. They obviously let themselves go when they started out, listing everybody they know. And between them, they know everybody in the valley. But they've cut the list by more than half, and your mom said we can also drop anyone who's unlikely to come." I gave him my most reassuring smile, which didn't work at all.

"When are we going to have time to address and mail ninety invitations, Rox? We've both got stuff to do."

My positive attitude was taking a bit of a beating, but I pushed ahead. "We can do it a chunk of names at a time. And remember, we can cut any of these people who aren't likely to come over the mountains for a wedding on New Year's Eve." We could probably get ninety guests into the barn, although I didn't know how comfortable they'd be. If we got it down to around seventy-five, it would be better."

Nate grimaced. "I've got a shitload of cousins we could start with."

"No cousins. I promised Madge I wouldn't let you

drop your cousins."

"Well, crap," Nate grumbled. "I was going to enjoy that."

We opened up Madge's list, which went on for several pages. Even I was stunned at how much space ninety names took up. "Let's work on them twenty at a time, so we don't get overwhelmed. We can do it tonight while you watch the game. The Nuggets are on."

Nate wasn't entranced with this idea, but he settled down with the printout of the first twenty names. "Holy shit, I don't know half of these people. How am I supposed to know if they're likely to come or not?"

Actually, I thought it would be easier to drop people I didn't know than people I did. "Let me see. They might be from Uncle Mike's list."

Many of them were, but they weren't that easy to eliminate. Other farmers from Shavano and Geary were friends, and I knew Uncle Mike would want to send them invitations even if they didn't choose to give up their New Year's Eve for The Wedding. I crossed out some of the commercial names, people who bought our produce along the Front Range. My guess was they weren't going to travel over the passes for a wedding in a barn. Although it might have been good business to invite them, they weren't as necessary as, say, Aram Pergosian, whose tomatoes we feasted on every spring.

Nate did the same with the café's suppliers, some of whom were old family friends but some of whom were just guys who kept the café supplied with, say, corn syrup. We cut five or six names before we sat down to dinner, which clearly improved Nate's outlook.

After we'd finished eating, we sat at the table, sipping the last of our bottle of wine. We'd managed to cut the list down, but we were just getting started. And we hadn't done the invitations yet. "We can't do this every night, Rox," Nate said. "It'll spoil my appetite if nothing else."

"The faster we get it done, the faster people will reply and the faster you'll have a menu to work with. There's a lot to be said for speed."

Nate groaned. "Okay, okay. Tell you what—you go through the next twenty, and then I'll go through them. And by the time we're both done, we'll have cut everybody we know doesn't belong on that list."

"Works for me," I said.

That night we propped ourselves in front of the television, writing out the addresses on the envelopes and stuffing in the invitations. Thank God Madge hadn't gone formal with double envelopes. I don't think even my determination would have lasted through that.

"Should I drop these in the mail tomorrow?" Nate asked.

"Let's send them all out at once. Otherwise, some people will be getting their invitations first, and other people will be wondering if they're going to be invited."

Nate sighed. "Good Lord, there's a lot more politics involved in this than I thought. Between this and the Pollack thing, we'll be lucky if we get through the winter without swearing off weddings altogether."

I produced an anemic smile. The whole question of weddings and our involvement therein was still hanging in the background, undiscussed and possibly undiscussable. Still, I'd prefer not to have weddings taken off the table altogether. I was happy for Madge and Uncle Mike, and I was curious about the Pollack wedding, which could be an interesting experience. But

I was still on the fence about Nate and me and what the future might hold. I wasn't rushing out to buy myself a bridal veil, but I'd just as soon not give up on the possibility completely.

One simple fact was always in the background—we loved each other. And people who loved each other got married eventually.

Or not.

Chapter 8

We had to set up in the afternoon for the Pollack engagement party that started at seven. The wedding was less than two months away, but maybe the engagement was recent. The timing seemed a little off to me, but needless to say, I wasn't in charge. And maybe Jennifer wanted to celebrate her engagement before they got into the weeds of the wedding.

According to Thalia, Pollack or, more likely, Jennifer decided to set the dinner up using several small tables rather than one big one for all the guests, a decision I thoroughly endorsed. A single table holding around fifty people struck me as totally unwieldy, although it would have given Emerson Pollack the chance to seat himself at the head.

No, I was not cutting him a break. The Emerson Pollack we'd seen at the tasting was probably the real deal, not just a one-time occurrence.

The menu was super simple, which it had to be since it was a last-minute order and Nate was already struggling to fit the Pollacks into the holiday schedule. We'd serve the stew in bowls along with Bianca's baguettes that could be torn into chunks and dipped into the gravy if people were feeling rustic. Jennifer had chosen to go with the salad before dinner rather than appetizers, but her father still ordered a couple of hors d'oeuvres to be passed among the guests as they arrived, including the mushroom tarts I'd been chopping cremini for earlier in the week.

Dessert would be another of Marla Purdue's cakes, which had yet to appear. Marla was responsible for delivering her own products, and I was hoping she'd get it over to the event center in time to serve. Maybe it was her way of commenting on the annoyance of creating a last-minute cake for an engagement party. At least she had a few more weeks before the wedding. Given that they had a simple menu for the reception, Marla's cake might be the centerpiece.

Thalia had worked her usual magic in decorating the event space. Discreet flowers perfumed the air; the tables were draped in gold and light gray, which I assumed were the bride's colors. Since they were also the colors for the University of Colorado Golden Buffaloes, they could have been a tribute to the groom's alma mater for all I knew. Or maybe they were just the color of money, which meant a lot to the FOB.

As I came into the room, I saw Thalia at the back, resting her hands on her hips as she gave the space one last going over. Her assistant, Beverly, stood at her side, frowning down at the notebook computer in hand. "It's lovely," I called as I placed the hors d'oeuvres along the table we'd set up for them. The servers would carry them around once the guests arrived, but the first on the scene could help themselves.

Thalia nodded absently, as if the room's loveliness was a foregone conclusion. "It'll do." She checked her watch. "The Pollacks should be here by now. The guests will start arriving in another fifteen minutes or so."

I checked my own watch. Five after seven, which wasn't so terribly late after all. Parties didn't always run on schedule although it would be bad form for the host not to be around when the guests started showing up. "We're ready whenever they are. Will somebody give us the high sign when they want to start service?"

"Theoretically, I will." Thalia sighed. "But who knows how long they'll want to stand around chatting. At seven thirty or so, I'll start moving them along. Who's the wait staff tonight?"

"Donnell and Jerry, two of our vets, who can handle just about anything, including Mr. Pollack having a bad evening."

"Good. I'll see what's holding things up."

Thalia pulled out her cell, but the door swung open before she could make a call. Loud male voices echoed from the hall, and three guys who were most likely the groomsmen ambled into view. Of course, given that I had no idea who the groom was, it could just as easily have been the groom himself and his chums.

I'm sure men who belong to fraternities get thoroughly sick of people like me referring to "frat boys" as if they all looked the same. But these three fit the frat boy stereotype more closely than anyone I'd seen before. All three wore khakis and knit shirts along with very expensive running shoes. All three bellowed at the top of their lungs, as if they were trying to outshout each other. And all three were already what Uncle Mike referred to as "three sheets to the wind."

Maybe they'd confused the engagement party with the bachelor party.

"Where's the bar?" one of the frat boys shouted. I wondered if they always talked at that volume level or if they were just reacting to the hush of the event center.

"There's no bar?" another of them rumbled. "What

kind of party doesn't have a bar?"

Well, crap. I hadn't anticipated that the groom and his cronies would be well-lubricated before we started serving. Judging from Thalia's expression, she hadn't either. Drunks usually didn't appreciate great food, but this wasn't a crowd who'd be interested in savoring the moment anyway.

Thalia appeared to be gritting her teeth as she marched toward the frat brothers. I didn't imagine anything connected with this wedding had been a barrel of laughs, given Pollack's nastiness, and now she had drunks to contend with. The brothers gave up on their search for a bar and advanced on the hors d'oeuvres table where they began piling food onto plates. Maybe a little sustenance would counteract the booze they'd consumed before the party started. .

At the moment, there wasn't any bar in sight, but that didn't mean one wouldn't open up as soon as all the other guests arrived. Liquor wasn't part of our contract. As far as I knew, the night's drinking would be confined to several bottles of mediocre Bordeaux that had been delivered to the kitchen earlier in the afternoon. But this kind of situation was what Thalia was paid to take care of. On the other hand, it wasn't part of my duties, in spite of the rate at which the hors d'oeuvres were disappearing, so I headed for the kitchen at a good clip.

Nate was setting out the salad plates so that we could distribute the greens. The greens themselves were in a couple of large plastic bags, waiting to be tossed with the vinaigrette that Nate had put together at the catering kitchen.

"Hors d'oeuvres are out on the table," I said. "Are the servers here?"

"Donnell is. Jerry called to say he's running late, but he should be here in ten minutes." Nate's jaw looked a little tense. He hated last minute glitches, but Jerry was reliable, and I was sure he'd show up as soon as he could. "Should I start putting out the greenery?"

"You finish putting out the plates. I'll do the greens, and then you can do the croutons."

We usually did plated dinners assembly line style, which made things a lot easier. The only problem this time would be finding enough room for fifty plates on the prep table and counters. We'd probably have to do it in shifts.

"Are you going to have Donnell put the salads out on the tables?" If she loaded up a tray of salads, that would reduce the number of plates we were dealing with.

"Yeah." Nate grabbed the bottle of vinaigrette and gave it a good shake to recombine the ingredients. Then he dumped the first bag of greens into an aluminum bowl. He tossed the salad before using tongs to put the salad leaves on the plates.

I grabbed the container of croutons and followed him around the table, sprinkling seven croutons over each plate. No, Nate hadn't told me to do that many. I'd just come up with that number over the many, many green salads we'd put together.

Donnell stepped into the kitchen as we were finishing up the first pass. "Jerry not here yet?"

Donnell is somewhere between forty and sixty. She's been working at the café since before Robert, senior, died, and she's Nate's first choice for a server whenever we have a catering deal. Which is to say, she knows her business.

"On his way," Nate said. "You can start putting

these salads out on the tables. Once we've got them in place, you and Jerry can pass some of the hors d'oeuvres until they decide to sit down and eat."

"Yeah, if we've got any hors d'oeuvres left. Those drunks have been sucking them up like they haven't eaten in a couple of weeks."

"What drunks?" Nate looked concerned, and I realized I hadn't filled him in on just what was happening in the event room.

"The groom and his buddies showed up soused," I said. "Thalia's dealing with it."

Donnell snorted as she lined the salad plates up on her tray. "Those boys are drunk as skunks. Don't know what kind of party this is supposed to be."

"An expensive one," I said. "As long as they pay us, we can put up with some disruptions."

"Guess that's right. Long as they don't puke at the table, things should be okay."

Nate and I exchanged a grim look. We'd once had a dinner party explode in a fit of what had first appeared to be food poisoning. It hadn't been a fun experience.

Donnell lifted her tray to her shoulder and headed out the kitchen door just as Jerry arrived. He was another pro, but he worked at one of the old-time steak houses in Shavano rather than the café. "Sorry, sorry. A sixteen-wheeler went off the road near Pine Leaf Street. Traffic backed up a mile or so."

"No problem," Nate said. "We're just putting out the salads. Then you can pass the hors d'oeuvres. Maybe load up the platters in here if there aren't enough left on the table." Fortunately, we had extra hors d'oeuvres in reserve if the frat boys had eaten everything I'd put out.

I was already laying out the plates for the next round

of salads as Jerry loaded up the last of the first round and made for the door. "Twenty-five down," I muttered.

"And twenty-five to go." Nate emptied the next bag of greens into the bowl, then sprinkled on the last of the dressing.

The second go-round always went more quickly than the first since we were in the groove. I finished up the croutons with only crumbs left in the container as Donnell reappeared.

"How are the drunks?" I asked.

"Still drunk." She started lining up the salad plates again. "They're off in a corner, wolfing down meatballs. Weird group overall, though."

I paused. "Weird how?"

"Well, I'm guessing the groom is one of the drunks. And the bride is obvious, along with a couple of bridesmaids. But just about everybody else is my age or older. And the bride's father is creepy."

"Yep," I said. "He is that."

Jerry swung into the kitchen moments later. "Seems more like a business dinner than an engagement party. Lot of guys in expensive suits and manicures. Hope that bride knows what she's doing. I sure wouldn't want one of my girls marrying into that bunch."

By then I was dying to see the guests myself. "How are the hors d'oeuvres doing?"

"Could use a refill," Donnell said as she lifted her tray to her shoulder again.

Jerry followed her out the door and I grabbed a platter to load with hors d'oeuvres. "Don't stay too long out there," Nate said. "We'll need to get set up for the stew."

"I'll be back directly." Or more or less directly. I

intended to spend some time checking out the guests.

The room was considerably more crowded now than it had been the last time I'd unloaded hors d'oeuvres. Thalia was moving around the room with dispatch, Beverly following at her heels. The level of noise had increased, but the volume was oddly muted now that the groomsmen had withdrawn to a far corner. Music played in the background from hidden speakers. Thalia had booked a musical group for the wedding, but the engagement party was using recorded music.

I saw what Jerry and Donnell had been talking about at once. The room was full of suits, most of them expensive. I didn't recognize anybody, but then I didn't run with the power elite in the county, and these guys looked to be big city types, probably visitors from the Front Range around Denver. Several women, most likely wives, were off by themselves or sitting together in twos or threes. Their clothes were probably designer, and I saw more than a few diamonds. But the women mostly looked bored, like this meeting wasn't their idea of a good time. The men were all gathered in groups, talking and laughing and ignoring the bride and groom, along with their own spouses.

The groom and his friends—I still assumed that's what they were—had taken over one of the small tables at the side and appropriated a couple of bottles of wine. They were still talking loud and hooting with laughter, but they were isolated enough so that they didn't appear to be bothering anyone.

I searched for Jennifer, the bride. She was sitting at a table with a few other young women, all of them sort of bored and sort of lost, much like the older women. For a minute I wondered if Jennifer's mother was among the group, but no one was paying much attention to her. No one was talking to the bride or her friends. I'm of the opinion that the bride is the star of the show at weddings and engagement celebrations, but for this one the bride was an afterthought. Which didn't seem right at all.

I carried the tray of hors d'oeuvres to their table, plastering on my best server smile. "Good evening. Would you ladies like some hors d'oeuvres? We have mushroom tarts and Asian meatballs and feta spinach pinwheels."

Jennifer blinked up at me, then took a mushroom tart. Her friends were more dubious, but they finally helped themselves to a couple of pinwheels. I gave them another smile and trotted toward the hors d'oeuvres set-up, avoiding the table with the groomsmen.

Donnell and Jerry were circulating with their platters. I replenished the trays of hors d'oeuvres quickly and hoped they'd start dinner soon because we were almost out of the preliminary stuff.

Apparently, I wasn't the only one who'd noticed we were running low. "When are you bringing out the dinner?" someone said at my elbow.

I turned to see Emerson Pollack glaring up at me. He was dressed like the other high rollers around the room, but it didn't do anything to improve his general demeanor. He still looked like a toad, only now he was a toad in a two-thousand-dollar suit.

"We're ready to serve whenever you and your guests are ready to take your seats." That wasn't entirely true since we hadn't plated the stew yet, but the salad was already on the table.

Pollack appeared ready to fume. I decided to direct his fuming where it might do more good. "Maybe you should talk to Ms. Rosenberg. Perhaps she can get people to sit down." *Sorry, Thalia, but better you than me.* I picked up the tray and went back to the kitchen. *Not my circus, not my monkeys.*

Nate was setting up the bowls for the stew when I got back, which meant we were ready for another go-round. This time Nate dipped stew into the bowls, and I sprinkled chopped parsley on top. Jerry swung through the door as we were about halfway through.

"They're just sitting down now," he said. "Ms. Rosenberg is playing sheep dog, herding them all to the tables."

"Are there place cards?" I asked, thinking of the table the groomsmen had already commandeered.

Jerry shook his head. "They're sitting wherever they want to. Bride and her friends are up front, but the groom's still drinking with his buddies."

Which confirmed my fears about the groom being one of the drunks. "Thalia will probably take care of it."

"Dunno," Jerry mused. "I think it'd be better to leave him in the corner. He's not likely to add much to the front table."

"Okay," Nate said, "take five. Once they finish the salads, you guys can start clearing. Then we'll do the stew and the bread baskets."

"Want us to put the bread out now?"

Nate sighed. "They'd just start on it before we could get the stew on the table. Wait until they're ready for the next course."

Jerry nodded and stepped toward the dining room again with an empty tray for the salad plates. I'd started loading the bowls on a tray so that we could free up some space on the worktable when the kitchen door swung open again. I glanced up, expecting to see Donnell.

Instead, I saw a very annoyed looking Marla Purdue. "Well," she said, hands on her hips, "where the hell are we supposed to put the cake in all this mess?"

Chapter 9

Marla didn't much resemble a baker at the moment. Her black slacks and sweater with white puffer jacket showed she was off duty. She and Nate exchanged the same sort of *Who the hell are you?* looks.

I cleared my throat. "I don't know if you two have met. Nate, this is Marla Purdue, the baker. Marla, this is Nate Robicheaux, the caterer." *And may the best person win.*

Neither of them seemed all that happy to meet the other. "You've got all the counter space taken up with your dishes," she snapped. "Where am I supposed to put the cake?"

I could tell Nate was considering just where she could put it, and things wouldn't end well. "I'll go get Thalia," I said. "She can tell you where the cake is supposed to go. I'm sure it's not going to be hidden here in the kitchen."

That was my clumsy attempt to keep Marla from sniping at Nate, which would result in him sniping back. As I stepped out the kitchen door, I saw him return to filling the bowls with stew, a much better use of his time than telling Marla Purdue she was an idiot.

No matter how much she might deserve to hear those words.

I found Thalia watching the guests demolish their salads. She didn't look happy, but then she hadn't looked happy at any point so far this evening. "Hey," I said. "Marla's in the kitchen. She wants to know what to do with the cake."

Thalia closed her eyes briefly, maybe in prayer. "Thank you, Jesus. I was afraid she wasn't going to show." She spun on her heel and marched toward the kitchen. I followed in her wake.

Marla stood with her hands on her hips, pointedly ignoring Nate as he filled the stew bowls. She narrowed her eyes at Thalia. "Where do you want the cake?"

"In the dining room. We might as well show it off before we cut it up." Of course, if Marla had brought the cake earlier in the evening, people could have admired it a bit longer.

Marla and Thalia made for the dining room again, and I grabbed my bowl of chopped parsley to catch up with Nate.

"What a jerk," he muttered.

I couldn't argue with him. Marla might have been the queen of wedding cake designers for all I knew, but she sorely lacked people skills. Maybe when you were a big-time wedding cake designer, you didn't need them, although I decided then and there that I'd never order a cake from her if I could help it.

Donnell swung through the door, carrying a tray full of salad plates. "They're finishing up." Jerry followed her, stacking dishes near the dishwasher.

"Yeah, we started loading the stew onto trays for you." Nate nodded toward the stew bowls. "You might want to take up the bread and butter first, so people have it when they get their stew."

"Got it. I'll take the bread and then come back." Donnell loaded the bread baskets and butter crocks onto her tray and departed.

"I'll get started on the main. We've got enough of the salad plates cleared away." Jerry hefted the tray with the stew to his shoulder and started toward the kitchen door just as it flew open from the other side.

Jerry staggered away, managing to keep his feet and keep his tray balanced on his shoulder, as one of the frat boys leaned into the kitchen and squinted at us. "Is the bar through here?"

Nate's jaw looked sculpted from granite, but he managed to keep his voice level. "This is the kitchen. There's no bar in here."

The guy looked confused. "Oh, yeah? Where is it then?"

Judging from Nate's expression, he was about to take a strip off the groomsman's hide, but Thalia's assistant, Beverly, appeared in the nick of time. "There's no bar tonight, Mr. Lukens. Like Ms. Rosenberg said, there's only wine."

Mr. Lukens scowled, which did nothing for his round moon face. "Not much of a party if it's just wine."

"It's your engagement party, Mr. Lukens. That's a different kind of event. There should be an open bar at the wedding reception." Beverly sounded like she was talking through clenched teeth, not that I blamed her. "Let's let these people get on with serving dinner. Everyone's hungry. I'm sure you'll enjoy the stew." She took Lukens by the arm and marched him toward the tables.

"Yeah," Jerry muttered. "Let's do that." He pushed through the door, his tray still balanced on his shoulder. So far as I could tell, he hadn't spilled a drop of stew. A pro.

Nate refilled the pot he was using to carry the stew around the worktable. "Groomsman?"

"Groom, sounds like. Beverly called it *your engagement party*." Jennifer Pollack seemed like a nice girl. She deserved better than Lukens. On the other hand, maybe he was a sweetheart when he hadn't been drinking for a couple of hours.

Nate blew out a breath. "Lord help us. We're going to have to deal with this crew again at the reception."

"Maybe."

There were over a hundred guests slated to be at the reception, so maybe it figured the same people would show up at both. At least Pollack had decided the reception would be a buffet, although Nate would have to take control of the carving station with the beef tenderloin, and I'd probably be serving the salmon.

Donnell swung through the door again with the last of the salad plates. "It's going good. Load me up and I'll get out there."

Nate and I placed bowls of stew on her tray, and she pushed through the door again. Fortunately for all of us, nobody tried to come into the kitchen as she was going out. Nate and I were both a little nervous about it, though.

Jerry and Donnell came and went a couple more times, and then we were down to the last few bowls. Jerry loaded up his tray with an ironic salute to Nate. "Looks like it's a success. Even the drunks are eating."

"Great," Nate said dryly. "Maybe it'll help them sober up."

"Doubt it. Those boys have been partying for a while."

Nate held the door open for Jerry as I started loading the salad plates in the dishwasher. Technically, the event center staff took care of cleanup, but we needed the space. Besides, I was enough of a neat freak to want the dirty dishes out of sight. I had the plates around two-thirds loaded when Thalia came in again. She gave Nate a smile that wasn't much more than a muscle twitch. "I need to impose upon you both. Again."

Nate leaned against the counter. "What's up?"

"I need someone to slice the cake and put it onto serving plates. I thought Marla was supplying someone, but she didn't."

Sometimes we served the wedding cake, but more often, the baker took care of cutting up the cake into even slices. After all, the wedding cake was sometimes an architectural wonder that needed careful slicing. In this case, Marla had dumped her cake and hit the road, which seemed to go along with the way she'd behaved so far.

Nate frowned. "We can do that, I guess. How complicated is the cake?"

"Not complicated at all. It's close to a sheet cake, in fact." Thalia grimaced. "Marla didn't put a lot of effort into this one, but then it was a very last-minute order."

I couldn't blame the woman for not knocking herself out. After all, she'd only had a few days to get everything ready. Even a jerk like Marla needed time to do her best. Still, Thalia would most likely be letting Marla know just what she thought of the decision to leave her holding the knife, so to speak. "Is there a slicing knife?"

Thalia nodded. "And a server. And plates. Everything is set to go if the two of you can do the slicing and plating."

"We can, I guess." Nate surveyed the room. "Everything we prepared is already out there. I don't think they'll be coming to us for refills."

"I'll make sure they don't," Thalia said grimly.

We followed her across the dining room, where everyone was eating and drinking happily enough. The cake had been set up on a table at the side of the room, which was covered with one of Thalia's beautiful cloths and sported an elegant floral arrangement.

And then there was the cake itself.

Thalia hadn't exaggerated. It looked a lot like a sheet cake with a more elaborate raised square layer in the middle. Granted, it was a sheet cake adorned with some gorgeous golden-brown frosting that had been piped around the sides and scalloped along the edges. There were yellow accents here and there, setting off the rich undertone of the brown. Clusters of sugared grapes and blackberries had been arranged around the inner layer and the corners of the outer sheet layer. It wasn't exactly gorgeous, but it was several steps above the kind of sheet cake you could get at a grocery store. Still, it reminded me vaguely of an Old West fort, with its outer perimeter and inner guard tower. Or maybe an adobe pueblo—all it needed were some miniature ladders.

Dessert plates were stacked near the cake, along with a silver slicing knife and a cake server. They resembled family heirlooms.

Nate sighed, studying the cake. "I guess we'll need to lift off the inner layer before we start slicing. Did they want to save it?"

We'd learned from working with wedding cakes that lots of brides saved the top layer for their first anniversary, particularly if it had a cake topper. I didn't know if that applied to an engagement party cake, though. There didn't seem to be much worth saving.

Thalia shrugged. "Nobody told me they wanted to

save anything. I think this one is strictly for on-site consumption."

"Right. Let's get to it then." Nate studied the cake, doing the mental math involved in slicing the cake up into fifty equal pieces. "How many people in the bride's and groom's families? They're the ones who should get the second layer."

I could see his point. The inner layer was more elaborately frosted and ornate, if you can describe a cake that way.

Thalia paused, doing some mental math of her own. "I'd say ten. That includes the bride and the groom, along with the parents and sibs."

"I'm thinking the groom may not be up to eating cake." Nate picked up the slicing knife. "But we'll cut them some slices just in case."

Between the two of us, we got the inner layer lifted off and removed the piece of parchment beneath it that protected the frosting on the sheet cake. Fortunately, the inner layer was also square, which made cutting equal-sized pieces a lot easier. Once we started cutting, we could see the cake beneath the frosting. It looked delectable—golden yellow with more mocha-colored frosting between the layers.

Thalia stood at the side and watched as Nate cut the cake with precision and placed each slice on a plate that I held for him. The inner layer made ten decent-sized slices that each had ample frosting, leaving the outer cake to be distributed among the lesser mortals.

Donnell stepped up as we were finishing, tray in hand. "Who gets those?"

"Bride, groom, parents, and family. I'll point everybody out." Thalia marched purposefully to the edge of the room and showed her where to place the best pieces. I saw Jerry beginning to clear the stew bowls.

"Do they want these now, or do they do speeches first?" Nate asked.

Thalia grimaced. "No one said anything about speeches. Let's go ahead and serve the cake. They can have speeches while they eat dessert."

And we'd be finished with the evening although neither Nate nor I pointed that out. It was obvious. We'd have to clean up and take our own equipment to the catering kitchen, but we'd be done with the business of serving Mr. Toad and his guests for the time being.

At least until the wedding reception.

Donnell and Jerry started clearing the tables with admirable efficiency. They were probably as eager as we were for this to be over. Normally, we might have expected a bonus, but Mr. Toad wasn't the bonus type. I doubted he'd tip the servers either. Fortunately, Nate had charged him a lot more than our usual fees to get this meal and the reception done in short order, and he'd already given them a healthy raise for this event.

Nate and I got a routine going quickly, with him slicing and me placing the pieces on the plates. Donnell and Jerry loaded the pieces onto their trays although she let him take over after the first few tables so that she could go to the kitchen and bring coffee for those who wanted it.

I kept expecting someone to stand up and be the host for this shindig, maybe tell a few jokes or share some maudlin anecdotes. Surely somebody from the families would have something to say about Jennifer and her groom. Of course, from what I'd seen, neither the groom nor his men were in any shape to be telling stories in mixed company. I wished Donnell would pour them some coffee, but I didn't know how much good it would do. Probably turn them into wide-awake drunks.

Finally, after most of the guests had been served their cake, Mr. Toad got to his feet. We were close to done with the cake cutting and serving, but I was curious to see what he'd say. Maybe Nate was too because he slowed down his pace with the final few pieces of cake. Thalia stepped up beside Mr. Toad and flipped on the microphone as the room gradually quieted.

Mr. Toad surveyed the room with his bulbous eyes, like he was searching for flies. "Thanks for coming," he said finally. "We appreciate it. All the best to Jennifer and Trent. Enjoy your night." He walked to his table as the volume of conversation rose again.

Nate turned to me. "That's it?"

"Apparently." I lifted the last two slices of cake onto plates. "How many more?"

Nate studied the stack of plates. "Judging from the plates, around ten more slices."

"I suppose Mr. Toad would hit the ceiling if we ate any of his cake." It really did look delicious.

"I doubt he'd notice. He hasn't even glanced over here since we started serving."

I placed the last few pieces of cake on the plates. The whole evening had been weird. The guests hadn't taken much notice of Jennifer and her groom, and neither had Pollack until he'd made his speech. It might have been an engagement party technically, but nobody had seemed particularly interested in the engagement.

I took another quick survey of the head table. Jennifer Pollack hadn't touched her cake, which still sat in front of her place at the table. Her friends were almost ignoring her. She raised her gaze for a moment and stared off at the snow falling beyond the windows. She looked less like a bride counting down the hours to her wedding than like a hostage who desperately wanted to get away.

"Oh, geez," I murmured.

"What?"

I took a deep breath. "Nothing. Let's get this cleared away so we can clean up and get out of here." Seldom had I been more anxious to get away from a job.

We left the slicing knife and the cake server on the table next to the remaining pieces of cake. We'd sliced everything up, and there were only a few pieces left. I figured anyone who wanted another piece of cake could take them. And whoever had provided the knife and server could come and get them.

I followed Nate to the kitchen. The dishwasher had finished the salad plates and the implements we'd thrown in, so we wouldn't have to pack them dirty. I started unloading everything, stacking the clean plates on the counter where the event center staff could find them since I had no idea where they were stored. "I'll load the stew bowls in and get this going before we leave. It won't hold all of them, but we won't leave the place stacked full of dirty dishes."

Nate gave me a dry smile. "My guess is that's what they expect to find after an event, but go ahead. I'll load up the pans in the SUV."

We'd take the pans to the catering kitchen, so that Tres could load them into the café's super-efficient dishwasher the next day. I checked my watch. We were getting away before ten, plenty of time to go home and put our feet up.

The kitchen door swung open, and Donnell entered, carrying a plate with a piece of cake and a fork. "Everything's breaking up in the dining room. People ate their cake and grabbed their coats."

"Not surprising. The snow's really coming down." Plus it hadn't been the kind of dinner where people wanted to sit around and exchange confidences after it was over.

"Yeah." Donnell put a bite of cake in her mouth, forehead furrowing.

"Is it good?" I asked.

"Sort of." She sounded like she wasn't entirely sure.

I grabbed a fork of my own and took my own bite. It was...flavorful. Sort of. I could taste almond and butter. But it was also sort of dry. The frosting was luscious, but the cake itself was disappointing. "Looked great, but texture's a little off."

"Yep. Tastes like it's been sitting around a while."

Jerry stepped into the kitchen with a load of dessert dishes. "Cleaning crew's in the dining room."

"Already?" They must have been waiting downstairs.

"It's just one guy. With one of those sweepers like a Zamboni." He grabbed a fork of his own, leaning toward the cake. "Glad you grabbed one of those. Looked like they were going to waste."

Donnell handed him the plate. "Nobody wanted a second helping, most likely."

Jerry took a bite. "Could be worse. Frosting's great."

Nate stepped into the kitchen, stamping his feet to knock off the snow. "Better get going. Looks like the snow's picking up." He reached into his pocket and pulled out an envelope of cash that he divided between them. "Here you go. We picked up a premium for doing this at the last minute."

Jerry smiled as he tucked the cash into his pocket. "Not bad. Not that much work for a last-minute gig."

"Got that right. I've had worse." Donnell nodded at us both. "Better get away yourselves. See you." She zipped up her parka and pulled on her gloves as she walked out the door to the parking lot.

"You ready to go?" Nate asked.

"Pretty much. Did you check to see if Thalia's still around? I saw her talking to Pollack. She might have some last-minute stuff to tell us."

Nate grimaced. "Grab your coat. We can check for her and then keep going out the front entrance. Thalia can always call tomorrow if she's got something to pass on."

I followed him into the dining room where the janitor was running the Zamboni-style sweeper around the room. I didn't see Thalia or anybody else. "Looks like she's gone."

"Probably," Nate said. "Everybody else has taken off. Let's take one more pass at the stairs."

He stepped out the doors that led to the stairwell. It looked pretty dark to me, but as I stepped onto the landing, I heard something that sounded like a sob. For a moment I pictured Jennifer Pollack staring out at the falling snow like she wanted to escape. I hoped she hadn't been left behind by mistake "Did you hear that?"

"What?" Nate turned to stare at me.

"That sound. It was over…" As I started across the landing toward the stairs, I heard another sob, much louder this time, coming from the stairs leading down to the lower floor. "Is anybody there?" I called.

"Roxy?" It sounded like Thalia, but a very different Thalia from the normal, terrifyingly efficient woman we'd been working with. I stepped quickly to the landing and peered toward the lower floor.

And saw Thalia Rosenberg leading over Emerson Pollack, who lay spread-eagled on the concrete floor.

From where I stood, he looked very dead.

Chapter 10

I ran down the steps, which is to say I went down quickly, not exactly running. The stairwell was very dark although the light from above streamed down on Pollack's body where it lay. Nate was at my heels.

Thalia knelt beside Pollack, her face the color of the snow still falling outside. "We need to call an ambulance," she said. "He's…hurt."

Judging by the way Pollack was splayed on the floor, I didn't think an ambulance would do much good. I put my hand on her shoulder. "Come on, Thalia. Step away from him now."

Nate had climbed up the stairs and was now speaking urgently into his phone. I heard the words "accident" and "serious injuries," which might well be true, as far as the "serious injuries" went. I was less certain about the "accident" part. Still, he was talking to the police, who were better equipped than us to figure out what had happened.

Thalia looked like she might faint or have hysterics, neither of which I wanted to deal with right then. A pool of blood spread under Pollack's body; some had soaked into the hem of Thalia's bright blue suit. I didn't think she'd noticed. I couldn't see any good reason for her to go on kneeling next to Pollack's body.

He obviously wasn't in any condition to need her help.

Thalia leaned toward me, her brown eyes huge in her pale face. "Oh my God," she whispered. "My God. He's dead, isn't he?"

"Looks like it." I pulled her a little farther away from the body just as I heard the sound of sirens outside. The Shavano Police Department had taken Nate seriously when he'd told them we needed help.

"Did he fall?" Thalia said, her voice trembling. "I didn't hear anything."

"Maybe," I said.

"He looks so…flat." Her voice was rising, and she sounded much closer to the faint or hysterics option I'd sensed earlier.

"The police will figure it out." I took her elbow and nudged her gently toward the stairs. "That's what they do."

One flight up, I heard someone banging on the front door. Nate was already undoing the front door lock, while the guy who'd been running the Zamboni peered out of the dining room. "What's going on?" he called. No one bothered to answer him.

Nate got the door open, and I heard a lot of voices, including Nate trying to explain what had happened. I edged up the stairs, still holding Thalia's arm. Then I heard a very familiar voice, one I'd been expecting. "Well, well. Nate Robicheaux and Roxy Constantine. Here you are again."

I've known Chief Ethan Fowler for a couple of years now, and he dates my best friend, Susa Sondergaard, off and on. I've also been involved in several murders he's investigated. Not as the murderer, of course. Sort of by chance. Unfortunately, I just happened to turn up at places where people were killed though I had nothing to do with their deaths.

"Evening, Chief," I said.

Fowler squinted over the stair railing, then back at me. "Who's the guy on the floor? Anyone you know?"

"His name's Emerson Pollack. His daughter's engagement party was here tonight. We catered."

"What happened to him?" Fowler's voice had that neutral tone that he used when he was dealing with witnesses.

"I don't know," I said. "We were just leaving when we heard Thalia scream. He was there on the floor when we came."

"Thalia?" Fowler raised an eyebrow.

"I'm Thalia Rosenberg. I'm the wedding planner in charge of the dinner tonight." She'd pulled herself together although she still looked like she could use a stiff drink.

Fowler had surreptitiously pulled out his notebook and was writing down Thalia's name. So far as I knew, he had no connection to weddings in Shavano, so he'd probably never heard of her. "You found him?" he asked.

Thalia nodded jerkily. "I was leaving. I happened to glance down as I was going to the door." She took a deep breath, very deliberately not looking toward Pollack.

"You were leaving without a coat?" Fowler asked mildly.

"I have a coat," Thalia said, then realized that she didn't. She was standing there in her bright blue bloodstained suit and nothing else. Looking a little desperate, she gazed around. "What happened to it?"

"Is that it?" I pointed to a dark puffer coat lying at the bottom of the stairs.

"Oh." Thalia closed her eyes. "Yes. I must have

dropped it when I got down there. I wanted to see if he was still…breathing." She took a couple of deep breaths of her own.

Fowler nodded as if that made perfect sense. "Did you touch him?"

Thalia closed her eyes, and once again I was afraid she might faint. "No. Once I got close to him, he didn't seem—"

"Good," Fowler said. "But you got close enough to get blood on your skirt."

Thalia stared down, horrified. "Oh, no. Oh, no, no."

I stepped forward, putting my arm around her shoulders. "It's okay. Don't worry. You can change after you get home." I didn't bother suggesting she could get the suit cleaned. Both of us knew she'd be throwing it into the trash.

"What happened next?" Fowler asked.

Thalia made a visible effort to get herself under control. "When I realized he was…that I couldn't help him, I guess I made a noise. And then I heard Roxy upstairs."

Fowler looked at me. "I heard Thalia scream," I said. "So I went to the stairwell and saw Pollack on the floor and Thalia next to him. I went downstairs, and Nate called you."

"Why were you up there?" Fowler gestured toward the first floor.

"We'd finished with cleanup after the dinner, and we were going home by way of the dining room. We thought we'd check to see if Thalia was still here or if she'd left for the night. We were going to go out the front door to the parking lot."

Fowler nodded. "Did you see anyone else around?"

"Just the janitor. He was running the vacuum cleaner in the dining room."

"Did you see anyone, Ms. Rosenberg?"

Thalia shook her head. "Just the man cleaning. Everyone else had left earlier."

"Except for Mr. Pollack. Did you see him leave the dining room?"

"No," I said. "We finished cutting the cake, and then we went to the kitchen while people were still eating. I didn't see him or any of the other guests after that." I could be positive about that. We'd been busy getting stuff packed away and cleaning up.

Thalia frowned. "I'm not sure. He made a speech—well, more like a few words—after dinner. And then he talked to a few people. I didn't see him after that. I was making sure we had everything from the dinner taken care of, and Jennifer had some questions. By the time she left, I thought he must have left, too. I thought they'd come together. Anyway, I didn't see him after that."

Thalia had turned her back on the scene at the foot of the stairs. There were several people around the body now, including a couple of medics who were clearly superfluous. The forensics guys were doing their thing, and I wondered if they'd want her shoes. Surely, they'd let her drive home first.

"Who's Jennifer?" Fowler asked.

"The bride," I said. "Pollack is her father. Was."

We all went quiet, realizing that someone was going to have to break the news to Jennifer Pollack. Probably Fowler. "Do you have her address?" he asked.

"In my purse." Thalia took a deep breath. "It's down there." She gestured toward her coat, still heaped on the floor near Pollack's body.

Fowler folded his notebook back in his pocket, then walked down the stairs to Thalia's coat. He gestured one of the CSI guys over and conferred with him for a moment, then leaned down and picked up Thalia's purse from where it had landed a foot or so away. He brought it to where we were standing. Thalia took it from him gratefully, digging through to find her planner.

"Do you need us to stick around?" I asked. I was even more anxious to get away from the event center than I had been before.

"I know where to find you." Fowler's lips edged up into one of his sardonic grins. Of course, he knew where to find Nate and me. He'd been through this before with us.

I turned to Thalia. "Will you be okay? Would you like us to drive you home?"

"Ms. Rosenberg needs to stay a little longer," Fowler said easily. "We'll make sure she gets home."

Thalia gave me an uncertain look. I guessed she wasn't sure why the police chief wanted to keep her around for a while longer when Nate and I were leaving. I wasn't sure either, but I knew better than to argue. "Okay," I said to Thalia. "I'll see you tomorrow, I guess."

Thalia closed her eyes. "I don't know. I don't know what's going to happen now. After—" She gestured toward Pollack.

Hard as it may be to believe, I hadn't really grasped all the implications of Pollack's death until then. If Pollack was dead, what happened to Jennifer's wedding? Did it go forward as planned? Was it postponed indefinitely? What about all the expensive food Nate had ordered? Pollack had paid for it, but what happened if the wedding didn't take place? Chances of cancelling the order were nil. We'd need to ask somebody for clarification very soon.

"Oh, hell," I murmured.

Thalia sighed. "Exactly."

Fowler's eyebrows went up, but he didn't ask us any questions. He probably had other things on his mind at the moment.

Nate put his hand on my shoulder. "Ready to go?"

"Sure." I turned to Thalia. "Call us if you need anything. We'll be up for a while."

She nodded a little absently, as if she was still trying to work everything out in her own mind.

We drove straight to the farm, without bothering to unload the pots at the catering kitchen. Neither of us was in the mood to be conscientious right then. "Do we need to call your mom?" I asked, leaving out the somewhat delicate point that she might well be at the farm herself, up at the main house with Uncle Mike.

"Yeah, I'll do it. This isn't likely to have any blowback on us. We were just the caterers, and there were a ton of other people involved. But I'd like her to hear about it from us before she sees it on the news."

"Plus there's Thalia. They're friends. Your mom might want to go over to her place."

"Maybe."

We didn't say much else before we got to the cabin. Both of us were trying to make sense of what we'd seen. Murder at an engagement party just didn't feel right. Of course, murder doesn't feel right in most circumstances, but weddings in particular were far removed from violence.

Except, of course, they weren't. How many times

had we wanted to throttle some members of a wedding party because they were being unnecessarily difficult? And we didn't do that many weddings. How many more times had it happened to Thalia, who dealt with weddings on a more or less daily basis?

She'd no doubt seen hundreds of bridezillas and outrageous wedding parents. She must know how to deal with them and how to keep herself from tipping over the edge into murderous rage. The idea that Thalia would kill Pollack was ludicrous. Really.

Nate went off to call Madge while I checked to see what kind of alcohol we had in the refrigerator. I wanted a glass or two. After a moment, Nate came up the hall. "Mom's going to call Thalia and see how she's doing." He dropped his phone onto the coffee table. "We'll need to talk to her tomorrow to see what's going to happen with the wedding."

I narrowed my eyes. "It can't be going forward. Not six weeks after the FOB was killed, possibly by someone at his daughter's engagement party. At the very least it'll be postponed. At worst, cancelled."

Nate paused. "You think it was murder?"

"I don't know." I bit my lip. "He might have fallen by accident. That stairwell is steep, and it was dark in the foyer."

Nate shook his head. "He'd have had to flip himself over the railing. It was above waist height on me and I'm taller than Pollack was."

Both of us were taller than Pollack, and I hadn't felt even slightly at risk of falling over the railing when I'd stood next to it. "Does that mean somebody pushed him?"

"If they did, they did it quietly, which doesn't seem

realistic. I mean, you have to figure Pollack would have made some noise if somebody was trying to shove him over the railing, and nobody heard anything."

"Nobody heard anything as far as we know," I countered. "If it happened after everybody left, the sound of the vacuum sweeper could have covered up any noise as far as we were concerned."

"True, although that would mean Pollack stayed later than everybody else for some reason." Nate headed toward the refrigerator and pulled out a couple of beers. "You want one?"

I sighed. "Sure." I was dead tired, but I was also sure I'd be wide awake if I tried to go to sleep just then. "What's going to happen to the food you bought for the wedding?"

"The stuff that's been delivered is frozen." He handed me a beer and took a swig of his own. "The deposit will pay for that. I ordered some fresh stuff for hors d'oeuvres and salad, but it hasn't been delivered yet, and I may be able to cancel it. The meat and the salmon won't go bad. I need to see if I can cancel the asparagus order, and I'll call Bianca tomorrow and cancel the bread order for now. At some point we'll need to confer with whoever will be in charge of this wedding, see how they want to proceed. But we haven't taken any financial hit. Yet."

"Did Pollack pay you for the rehearsal dinner?"

Nate dropped onto the couch beside me, sliding his arm around my shoulders. "Oh, yeah. That's what that envelope of cash was that I used to pay Donnell and Jerry. He passed that to me after dinner."

"He paid the balance in cash?" It went without saying that we seldom got paid that way. Mostly we got credit cards, payment apps, and the occasional check. The only time we got cash as a rule was when somebody gave us a bonus or tips for the servers.

"It wasn't just the balance of the rehearsal dinner," Nate said. "He paid for *everything* in cash—deposits, payments, everything. I've been running it to the bank every few days."

"That's weird." It also sounded faintly shady, but I couldn't think of any law we were violating by taking cash payments.

"It's unusual." Nate shrugged, pulling me closer. "I didn't care how he paid us as long as he paid. I've had credit cards get declined, checks bounce. Cash doesn't bounce. That's the main advantage." He gave me a tired smile.

"Right." I dropped my head to his shoulder and tried to relax. But it still struck me as odd. This last-minute wedding was costing a fortune, a fortune the FOB had on hand. He was paying out thousands of dollars in cash, assuming that Thalia and people like Marla Purdue were getting paid the same way.

"Could somebody have tried to rob him?" I mused. "He was carrying a lot of cash around if he was paying everybody tonight. If somebody saw him paying you or Marla, they might have decided to stick a gun in his ribs or something."

"No one was around when he paid me. We were out in the front hall, and everybody else was still inside the dining room."

Nate paused, and I guessed we were both thinking the same thing. The front hall was where Pollack had been killed. Maybe he'd tried to pay someone else, and they'd decided to take more than they were owed.

"I think I was the only one he was paying tonight, unless he owed Thalia for something she'd picked up for him." Nate picked up his beer again. "I'm guessing Purdue wouldn't have brought the cake if it hadn't been paid for in full. No advance deposits for a baker."

"No, she'd have expected to be paid before she created the cake." I settled a little lower on the couch. "Besides, I doubt Pollack even spoke to her. She came into the kitchen and then she and Thalia carried the cake to the serving table. And the serving table was at the side of the room, away from the guests."

Nate took another swallow of his beer. "We're both leaping to a lot of conclusions here. We don't even know for sure that Pollack was murdered. It could have been an accident."

"Could have been but probably wasn't," I said. "Murder makes more sense."

Nate narrowed his eyes. "Are you just saying that because you thought he was obnoxious?"

"You thought so, too." I put my beer down on the table. "And I'm saying it makes more sense because we both agree it would be tough for Pollack to go over that railing unaided. And it's a nasty way to commit suicide, not that I think anyone would believe he did that. He was busy with too many things to leap over that railing on his own."

Nate settled farther into his chair. "You want something to eat? It's late for delivery, but I could do some eggs."

"How about just some chips and salsa? I don't need a full meal tonight." Plus I didn't think either one of us was up to cooking one.

"Good idea. I'll warm up some queso." Nate started

for the kitchen, and I stepped into the pantry to locate a bag of chips. "You think Fowler's going to want to talk to us? I don't know what more we can tell him than we've already passed on."

"He'll probably want to know what we know about Pollack, but that won't be much." Nate dumped the jar of queso into a bowl. "As far as the murder's concerned, we weren't anywhere near where it happened, and we were together in the kitchen. My guess is, this is one murder we won't have any connection to besides being in the same building where it took place."

"Always assuming it's murder," I added. "This one might actually be an accident, even though it doesn't seem likely."

"Right." Nate put the bowl of queso into the microwave to heat. "For once I think we're out of the loop."

I rapped my knuckles on the wooden pantry door. "Here's hoping."

"Here's hoping," Nate repeated and smiled at me.

I did hope we were out of the loop this time.

But I knew better than to count on it.

Chapter 11

The next morning, we had a load of dirty pots and pans in the back of the SUV that needed to be taken to the catering kitchen. I volunteered to drive in behind Nate and then help him unload. I had a case of jam I needed to take to Bianca Jordan's bakery, but then I'd drive to the cabin to do some more jam-making, given that I hadn't done much for the past few days.

We were carrying the cartons of equipment into the catering kitchen when Madge stepped through the connecting door from the café. "Is that from last night?"

I nodded. "Yeah. We decided we'd bring it in today rather than coming here after we finished."

"Of course you did," Madge said staunchly. "You needed to go home and relax after everything that happened."

"How's Thalia?" I asked. Madge would most likely have called her last night, which might give us some idea of whether she'd be up to figuring out the wedding disaster today.

Madge's jaw firmed. "They made her stay for an hour, can you believe it? And then Ethan sent a policewoman home with her to take her shoes and her suit. Outrageous!"

"Well, she stepped in Pollack's blood, and she got some on her skirt. They probably just wanted to match them to any marks around the body." That sounded a lot more authoritative than I felt. In reality, I wasn't sure why they'd need Thalia's stuff, but I guessed Fowler was making sure he didn't let any detail slip by.

Madge looked properly horrified. "This whole wedding has been a disaster from the get-go. I'll bet Thalia wishes she'd never gotten involved with that awful man."

"Probably. Although she must have a lot of experience dealing with awful customers," I said. "Weddings can bring out the worst in some people."

Madge sighed. "Yes, she has. But Pollack wasn't just a customer."

I paused. "What was he?" I couldn't believe Pollack and Thalia had any romantic connection. Thalia had better taste.

"He was one of the original investors in Thalia's business," Madge explained. "That's one of the reasons she was willing to take on this wedding at the last minute."

"He was? Thalia never mentioned that." Which seemed odd, given the number of times we'd complained about Pollack.

Madge shrugged. "I don't think she wanted people to know about it. I thought she'd paid off all the investors by now, since her business is so successful. But she may not have paid him in full yet. I guess that means his daughter will take over whatever is left of the original loan he made to her. Assuming the loan hasn't been entirely paid off."

"I guess." I was still trying to decide if this was important news or just an interesting sidelight.

"So anyway," Madge went on, "I think I'll ask Thalia to help with The Wedding. It'll give her something to do."

I stared at her. "Why would Thalia need something to do? She's usually up to her ears in clients."

"She had to cancel all her December clients to deal with the Pollack wedding. He insisted on it."

That news qualified as more than just an interesting sidelight. "December's a huge wedding month. She would have lost a lot of money doing that."

"Which is why I want her to take over The Wedding," Madge said firmly. "It may not be much, but it's still a paying job. And it'll help keep her mind off everything else."

I was still trying to decide if this was a good idea. On the one hand, it would take the pressure off Madge and should get the wedding moving again. On the other hand, I wasn't sure Thalia would want to get involved in the mess that was The Wedding. Still, she could always say no.

"Okay," I said. "Let me know what she says." At which point I would gladly turn everything over to her, including the still-evolving guest list. We'd gotten most of the invitations sent out, but we were still getting last-minute additions from Madge.

After we'd finished unloading the pots, I walked over to Bianca's bakery to deliver the jam and to tell her the wedding order was currently on hold. For once Bianca was out at the bakery counter, along with the ever-cheerful Sharon.

Only Sharon wasn't particularly cheerful at the moment. Bianca was holding two loaves of bread in her hands. "This one is Swedish rye," she said. "This one is pumpernickel. Just check the tags. Plus the pumpernickel is darker than the rye."

"They taste sort of similar to me," Sharon said stubbornly.

"They're both varieties of rye bread, but they're not the same rye bread." Bianca sounded like she was working hard to keep calm. "And believe me, people who want pumpernickel won't be happy with Swedish rye. It's lighter and sweeter than pumpernickel. That's why you need to keep them in separate bins."

Sharon's expression became mulish. "All I did was offer Mr. Dietrich rye bread when we were out of pumpernickel. I didn't try to deceive him or anything."

Bianca blew out a long breath. "Right. Okay. Just don't do it again. If we're out of pumpernickel, we're out of pumpernickel." She turned toward me. "Hey, Roxy, you here about that wedding order?"

"And I brought you some jam." Maybe that would take some of the sting out of the possibly cancelled order.

"Put it on the counter. Sharon can add it to the display and update the database." Bianca gave her a narrow-eyed glance, and Sharon got to work on the case.

Back in Bianca's workroom, she gave me a receipt. "Here you go. Everything's moving well for the holidays, so I should need another case in a couple of weeks. Assuming Sharon gets it all out on the counter."

"Sharon having problems?"

"She means well." Bianca's tone of voice made it clear that *meaning well* was not necessarily a plus. "What's up with this wedding? Somebody got killed last night?"

I nodded. "Father of the bride. Everything's on hold for now until we know if and when the wedding's going to happen. Nate says he'll let you know on the bread."

"Figured as much." Bianca shrugged. "No big deal.

I've got holiday orders out the wazoo anyway. So who killed him, anybody know?"

"No idea. I don't even know if he was killed or if he fell down the stairs by accident." That was my story, and I was definitely sticking to it.

"Thalia was there?"

"Yeah. So were Nate and I. She found him and we called the cops."

"Tough. What does Fowler say?"

"I haven't talked to him about it." Although I was pretty sure I would be talking to him about it soon.

"Whole town's buzzing, but it'll die down." Bianca grinned. "At least it's distracted people from the usual Thanksgiving nuttiness."

Which reminded me—we were supposed to be in charge of a large part of this year's usual Thanksgiving nuttiness. "Everybody all set for the big feed?"

Bianca nodded. "By my count we've got around fifty people coming, but I'd figure on seventy just to be sure. Lots of sides. Are you keeping tabs on who's bringing what?"

"Coco is." Theoretically, anyway. Coco was supposed to have a spreadsheet somewhere around the café's kitchen where she wrote down what people told her.

"I'll make enough rolls for the multitude. And Marcus is bringing sausage dressing." Bianca's son, Marcus, was the town's leading artisan butcher. Also Coco's main squeeze.

"Okay, I'll let Nate and Bobby know about the numbers, so they can make sure we've got enough." The two of them were in charge of the turkey and ham part of the meal.

"Do that." Bianca was glancing at her worktable as if she had things to do, and I had jam to make myself.

"See you later," I said. "I'll let you know what happens with the wedding."

Bianca began pouring ingredients into one of her massive bread bowls. Time to get going.

Back at the cabin, I had a double purpose. On one hand, I needed to make more raspberry jam along with some peach preserves. Dolce had put up a goodly supply of strawberry, and I didn't have enough apricots to do anything with them yet. At the same time, I needed to start working on the red wine jam so I could start filling the miniature jars I was using for the wedding favors.

Multi-tasking looked to be the order of the day. I decided to stir up the red wine jam first since it needed to steep for a while before I put in the pectin. I'd just poured everything together in a jam pot when someone knocked on the front door.

I wasn't particularly surprised to see Fowler standing there. I'd figured he'd show up at some point to ask me questions about the engagement party and Emerson Pollack. "Come on in," I said. "You can sit at the kitchen table while I get some jam going."

Fowler has been to my place often enough not to be annoyed by my making jam while I talk. Incidentally, I don't necessarily recommend doing this most of the time since distractions can mean you leave out something vital, but the red wine mixture just had to boil and then steep, which didn't take much of my attention. After that, the raspberry was so straightforward I could do it in my sleep.

Fowler took his seat at the kitchen table well out of my way and pulled out his notebook. "About that engagement party."

"What about it?" I asked dutifully.

"How'd it go?"

I paused, giving the red wine mixture a quick stir. "Okay. There wasn't much to it. We put out hors d'oeuvres while people were coming in, and then we served the dinner. We had a salad first, and then bowls of stew with some baguettes from Bianca Jordan."

Fowler wrote some notes. "No dessert?"

"Dessert was cake. Marla Purdue made it, or anyway it came from her shop." The cake had been so uninspired I was willing to believe Marla had given the assignment to one of her interns.

"Right. You and Nate had to slice it. Was that unusual?"

"A little bit. With wedding cakes, the baker often supplies somebody to do the slicing, or sometimes the wedding planner does. But this wasn't a wedding cake, so I guess Marla just assumed we could take care of it for her." I dumped the bags of frozen raspberries into my oversized colander to drain in the sink.

"No problems with the slicing?"

I shook my head. "It was a lot like a sheet cake. We got it done in fifteen minutes or so."

"No altercations or anything during the dinner?" Fowler asked hopefully.

"Not that I heard about. I was in the kitchen most of the time." I paused. I needed to fill in a few more details. "The groom and his buddies were plastered, but they didn't cause any trouble for us. Except the groom wandered into the kitchen looking for a bar."

Fowler narrowed his eyes. "He thought you guys were bartenders?"

"I don't know. Like I say, he was pretty plastered. Thalia's assistant took him to the dining room before he could cause any problems."

"How long have you worked with Thalia Rosenberg?"

"A few months. Nate's been trying to break into the wedding business because it's a big deal for caterers around here, but it's tough. A lot of the wedding planners in the area already have a list of favorite caterers, and it's hard to get added."

Fowler paused. "But Ms. Rosenberg added you to her list?"

"Thalia's a friend of Madge's. I think she added Nate to her list because she knew the café."

"Nice of her." Fowler had shifted into deadpan mode, but I decided not to call him on it. On the other hand, I wasn't going to let him get away with any implications.

"Nate's a great chef. Thalia knows it. Putting him on her list of caterers is an advantage to her, not a favor."

I gave him my best steely stare, and he raised his hands, smiling easily. "No argument. Moving on. Was it Ms. Rosenberg who got you the job with Pollack?"

I nodded. "Sort of. Thalia recommended us, but we were probably the only caterers who could handle the assignment."

"How's that?" Fowler was back to jotting down notes again.

"This whole wedding was last minute. We found out about it couple of weeks ago. Most of the big wedding caterers would already be booked, but Nate could fit it in. Barely. We're dealing with the same holiday rush as everybody else." I remembered Nate juggling jobs so that we could do the party for Pollack and company. If it had been anyone but Thalia, he might have said no.

Fowler wrote another note. "Pollack paid extra?"

"He paid through the nose. But it didn't faze him." In fact, paying through the nose had seemed to make Pollack feel more powerful.

"What was he like to work with?"

I switched off the burner under the red wine mixture and set it aside to cool and steep. "He was a jerk. We had a tasting of the dishes he'd chosen for the reception, and he sneered at beef tenderloin with burgundy sauce. I thought Nate might quit right there, but Pollack backed down when Nate stood up for his food."

Fowler glanced up from his notes. "Would you say Pollack was a bully?"

"Maybe." I bit my lip. "It's weird to call somebody that short and dumpy a bully, but he did like to make a point about how powerful he was, or anyway how rich he was. Sort of the same thing, I guess." I got the raspberries into a jam pot along with some sugar and lemon juice, then used a potato masher to break them up.

"Last night at the rehearsal dinner, when did you last see Pollack?" Fowler asked.

I stopped to think. "The only time I talked to him was just before dinner was served. I was out in the dining room, and he came up to me to complain about dinner not being on the table. I told him we'd serve as soon as his guests were seated. A standoff."

"Any guesses about when that was?"

"Maybe seven-thirty. People were slow getting into the dining room." I gave the raspberry mixture another quick stir, trying to get the sugar to dissolve.

"Was the party in the big room?"

"Yeah. The wedding reception's going to be there, too." I paused. "Well, it was supposed to be there. I don't know what the plans are now."

Fowler nodded. "Wedding's on hold, I guess. How big was this party?"

"There were over fifty guests, along with the bride and groom and their friends."

"Do you do a lot of these engagement parties? Was it a typical one?"

"We haven't done any others that I recall. But the people at this one didn't look like the kind of guests I expected. They were older and more like business associates of Pollack's than family. And it was a big group."

Fowler looked like he might have something else to ask, but then he let it go. "You said that was the only time you talked to Pollack. When did you actually see him last?"

"After we finished cutting the cake and people were served, he got up and thanked everybody for coming. After that people started to leave, and I lost track of him." Not that I was trying to keep track of Pollack at all. "Nate saw him later when he paid us the balance for the engagement party. I don't know exactly when that was, but Nate could tell you. He came into the kitchen and paid the servers from the money Pollack gave him."

Fowler stopped again. "From the money he gave him? You mean he paid him in cash?"

"Yep." I got the burner going under the raspberry jam mixture, giving it another quick stir. "And before you ask, no, that's not common. It happens occasionally, though. More often they pay any bonus and tips in cash."

"So tell me about walking out of the dining room

when you were done. What did you see?"

I paused to work it out in my mind. "Well, around nine-thirty Nate paid the servers, Donnell and Jerry, and they left."

"Did they walk out through the dining room?"

"Nope. There's a door from the kitchen straight into the parking lot. They took that."

Fowler glanced up again. "Why didn't you take that one?"

"Because we wanted to see if Thalia was still around. We needed to check with her to see if there'd been any changes in the wedding schedule." It was always possible Pollack had decided he wanted a Cinderella carriage ride through Shavano or something.

"Did you see her in the dining room?"

I shook my head. "The only person in the dining room was the guy who was running the vacuum sweeper. We just walked out the door that led to the foyer and the entrance."

"And you heard what?" Fowler seemed very concentrated.

"I heard Thalia gasp or sob a couple of times. Then after I called to her, she said something like 'Oh my God' or 'My God.' So Nate and I went over to the stairs to see what was going on. And we saw Pollack stretched out on the floor." Not something I was going to forget any time soon.

"Did you see Ms. Rosenberg?"

"She was kneeling next to Pollack. Like she was trying to see if he was still alive." I swallowed hard. It had been clear that Pollack was beyond help at that point.

"So what did you do?"

"Nate and I both went down the stairs. I went to

Thalia to get her away from the body. I mean, her skirt had blood on it by then, and so did her shoes." I stopped, swallowing again. "Anyway, I got her to step away, and Nate called you guys. That's everything until you showed up."

"Was there anyone else in the foyer area besides you three?" I started to answer, and Fowler held up his hand. "Take a minute. Think about it."

The foyer area was a large open space, stretching up to the top story, with stairs along the sides. It was impressive in daylight. At night it had been full of shadows only partly contained by the spotlights shining down onto the floor at the bottom of the stairs. I closed my eyes for a moment, trying to picture it last night. "I wasn't aware of anybody besides us. And Pollack. The janitor came out of the dining room when y'all pounded on the door, but he wasn't there before." I took another breath. "But it was dark down there, with lots of shadows. I could have missed someone."

"Okay." Fowler sat for a moment longer staring down at his notebook. "Where did you leave the knife you used to cut the cake when you were finished?"

I frowned. That sounded like a question out of left field. "Where? We left it on the cake table. I didn't know whose it was, but it wasn't ours. The owners should have picked it up."

Now it was Fowler's turn to frown. "What do you mean you didn't know whose it was? Didn't it belong in the kitchen?"

"It was a fancy slicing knife and server set. I'd never seen that one before, but they usually have special knives and servers for wedding cake. Sometimes they belong to the bride's family—family heirlooms or something. Or this one might have belonged to Marla Purdue. She's the one who baked the cake." A drip of ice slid down my backbone as it occurred to me the question might not be as irrelevant as I'd thought. "Did someone use that knife on Pollack?"

Fowler ignored my curiosity, as usual. "Could the knife have belonged to Ms. Rosenberg?"

"I doubt it. Thalia isn't usually involved in cutting the cake. She could probably tell you who the knife belonged to, though. That's the kind of thing she keeps track of."

That drip of ice felt even colder. Thalia could tell him who owned the slicing knife. Nothing was weird about that. She was a wedding planner, after all. Her job was to keep track of details. Such as where the FOB had gone after the guests had all left.

Well, crap. I hoped I hadn't just made things worse for Thalia.

"One more thing." Fowler reached into his jacket and brought out a plastic evidence bag. "Do you recognize this?"

I leaned over the table to study it more closely. It looked like a piece of paper, maybe the corner of a sheet that had been torn off. There was some printing at the top that I couldn't read, but the word *Gan* was right at the edge of the tear. I narrowed my eyes, but I couldn't read anything else. The paper was too badly stained.

Stained. I suddenly identified the large brownish-red blot at the top of the page, and stepped away from the table, my hand on my chest. "Is that…?"

"It was underneath Pollack's body," Fowler said flatly. "Ever seen it before?"

"I don't think so. It doesn't look familiar." Although

it sort of did, now that I thought about it. I just couldn't fully identify it. "What's the word?"

"Something that starts with *g-a-n*. Beyond that, I don't know. We may try to get this scrap enhanced, see if we can read the stuff at the top." He put the bag with the paper back in his jacket, then folded his notebook closed and tucked it in his pocket. "Okay, that's all for now. If you think of anything else about the dinner or about Pollack, give me a call."

I nodded. "Right."

I wanted to ask him if Pollack had been stabbed. I wanted to ask him if Thalia was under suspicion. I wanted to ask him if he knew anything about Pollack's background that might make him a murder victim. But I knew better. Fowler never passed along details unless he had to. And right then, he didn't have to.

He gave me a quick dry smile, as if he knew what I was thinking. "See you around, Roxy."

"Oh, yeah, see you around." But then I thought of something, although not anything that could get me more information about Pollack. "You coming to the big Thanksgiving dinner at the café?"

Fowler paused at the door. "I don't know. Me and the other singles usually work Thanksgiving so the married guys can be home with their families."

That sounded sort of depressing. "Come on by when you get a break. All of you. There'll be lots of food."

"I can do that," he said, and his smile was more genuine this time.

Thalia would be at the Thanksgiving dinner, too. But given the number of people who were likely to show, we could keep the two separated.

Provided the chief hadn't thrown her in the slammer by then.

Chapter 12

Nate got home around six. I hadn't called him during the afternoon although I'd been dying to talk to him. "Did Fowler find you?" I asked.

He paused, then hung up his parka on the coat rack. "Yeah, he came by the kitchen while we were finishing up. We've got that party on Friday."

I'd forgotten all about the other jobs Robicheaux Catering had to get ready. The Pollack wedding had expanded to fill all the available space on our mutual schedule before shrinking down to nothing again. I wouldn't be involved in most of the other jobs—Nate and Dex could take care of both the prep and the service.

I heard the clicking of claws as Herman came into the living room. He'd been spending most of his time in the kitchen since the stew had begun to smell terrific.

"Hey, dog." Nate reached out to scratch Herman's ears. We didn't see as much of him as we once had. In fact, he'd become Uncle Mike's full-time dog since he and Madge had more or less moved in together. But tonight was Uncle Mike's poker night, so I'd volunteered to Herman-sit.

Herman bonked against Nate's thigh, clearly delighted to be the center of attention once again.

Nate turned to me after a moment. "Did Fowler come by here?"

"He was here for a while this afternoon, getting all

the information he didn't get last night."

Both of us seemed to be waiting for the other to say what Fowler had been after when he talked to us, as if we were afraid one or the other of us would ask a leading question. But it was a leading question that needed an answer. "Did he ask you about the knife?"

Nate blew out a breath as if he'd been holding it. "Yeah. I couldn't tell him anything. As far as I could remember, it was still on the table when we left."

"I don't know who it belonged to. I don't think anybody ever said."

"No, we were too busy getting the damned cake cut to ask about the implements we were using."

"Did he show you that piece of paper that was underneath Pollack's body?"

Nate nodded. "I didn't recognize it. Did you?"

I shook my head. "There wasn't enough there to identify. It didn't mean anything to me."

Nate started for the kitchen, and I trailed after him, holding onto Herman's collar to keep him in check. "I've got a chicken stewing," I said, "one of the ones I got from Aram last week."

Aram Pergosian, of the wonderful summer tomatoes and the terrific honey, also had a flourishing business in free-range chickens and eggs. Like most chicken farmers, he wasn't particularly sentimental about them, which meant when the hens aged out and couldn't lay eggs anymore, he sold them for stew. Believe me, the stew they make is sensational.

"Okay, great," Nate said. "We've got that leftover bread in the freezer."

"Right. It's thawing as we speak."

Nate paused. "Do you think he fell? Or did someone

stab him?"

Clearly, we weren't talking about the hen. I pushed the jars of raspberry jam on the counter that were my afternoon's production into a straighter line. "I don't know what to think. I saw a lot of blood underneath him. I don't know if that's normal when someone falls down a couple of flights of stairs."

Nate opened the refrigerator and pulled out a bottle of white wine. "The fact that Fowler asked both of us what happened to the knife when we were through slicing makes me think something's going on."

"You think somebody took the knife and stabbed Pollack? If so, did he fall from the foyer or was he down on the ground floor for some reason and someone took advantage?"

Nate poured us both a glass of wine. "Did he ask you about Thalia?"

I had to think back over what Fowler and I had talked about. "It was more about timing—when I saw Pollack last, that kind of thing. He was shocked over Pollack paying you in cash."

Nate grimaced. "I was pretty shocked myself. It was a lot of money."

"So did Fowler ask you a lot about Thalia?"

"He wanted to know how she'd gotten mixed up in the Pollack wedding, but I couldn't tell him much. She just treated him like a client. Not someone who was on a different level from her other clients."

"But your mom said Pollack was one of her investors. When she was getting started. So they must have had some kind of relationship, even if it was just business."

Nate blinked and reached down to scratch Herman's

ears as the dog settled beneath the table. "Pollack was one of Thalia's investors? She never mentioned it."

"Not to me either. But your mom knew about it."

"Yeah, well, Mom and Thalia go way back. She knew my dad, too." He took a sip of his wine, frowning. "Mom's going to be really upset if Fowler goes after Thalia."

I frowned back. "You think he would? I mean, she was close to hysterics when we found her. I can't picture her killing Pollack and then being able to pretend she was that upset. She's never struck me as much of an actress."

"Right. Thalia was in a state when we found her. Of course, killing somebody would probably put you in a state, too."

I was beginning to have a very unpleasant feeling about this. "Surely there are other suspects. I mean, to know Pollack was to loathe him from what I saw. And that event center was full of people who knew him, people other than Thalia."

Nate stared down at his glass. "Look at it from Fowler's point of view. Thalia was there, and her clothes had Pollack's blood on them. If she'd just stabbed him when we came out of the dining room, she'd have had to come up with a fast excuse. Telling us she'd just found him and was trying to see if he was still alive would explain why she was there and why her clothes were such a mess."

"It would also explain why she was there and why her clothes were a mess if that was exactly what happened," I said flatly. But he'd started an unpleasant train of thought. One I didn't want to consider. I liked Thalia, and I didn't like thinking she might have killed somebody, even somebody as obnoxious as Pollack.

"Hold the thought." Nate sighed. "I don't want it to be Thalia, but that's where the evidence may point."

I took a breath. Might as well go through all the unpleasant topics at the same time. "Any news about the Pollack wedding—whether it's going to happen or not?"

Nate shook his head. "Eventually, I'll try to get in touch with Jennifer Pollack, or whoever is in charge of things now her father isn't around. I thought I'd give her a day or two."

"Right." I took a moment to think about the diminutive Jennifer Pollack. Who probably was now in charge of this train wreck wedding that might or might not actually happen.

Nate turned toward the stove. "That stew smells great. Did you throw in those onions from Barry's place?"

I had to admire his determination to get off the subject. I was ready to move on myself. "Yeah, plus some of Luca's potatoes that were a little elderly. And some red dragon carrots. Should be tasty."

"Should be very tasty." He nodded. "Let's eat."

Herman pushed to his feet and gave us a doggy grin. *Eat* was one of his favorite words.

****

The next day I stirred up some more wine jelly, but it was becoming obvious that I needed more wine if I was going to make enough for all the wedding favors. I decided I'd go with a decent boxed wine rather than multiple bottles so I wouldn't have to visit the liquor store quite so often. At the same time, I'd swing by the café to check in with Madge. Bianca had close to a final count for Thanksgiving, and I decided to pass it on. Plus I could find out what was going on with The Wedding.

And Thalia, but I wasn't ready to admit that to myself quite yet.

I timed my arrival for the end of lunch service at the café, entering through the catering kitchen so I could say hello to Nate and Dex. In the café kitchen, Coco was chopping tomatoes for tomorrow's salads. "Hey there," she said, glancing up. "What's happening?"

Quite a bit. But I didn't want to get caught up in conversation when I still needed to talk to Madge. "Do you have any count on what dishes people are bringing for Thanksgiving?"

Coco grimaced. "Yeah, the spreadsheet's over by the phone. At the moment we're heavy on carbs, but I guess that's the nature of Thanksgiving."

"It is indeed." I went to the phone and tried deciphering Coco's scrawled entries. Lots of potatoes, both sweet and not, corn, and a fair amount of dressing. A couple of people were doing green bean casserole, and since they were chefs, most likely there'd be a lot of cream and butter involved. By the end of the meal, we might all be in a coma.

I glanced at Coco. "It's going to be quite a spread."

"Oh, yeah." She sighed. "If anyone asks for suggestions, I'll probably tell them to bring antacids."

I walked through the kitchen toward the door to the café. Bobby and Marigold were side-by-side at the flattop, although Marigold was taking up a bit more than her side, given her current size. She saw me and grinned, pausing to flip a burger like the pro she was. "Want lunch?" she called.

"I'm good," I said, sliding through the door into the café dining room.

Madge was at the hostess station, stacking menus.

She gave me a guarded smile. "Hi, Roxy, what brings you to town?"

"I needed to buy wine for the jam," I said. "And I thought I'd give you an update about Thanksgiving."

"Oh, Lord, I forgot all about that. Is everything all right?" She gestured toward an empty table at the side.

I dropped into one of the chairs. "It's going great. Bianca's been collecting RSVP's, and Coco's got a list of what everyone's bringing. It's going to be a real feast, as usual."

"Oh, good." Madge gave me a tired smile. "How's the wine jam?"

"Great," I said staunchly. "I've got around thirty-five jars done, and I'm buying wine by the box now so it should go smoothly. How's The Wedding?" I checked Madge's expression for any telltale signs of panic.

"Thalia's taken over, thank God." Madge relaxed in her chair. "She says it will give her something to concentrate on while this whole mess with Emerson Pollack works out. Honestly, I can't believe she has anything to worry about. Can you?" I took maybe a second too long to answer, and Madge frowned. "Oh, my. I don't like that look. What do you know that I don't?"

"Fowler came out to the farm to talk to me yesterday. He talked to Nate at the catering kitchen. I think he's still concerned about Thalia being next to Pollack's body. She had his blood on her clothes." I watched Madge's eyes widen. Maybe she hadn't heard that part. "But I don't think she has any motive to kill him, so there's that," I added hurriedly.

"Damn," Madge said softly. "I told Thalia everything would work out in a few days. That's not entirely true, is it?"

"I'm afraid it probably isn't. I don't know what Fowler's searching for, though."

Madge shook her head. "Thalia's upset about this. I mean, it was bad enough she found the body, but now it's like the police are zeroing in on her just because she was in the wrong place at the wrong time."

"I don't think Fowler would do that," I said. "He's very good at his job overall."

"Oh, I know. I like Ethan. But I worry about Thalia. Even if she's not accused outright, her business could suffer. A murderous wedding planner isn't a good look, although it might help to keep some of the bridezillas in line." She fixed me with a level glance. "Roxy…"

I knew what she was going to ask me, and I knew I needed not to let her. "I'm sure it will all work out. Thalia's the best. People won't listen to gossip." I sounded a little desperate, even to myself.

Madge nodded. "Thalia is the best. But even the best can take a serious hit over something like this. Could you possibly…"

I bit my lip. No. No, I couldn't possibly…

Madge leaned forward, placing her hand on mine. "I know it's an imposition. It's just that you've done this before. You've had some real success investigating things like this."

Things like this meaning murders. And I'd seriously annoyed Ethan Fowler investigating things like this. And I'd gotten myself into some real scary situations investigating things like this. I really didn't like having my life threatened. I took a breath. "Madge…"

"I'm not asking you to solve the crime, you know, sweetheart. Just maybe find out some more about

Emerson Pollack, the way you did with Brett Holmes. He was the kind of man who'd have lots of enemies." Madge patted my hand again. "Just give Ethan some alternatives to consider."

We both knew only too well how Fowler would react to my finding him some alternatives. I'd been told enough times to stay out of his business. On the other hand, a couple of times I'd been able to help. I hoped this was one of those times because it looked like I was going to be doing it.

"I'll see what I can do," I said reluctantly. "But don't count on me for much, Madge. I've got a lot of irons in the fire right now."

"Oh, of course, you do." Madge gave me a brilliant smile. "But I'll appreciate any help you can give us. So will Thalia, believe me."

I did believe her, but it didn't make me feel much better. "Okay, I'll talk to a few people. You know, Thalia will have to be one of them." Given that Thalia was the only person I knew who'd had a professional relationship—any kind of relationship, really—with Pollack, she might well be the first person I talked to.

"Oh, dear, I suppose you will have to do that, won't you. But you won't upset Thalia as much as the police did. You know Ethan can be a little imposing."

I knew that only too well. "Speaking of Fowler, I invited him to Thanksgiving. Well, him and the other Shavano cops on duty on Thanksgiving."

Now Madge looked disconcerted. "All of them?"

"There probably won't be that many. Fowler said he and the other single people take Thanksgiving duty so the married cops can be home with their families."

"Oh, that's nice of him." Madge still didn't seem

delighted. "The thing is, I asked Thalia to come to Thanksgiving, too. You don't think Ethan would say anything to her, do you?"

"I can almost guarantee that he won't," I murmured. In fact, seeing a prime suspect at the dinner might be enough to make Fowler decide he wasn't hungry.

"I suppose you're right. It would be out of character for him to do that." Madge managed to smile again. "Thanks for doing this, Roxy. I really appreciate it. So will Thalia."

I certainly hoped that was true, but I couldn't guarantee it. As Nate had pointed out, Thalia didn't have a rock-solid alibi. And some circumstantial evidence pointed to her. Still, she was my friend, and I'd do what I could to find out some details about Emerson Pollack.

And hopefully those details wouldn't point me to Thalia's front door again.

Chapter 13

After I thought about it, I realized I needed to talk to someone other than Thalia about Emerson Pollack. Specifically, I needed my friend, Susa.

Susa Sondergaard and I have known each other since second grade. In a lot of ways, we're unlikely friends. As I may have mentioned, I'm a very big girl, over six feet tall and, shall we say, sturdy. Susa, on the other hand, is around five feet two. I'm a Greek American, with a lot of brunette curls, although fewer than I used to have at the moment. Susa is Norwegian American, with bright golden hair and big blue eyes. Usually, dainty little girls make me feel clumsy and oversized, which is why I don't hang out with them much. But Susa has never made me feel that way. Possibly because no one who knows Susa would call her *dainty.*

Even when we were kids, Susa was a dynamo, someone who'd happily run up the nearest trail if she thought she had a chance of seeing a bear at the top. Most of us in Shavano do some outdoorsy things. I bike and snowshoe and occasionally ski. Susa does it all—hike, climb, snowshoe, snowboard, cross country ski, downhill ski, mountain bike, and horseback ride when she has the time.

Which she doesn't anymore. Susa runs the town's best computer services company. She's responsible for most of the county government's technology, as well as most of the business technology in the area. Over the years, she's hired her own stable of geeks, who can do just about anything with a computer although Susa keeps them on the right side of the law for the most part.

She does that, partly anyway, because she and Ethan Fowler are an item. Off and on. Susa has had more boyfriends over the years than I have canning jars; still, she and Fowler do seem to have a special understanding. But both of them are wary when it comes to commitments, so I'm never sure whether they're together or on a break.

If they were together, that would limit how much Susa might be willing to help me out on my extremely limited Emerson Pollack investigation. She had a sort of unwritten rule that she wouldn't mess around in anything that would screw up one of Fowler's cases. Of course, this time around, all I needed was advice, which she might be willing to pass on without violating any confidences originating with the Shavano police. I didn't know how far along Fowler was in the investigation, and I doubted he'd share many details with Susa. But I'd do my best to stay out of his way.

Susa's business, SS Systems, is located in Old Shavano, the part of town that dates to its rough and tumble beginnings as a mining town in the nineteenth century. A lot of the historic houses there have been renovated and go for several million when they occasionally come on the market. Susa's office building is a lot smaller than the mansions. It's a former miner's cabin, what they call shotgun style, meaning that if you stood in the front room and fired a shotgun it would go straight through the whole house. She's added on to the original small cabin, which was great for her when she was a one-woman office but not so great for the geeks who do her bidding. Along with a few rooms partitioned off from the main part of the cabin, she's also renovated what used to be a small barn/garage/stable in back so that her crew has more workspace. It's a sort of eccentric layout, but it's effective for Susa and the geeks, who like to keep things a little off center.

Carly Silverman was at the front desk as I walked in. She started off as one of the geeks but has become Susa's number one assistant. I wasn't sure why she was at the front desk rather than the occasional receptionist, who was usually a geek in training.

"Hey, Carly."

She glanced up. "Oh, hi, Roxy. Did you bring any jam for tasting?"

This last was delivered with a hopeful gleam. I have occasionally brought some experimental jams by to get Susa's opinion and shared them with the geeks. Unfortunately, many of the geeks are perennially hungry, which means reasoned evaluations aren't their specialty.

"Not this time," I said. "Have you guys gotten the word about Thanksgiving at the café?"

Carly nodded enthusiastically. "Wouldn't miss it. We're bringing chips and salsa."

That made sense since chips and salsa constituted the base of the geeks' diet. "Good. Did you let Coco know?"

"We did. She sighed, but I guess it's all right."

"It's terrific," I said resolutely. After all, we needed some non-chefs to supply normal, run-of-the-mill stuff. "Is Susa around?"

"She was in her office the last time I checked. Let me buzz her to make sure she's still there."

I expected her to use some kind of state-of-the-art intercom, but that wasn't the geek way. Carly pulled out her cell phone and sent a text. A moment later my own cell pinged.

—*Come on back,* the text read, *I'm bored out of my skull anyway.*—

At least I had things to ask Susa that wouldn't bore her.

Susa was at her desk, peering at one of her multiple monitors and frowning. When she saw me, she leaned back in her chair, rubbing her eyes. "Hi," she said. "What's up? I did phone Coco and tell her I'd bring some wine—if you're checking up on me."

"I'm not, but good for you. If anybody asks, we could use a few salads. We're heavy on carbs at the moment." I dropped into a chair beside her desk.

"Of course we are. It's Thanksgiving. I intend to be in a carb daze by the end of the afternoon. Anything else going on?"

I took a breath. "Well, Nate and I got pulled into this thing…"

Susa gave me a shrewd look. "You mean you ended up in the middle of another murder."

She made it sound like it was a regular occurrence. "Well, yeah. But it wasn't like we planned it."

"No, I know. It sounded like a mess, though. I don't even know the guy who got killed. Is he from around here?"

"He was one of those rich out-of-towners who bought himself a mountain retreat in Geary," I said. The *mountain retreats* around here are like the *summer cottages* in Newport, ridiculously outsized and opulent, built by the same kind of people a hundred years later.

"Which means there are probably a lot of people who wouldn't have minded pushing him off a balcony," Susa mused. "Or down a stairwell."

"You'd think so. Unfortunately, the investigation is zeroing in on Thalia Rosenberg." I watched Susa's reaction, trying to see if she had any inside information from Fowler.

Judging from her expression, she didn't. "Thalia? I have a hard time picturing her pushing anybody over a balcony. The woman wears three-inch stilettos. She's more likely to fall over the balcony herself."

"I agree, totally. But Madge is upset about it. Thalia's one of her besties."

Susa arched one golden eyebrow. "And she wants you to investigate it, right?"

I nodded. "Honestly, I don't know what I can do. I don't know anything about Emerson Pollack, except he was a creep. There may have been a lot of people who didn't like him. Hell, there were undoubtedly a lot of people who didn't like him, given his personality. But Thalia and Nate and I were the only ones around the event center at the end of the evening. So if one of his enemies did him in, they also did a great job of disappearing into the snowstorm before he was found."

"Tell me about Pollack," Susa said. "All I know is what I saw on the news. And before you ask, no, Ethan hasn't said anything about it. And he won't. When it comes to his cases, he's like a steel trap."

Susa was pouting a little, and I could see her point. What good was having a first-rate source of information if that first-rate source didn't feel like sharing?

"Like I said, I don't know much about him except that he was rich. He set up this whole wedding on the fly, maybe because his daughter wanted it, which means it must have cost a mint since he had to pay everybody for a last-minute job. Nate certainly charged him premium rates, and according to Madge, so did Thalia. He was obnoxious when he did a tasting with Nate and me, complaining about everything, even the prime beef tenderloin. Nate finally stared him down and his daughter pleaded with him, so he approved the menu. Then he hired us to do this engagement party, too, which was even more last minute, so there was no haggling over the food."

"I thought the wedding was in January. Isn't it late for an engagement party?"

"Maybe, but I'm not sure it had much to do with his daughter's engagement. Most of the people there looked more like business associates. And Pollack made the only speech of the evening, although it was more like a couple of sentences than a speech. He thanked everybody for coming and told them to have a nice night."

Susa frowned. "Weird. What's the groom like? Was his family even there?"

"The only time I saw the groom was at the party, and he was plastered, along with his buddies. They had their own table at the back. I think they were confusing the engagement party with the bachelor party." The more I thought about the drunken frat boys, the more unpleasant they seemed.

Susa snorted. "Jerk. The bride and groom are supposed to be together at the engagement party. At least they were at every engagement party I've ever been part of. If her father was running everything, he should have taken care of that."

Yet another thing Emerson Pollack had let slide. "He wasn't paying much attention to his daughter or to her fiancé, for what it's worth. He had other irons in the fire." I remembered Pollack talking to some of the guests at the engagement party, but I don't think I ever saw him speak to Jennifer.

"Do you think there was some kind of problem between the two families? Was the groom's family even there?"

I shrugged. "Like I said, so far as I know, I never met the groom's family. And I didn't hear any gossip about them either. I couldn't tell you whether they were there or not." But it was something I needed to ask Thalia about. A family feud could be a very good motive for killing Pollack.

Susa settled into her chair again. "Okay, as you've pointed out, Pollack was a creep with lots of people who might have potentially wanted to kill him. How do we zero in on the one who actually did it?"

"I figure that's Fowler's job." Susa narrowed her eyes at me, but I shook my head. "All I want to do is find out who Pollack really was and maybe what he was up to. If I can find that out, maybe I can show that someone other than Thalia might have been involved."

Susa sighed. "The usual. What do you want me to do?"

"I was thinking maybe we should talk to Alice," I said carefully.

Susa bit her lip. "Alice Hoover?"

"Right."

Alice Hoover was a financial guru who'd retired to

her hometown of Shavano after making a fortune in Denver. She'd given Susa advice when she was just starting out, and she was a tremendous source of information about anything financial. She was also one of the most terrifying old ladies I'd ever met. To put it mildly, Alice did not suffer fools gladly. No way would I go to Alice's place on my own. "I thought maybe since she was your friend…"

Susa sniffed. "Alice is many things, but she's not a friend. Advisor, mentor, even tutor. But I wouldn't presume to say she's my friend. She'd slap me to my knees if I tried it."

I squared my shoulders. "Nonetheless, I'm guessing if anyone around here knows what Pollack was up to in a business sense, it would be Alice."

"Probably true." Susa frowned. "Actually, I'd like to hear what she has to say about this. If nothing else, it'll be entertaining."

I couldn't do it myself. I didn't even have Alice's number. "So will you call her and try to set something up?"

Susa nodded. "I'll do it. No telling if or when she'll see us, though. She might even be going away for the holidays."

Both of us must have looked a little doubtful over that. Alice had always struck me as the type of person others came to visit, not the type to do the visiting herself. "Well, we can ask, anyway."

Susa was beginning to get that restless expression that usually meant she wanted to get to work. "We can at that. I'll let you know what she says."

"Okay." I pushed myself to my feet. "You want to get together for dinner sometime? If you come to the cabin, you can taste the red wine jam I'm making for The Wedding favors."

Susa grinned up at me. "How can I resist? We'll set something up."

I gave her one last smile and then went up the hall toward the front door. I'd made some progress in my hunt for Pollack's killer. Maybe.

I knew I still needed to talk to Thalia, though. Nobody else around Shavano knew Pollack beyond having sold him stuff. And as we now knew, selling Pollack stuff wasn't a fun experience. If Madge was right, he'd been one of Thalia's backers, which meant she had to have talked to him about her business.

As I drove to the farm, I ran over all the possible reasons I could come up with for visiting Thalia. It didn't strike me as a great idea to barge into her office and tell her I was trying to find Pollack's murderer because Madge was worried about her. Getting information about The Wedding seemed like my best bet. I could tell Thalia that Nate and I had taken care of the invitations, and I could reassure myself that The Wedding was on a firm footing again.

Not that I ever thought The Wedding itself was on shaky ground, but, yeah, I sort of had thought that. Given how long Uncle Mike and Madge had circled each other before finally deciding to go for it, I didn't want anything to get in their way now.

Nate's SUV was parked in front of the cabin when I got there, which probably meant he was going to grab supper before heading off for the latest catering job. Thank God most of these events only called for heavy hors d'oeuvres, which could all be made in advance. Otherwise, I wouldn't have seen him again until January.

We were spending a lot of time apart these days.

Inside, I found Nate dressed in his chef's pants and a T-shirt, stirring up a pot of ramen with leftovers, our usual last-minute supper. "Hey, babe, I didn't know if you'd make it home before I left." He gave me a quick grin as he dished the ramen into a two bowls and grabbed some chopsticks.

Nate is an expert user of chopsticks. I'm not. I grabbed a fork and took the chair across from him at the kitchen table. "What event are you doing tonight?"

"Office party down at Rinderknecht's Furniture. I shouldn't be long. It's just hors d'oeuvres and drinks. And Carey Rinderknecht said that they'd kick everybody out by eight."

We frequently got promises like that, but this time the people in charge might make it stick, given that the furniture store would be open tomorrow, and they'd want to make sure no traces of the party remained to upset the customers. "I'm surprised they aren't having the party somewhere else. Surely, they don't want anybody sitting on the sample furniture with food."

"Got me. I just go where I'm told." Nate dredged up a couple of bites of ramen.

"Just you and Dex?" I asked.

He sighed. "Dex can't make it. His kid's got a school program. Just me and Val."

Val was one of the newer servers, very hard-working but not as experienced as Donnell. Still, she'd just be passing hors d'oeuvres. She'd be fine. Probably.

Nate paused, tapping his chopsticks on the side of his bowl. "You want to come and find out how they handle the furniture? I could use some company."

I started to say no, not tonight. I was tired and

looking forward to a night with my feet up in front of the TV. But we hadn't seen much of each other for the past month. We'd both been busy, and the Pollack wedding and rehearsal dinner—along with Thanksgiving and The Wedding—had sucked up a lot of the time we normally spent together. Suddenly, I wanted to spend the evening with Nate, no matter how broken up that evening might be. "I could use some company myself. You want another pair of hands?"

He reached across the table and took my hand in his. "As long as they're yours."

My face warmed. "Well, all right then. Give me a minute to change. Can I get by with jeans and a T-shirt?"

"Sure." His grin turned slightly devilish. "Won't be anybody in the kitchen except us."

That produced another flush a little lower down, and I decided to go pull on my working clothes before things got out of hand.

As I brushed my hair into some kind of acceptable shape, I considered what I should tell Nate about my deal with Madge. He wasn't crazy about having me dig around Fowler's cases. There had been one or two close calls, and he was all for leaving things to the professionals. I could see his point, but this was a special situation.

And I liked Thalia. She'd come through on getting Nate into the wedding business, and she'd never struck me as the type to make trouble. It was possible that she'd killed Pollack in an angry moment, but I didn't think she had. She was far too calm for that. And Madge, my future aunt by marriage, was upset about what was happening to her friend.

Surely Nate wouldn't mind if I did a little digging

under these very special circumstances. And, I considered, he'd mind even less if I didn't actually tell him what I was up to. That possibility started an uncomfortable feeling between my shoulder blades, but I ignored it. *Ask for forgiveness rather than permission* had become my motto over the years.

This so-called investigation was all very low-key and unlikely to cause anyone any trouble. Or so I told myself.

Chapter 14

All expectations to the contrary, the party at Rinderknecht's turned out to be a lot of fun. It took place on the floor above the sales area, so I needn't have worried about people spilling meatballs on some expensive leather upholstery. Val was game to learn the ropes, even if she was still new at being an event server rather than a café server. The food was enthusiastically consumed and, true to his word, Carey Rinderknecht kicked everybody out by eight. A good time was had by all—even the caterers.

And Nate and I had an evening together. True, we were working part of the time, but it was the principle of the thing. We went home after the party and split a bottle of pinot noir, and then went to bed. Together. A great day and night, y'all.

The next day I spent the morning cooking up more red wine jelly, along with some of my perennial jam favorites for my mail order customers. A lot of those perennials were currently being handled by Dolce, who knew my basics almost as well as I did. Bridget was there getting the mail orders finished although she had to leave early because they needed her at High Country. Dolce would breeze in after school and stir up some raspberry and peach, which should put us nicely ahead.

I'd already sold a lot of my summer specialties at the winter market that took place before Thanksgiving, but I hadn't bothered with anything beyond the ordinary. I wasn't in the mood to produce a specialty jam this year, given how much jam I was producing for The Wedding. If I had any wine left over, I might offer wine jelly for January's monthly special although I wasn't sure if people would be interested after the New Year's Eve vibe wore off.

After lunch, I changed into a nicer top and cleaner jeans and set off for Thalia's office, leaving Bridget to lock up after me. I planned to lead off with questions about The Wedding, then segue into Pollack, assuming I could make that transition. I had no idea whether Madge had told her about my little investigation. I doubted I'd mention it myself.

I'd expected to find Danielle in the outer office, but Thalia herself was behind the desk, working on the computer. She glanced up when I walked in. "Oh, Roxy, if you're here to find out what Jennifer Pollack has decided, I can't help you. She hasn't told me anything yet."

She didn't sound upset, just resigned. "That's not why I'm here, but thanks for the information. I'll pass it on to Nate."

Thalia narrowed her eyes. "Why are you here, then?"

"I wanted to check with you about The Wedding."

Thalia stared at me as if she was trying to figure out just what the hell I was talking about. *Oops.* "I'm sorry. We're so used to talking about Madge and Uncle Mike's wedding as *The Wedding* that I forgot other people don't have the same frame of reference."

She gave me a tired smile. "I can see why you'd talk about it that way. I'm still trying to find out what Madge has finished and what's still to be done. Maybe you can help me."

We spent a pleasantly confused half hour over one of Thalia's printed wedding checklists, trying to decide where we were in getting The Wedding ready to go. I helped her check off some things, like the venue and the seating arrangements. Uncle Mike had finished the renovations on the barn a couple of weeks ago. And I knew he'd already arranged to rent both tables and chairs for the wedding and reception. Thalia wasn't especially pleased with the idea of having the guests seated at tables while the ceremony took place, but it was easier than trying to get everything rearranged after the ceremony was over. Particularly since that might require sending the guests to stand out in the snow while the chairs were moved around.

"What about the menu?" she asked. "I assume you and Nate are in charge of that."

"We are, but we haven't made much progress in getting Madge to come up with a final decision on what she wants to serve. If worse comes to worst, we've got all that salmon and tenderloin for the Pollack wedding, which may or may not be an option. If Jennifer doesn't want it, maybe she'd let us pay her for it."

Thalia grimaced. "That doesn't sound like Madge's style. Plus it feels like bad luck. What menus has Nate sent her? Maybe we should just choose something. Honestly, I think she would appreciate having someone take all of this off her hands."

She had a point there. And by now I had a pretty good idea of Madge's favorite foods. "We talked about several possibilities, and I know she wants a vegetarian dish, maybe pasta. We could even do a vegan version if you want. —We've got a lot of vegan entrees now. And we'll be serving buffet style because we absolutely won't have time to do a plated dinner. Plus there's no working kitchen in the barn. We thought we'd have hors d'oeuvres set up when people came in, so they could take them to their tables. And we'd get bread from Bianca, and probably a salad. Coco can help with that."

"What about dessert? Wedding cake?" Thalia raised an eyebrow.

I sighed. "I don't think we'll have one. Coco doesn't do cakes, but she does divine fruit tarts and galettes and small pastries like pecan tassies. Or she's talked about cupcakes in the past." Actually, now that I thought about it, Coco might be willing to do wedding cupcakes since they wouldn't take as much decorating as a wedding cake.

"Why not order from Marla?"

I blew out a long breath. "You mean there's actually a chance Marla might have an opening on her schedule so she could bake Madge's cake for New Year's Eve? I thought she was booked months in advance."

"She might be willing to do something as a favor to me. I'll ask her myself if you're interested."

I paused to think about it. Marla's cakes were exquisitely designed, but the cake at the Pollack engagement party hadn't tasted like much. And was this a situation where we wanted to go for fashionable rather than delicious? Would Coco be hurt if we called in a wedding pro? "I'm not sure how that would work for Madge. She might want Coco to do something to prevent hurt feelings."

Thalia nodded. "I can see that. But check with her anyway, just in case. I can talk to Marla and set something up if we get going on it soon."

"I'll do that." But I might also be honor bound to tell Madge that Marla's cake at the party had been disappointing.

Thalia rubbed a hand across the back of her neck, stretching her shoulders. "I'm so glad you came by, Roxy. I was putting off doing any work on The Wedding because it was so confusing."

Apparently, Thalia had decided to adopt our way of referring to Uncle Mike's and Madge's extravaganza. "Glad I could help. And thanks for taking over the coordination. I'm sure Madge appreciates it."

"No problem. I cancelled my December schedule to accommodate planning the Pollack wedding, so now I've got nothing pending until January. I gave Danielle and Beverly time off so they can get themselves ready for next year. We've got a bunch of events coming up in late January."

That was likely the best opening I was going to get to switch the topic to Pollack and company. "Madge said you cancelled everything to work for Pollack because he was one of your early investors."

Thalia's expression immediately shut down. "I didn't remember I'd told her about Emerson."

"I'm sorry," I said. "Were you friends? I didn't realize."

"We weren't friends. We were…business associates." Thalia paused, staring out at the traffic. "When I wanted to set up my business, I couldn't convince any of the banks around here to back me. The loan officers were all men, you see."

I did see. "They didn't know what event planning was?"

"Not really. If their daughters or granddaughters had gotten married, their wives did all the work. They couldn't understand why you'd hire an 'outsider' to put a wedding together."

"Were you the first in the region? I didn't realize that."

"I wasn't the first, but I was the first who put weddings ahead of all the other events. A lot of the planners around then were like Amy Luria—all-purpose event planners with a sideline in renting tents and tables. That made sense to the bankers because they were also sure there weren't that many events happening around Shavano and Geary."

Thalia's business went well beyond Shavano and Geary. Having spent several years building up her clientele, she was now the most successful planner in the Collegiate Peaks area. "How did Pollack get involved?" I asked. "I didn't think he was from this area."

"He wasn't," Thalia said. "His business was located in Denver, but he had connections throughout the Southwest."

"What was his business?"

Thalia got that closed look again. "Finance. He managed investments for several private individuals and some corporations."

"And he decided to invest in your business? How did he hear about it?"

Thalia leaned back in her chair. "One of the bankers who turned me down for a loan suggested I talk to Emerson. He said he was considering investments around here, and his standards weren't as tight as the banks. I called him, and he invited me to give him a presentation at his Denver office. After I'd finished,

Emerson agreed to advance me the initial amount I needed to get started. And he brought in other investors after that so that I could expand my reach. And he referred customers to me over the years. He was very active in the business."

"How long did it take to pay the investors off?" I asked.

Thalia looked uncomfortable. "I hadn't entirely paid Emerson off yet. The interest rates he charged were very high, probably because he was backing riskier businesses. I suppose I'll need to find out who'll take over the loan now."

That *high interest rates* comment set off some alarm bells in my mind. It made me think of phrases like *loan shark* and *predatory lending*. "Was the wedding for Jennifer going to pay off part of the loan?"

Thalia's eyes widened, but then she shrugged. "I was charging him quite a lot of money for my services. It would have cut into the loan."

Which didn't answer my question. Or maybe it did. Apparently, Thalia hadn't suggested using the wedding to pay off the rest of her debt. Maybe because that debt was still sizeable.

Thalia gave me a sort of artificial smile. "Well, I think we've taken care of everything we can do on The Wedding, for the moment anyway. You'll talk to Madge about the wedding cake?"

"Sure. I'll see her today or tomorrow." Which reminded me of one more thing I needed to pass on to Thalia. "I've taken care of the wedding favors, too. Or part of them anyway. I'm making red wine jelly to hand out in half-cup jars. I had labels printed up with the names and date."

Thalia nodded absently. "That should work very well. And it's personal, which I always recommend."

It was definitely personal. Also, definitely a pain in the neck, but I'd volunteered, more or less. Thalia was clearly through for the day, and I'd gotten some information I could pass along to Alice and Susa. "I'll let you know what Madge says."

"Yes, do that." Thalia was peering at the computer as I headed out the office door.

I decided to swing by the café to see if Madge was still there. It was around three-thirty, and she often stayed late to make sure everything was ready for breakfast the next day. Nate's SUV was parked in front of the catering kitchen, so I decided to say hello on my way to find Madge.

Finding her turned out to be easier than I'd expected since she was in the catering kitchen herself, watching Nate chop carrots. I'd often done that, too. There's always something soothing about watching a chef do his thing.

Nate glanced up as he heard the door open. "Hey, Rox," he called. "Mom wanted to ask you about the jam."

I slid into a chair next to Madge. "Which jam?" Because, of course, I had lots around my cabin.

"The wine jam," Madge explained. "I wondered if you'd made all the jars yet because I think a few of the RSVPs are squishy, and I don't want you to be stuck with a bunch of unclaimed jars."

Nate grinned. "Other people will claim them. If there are extras, you can just leave them out for people to take home. Trust me, they'll be gone by the end of the evening."

He was right, but I'd just as soon not spend time making jam that wasn't needed. "How many do you consider squishy?"

Madge shrugged. "Maybe ten or so. They're all people over on the Front Range, and if the weather's at all dicey, they probably won't come."

I hadn't even thought about the threat of bad weather, always a factor at this time of year. I was still dealing with day-to-day stuff. "Okay. I'll hold off on the last ten until we have a better sense of what's going to happen. But while I've got you…"

Madge looked apprehensive, and I shook my head quickly. "It's nothing bad. I talked to Thalia this afternoon, and we got some things settled."

"Such as?" Madge looked even more apprehensive.

"Dinner, for one thing. We talked about the menu." I gave Madge a bright smile, but Nate narrowed his eyes at me. We'd been trying to get Madge to settle on a menu for weeks with no luck.

"Oh." Madge closed her eyes for a moment. "Thank God that's settled. What are we having?"

Across the kitchen Nate seemed about to say something cutting that would throw everything into chaos. I just hoped he'd keep quiet for a little while longer. "I'm going to discuss some alternatives with Nate to get his input, and we'll need something for the vegetarians. Have you heard anything about vegans coming? We can make some special alterations for them if there are any."

"Oh, vegans?" Madge bit her lip. "Cora Runyan and her kids are vegetarians, but I don't think anyone's vegan. I'll have to check with Mike."

I could almost guarantee that Uncle Mike didn't

know any vegans, but he could always confirm it to be sure. "And we'll do bread from Bianca and a salad. I'll leave that to Coco."

Madge nodded. "That sounds lovely, sweetheart. Tell Thalia thanks for me."

I swore I could almost see steam coming out of Nate's ears. Of course, he could have set all of this up weeks ago if Madge had only cooperated, and of course he was righteously annoyed. But I hoped he could hold his peace. This was major progress, after all.

"We'll do hors d'oeuvres as the guests come in so they can munch while they wait. Did you want place cards? A seating chart?"

Madge got that apprehensive look again. "Oh, I don't think so. Do you think we need them?"

"Not if you don't want them," I said resolutely. "We can just let people find their own tables and sit with whoever they want." And no one would have to worry about getting place cards written and in place. To me, that was the major advantage to this plan.

"Oh, my." Madge blinked a few times, pressing her hand to her heart. "It's all coming together, isn't it? I've been so stressed, and now that Thalia's in charge, it's just falling into place. I should have gone to her weeks ago."

At that point, I knew just how Nate felt. Thalia hadn't done a lot with this, other than just deciding to go ahead and firm things up. But she'd done that much. And we were that much further along.

"There is one thing we need a decision on." I settled in my chair and folded my arms. If Madge was happy with our progress, she could help keep it going by making some fast decisions of her own.

She bit her lip. "What?"

"The cake. Thalia thinks she could get Marla Purdue to make a wedding cake, but I didn't know if you'd want that. And I didn't want to hurt Coco's feelings by bringing in another baker. Though Coco doesn't really do cakes." I sat back to wait. *Come on, Madge. You can do this.*

"Oh. A cake." Madge was blinking again. "You've seen Marla Purdue's cakes. What did you think of them?"

I glanced up at Nate, but he was chopping again, clearly leaving this one to me. "They're certainly gorgeous. She's a gifted designer." Then I thought of the engagement party sheet cake. "When she's motivated."

Madge narrowed her eyes. "Do you think she'd be motivated with our cake?"

"I think Thalia would make sure she was." I was certain about that. Thalia wouldn't let Marla get by with a half-assed cake this time.

Madge bit her lip. "Did you get to eat any of the cake she made for that rehearsal dinner?"

Well, damn. I'd hoped Madge wouldn't ask me that. "Yeah, I had a piece."

"And?"

I took a breath. Honesty was called for here. I didn't want Madge to end up with a cake that tasted lousy. "It was okay. The decoration was good, and the frosting was outstanding. The cake tasted sort of ordinary."

Across the kitchen Nate gave me an approving smile. He wouldn't have let me lie to Madge, no matter how much I would have liked to.

"So basically, this cake would be for show rather than for eating." Madge folded her arms, too. "On the other hand, I guess that's true of a lot of wedding cakes."

"Honestly, her regular wedding cakes may taste fine," I said quickly. "This was a rush job, and I don't think she liked Pollack any better than we did."

"Right." Madge nodded. "Well, tell Thalia to do her best. And, as you said, Coco doesn't do wedding cakes, although she might do cupcakes for the rehearsal dinner if I asked her."

I stared at her. So did Nate. "We're having a rehearsal dinner?" Visions of more planning battles marched through my brain. *God, what could we make in my kitchen?*

Madge's lips edged up in a grin. "Catered by Moretti's Pizza. I'm not pushing my luck."

Nate laughed, and my shoulders relaxed. At least that was one less thing on the checklist.

Chapter 15

I decided I'd check with Coco just to make sure she didn't mind having Marla do the wedding cake, but I needn't have worried.

"Tell her to have at it," she told me. "I could have done a bunch of cupcakes or several dozen fruit tarts, but I wasn't happy about it. I'll come up with something in the way of a salad, and that will be my contribution to this epic production."

Thalia said she'd call Marla and get back to me, but she was still certain she could talk her into it. I hoped we wouldn't end up with another glorified sheet cake, but that decision was off my plate.

I did talk to Nate about the menu, but basically it was just to tell him to go to it. He knew what the drawbacks were at the barn—the fact that we had no kitchen, so we'd be doing the prep work at the café and then trying to keep the food warm at the cabin. My guess was he'd go for something low stress like pasta, but knowing that the cooks would be Nate and Bobby, that pasta would be Best of Breed.

Susa had set up a file sharing site for us when we'd been investigating a murder where I was a chief suspect. I'd learned the advantages of writing out anything I learned that was relevant to the case, so I wrote up what Thalia had told me about her deal with Pollack. I didn't see how it helped much, but at least it was information about Pollack's business.

Susa called me a couple of hours later. "Saw you posted stuff to the site. Good for you, kid. You're learning."

"Yeah, I don't know how much help it'll be, though. It's just details about the deal Pollack had with Thalia. Given that I'm trying to show Thalia couldn't have done it, the fact that she still has a loan with Pollack's estate isn't helpful."

"Sure, it is," Susa said. "It shows she didn't have anything to gain from killing him in terms of money. He made her a business loan, and I think we can assume he had a record of it somewhere so whoever takes over his business can go on collecting on his loans. Killing him wouldn't get her anything."

"Except relief from his presence," I muttered.

"Be that as it may, now you know a little about his business. Which means you've got something to tell Alice."

I paused. "You called her?"

"I called her. She said Sunday afternoon."

"This Sunday?" Sunday was usually a low stress day I spent with Nate. He helped with brunch at the café in the morning, and then we had the rest of the day to ourselves. And since the café was closed on Monday, we could sleep in.

"Of course, this Sunday. Don't tell me you can't make it. If we ask her for another date, she'll never talk to us again."

"No, no, I can do it. I just wish I had more to tell her." Considering what I had at the moment, Alice would probably sneer at us. "Did you say what we wanted to talk to her about?"

"Yeah, I told her you were working for Emerson Pollack the night he got killed, and now you were trying to figure out who might be a suspect besides Thalia."

"Okay, did she say anything?"

"Not really. She sort of muttered something about 'Their name is legion.' "

That sounded vaguely threatening. "What time does she want us?"

"One o'clock. At least she won't make us drag ourselves out of bed early."

"That's something. I'll come get you at twelve-thirty or so."

"Twelve-forty-five. No point in getting there early."

I hung up with an uncomfortable feeling. If I was going to spend a Sunday afternoon with Alice Hoover, I'd need to tell Nate why. So far, I hadn't let him know I was checking up on Pollack. I was pretty sure he wouldn't approve, even though I was doing it because Madge had asked me to. Still, he could give me some suggestions, assuming he didn't decide to tell me I was nuts for getting involved.

I decided to explain during supper. We were having a very nice bowl of tuna casserole that had been left over at the café, along with a bottle of muscadet that had been hiding in the refrigerator. We were as relaxed as we were likely to be for the rest of the evening.

"So," I said, "Susa and I are going to talk to Alice Hoover on Sunday afternoon."

"Alice?" He raised an eyebrow. "Why do you need to speak with her?"

I took a deep breath. "We need to find out more about Emerson Pollack, and she's the logical person to ask."

Nate started shaking his head as soon as he heard the name, Emerson Pollack. "No," he said. "Please no. You don't need to do that at all."

"Actually, I do," I said. "Madge asked me to. She's worried about Thalia."

"I don't know whether she needs to be worried about Thalia or not, but she doesn't need to pull you into it. This is none of our business, Rox. You know that. I like Thalia, but I'm not happy about you investigating Pollack's murder just because Thalia's under suspicion. Neither of us thinks she's guilty. And if she's innocent, she'll come out from under suspicion when Fowler finds the real killer."

I thought that was a little overoptimistic, but it wasn't the point here. "I'm not looking for the killer. I've got no way of knowing who all the people were at the dinner, and any of them could have been the one who killed Pollack. All I'm trying to do is find out who the man really was. Don't you want to know why this might have happened?"

"Not particularly." Nate sighed. "He was a nasty piece of work, and he probably had enemies wherever he stayed for any amount of time. I don't care which ones did him in."

"Okay," I said, "how about if I promise talking to Alice is the end of it? We've got a lot on our plate right now. Thanksgiving and the holidays and, God knows, The Wedding. I'll get a little information from Alice, and if it seems like something Fowler needs to know, Susa can pass it on."

Nate gave me a long look. "I know better than to think I can talk you out of this. But I'll hold you to that promise. Talking to Alice is the end of it."

I nodded. "Talking to Alice is the end of it. Absolutely." And I meant it. At the time.

Alice's house was also in Old Shavano. It had actually been her family home from when she'd grown up in town, but she'd had it renovated and brought up to date when she'd retired from her job as a financial guru in Denver. It was in the part of Shavano where the property values were rising steeply as more people bought the old houses and turned them into showplaces. Alice had been ahead of the trend, but I doubt she thought much about trends anyway.

Trends followed Alice, not vice versa.

She met us at the door wearing her usual style that was a cross between upscale lumberjack and wealthy retiree. Her jeans were well worn, as was the flannel shirt she wore over her olive-green turtleneck. But that turtleneck was cashmere and the diamond studs in her ears were most likely real, as were her olive suede booties. Alice was the embodiment of knowing just who you were and not giving a damn. I very much hoped I'd be a bit like her when I hit my seventies.

"Come on in." She marched down her entry hall, obviously expecting us to follow her. Which we did. She paused at the dining room, pointing to her oak dining table. "Sit. I'll bring the tea."

I don't drink much tea, but I do when I'm at Alice's house. It's not a matter of choice. Susa and I sat opposite each other, waiting, while Alice puttered around in her kitchen, finally emerging with a tray that held a bright blue teapot and a couple of mugs. "It's Irish breakfast," she said. "All I have on hand until the next shipment arrives from Boston."

"Sounds good," Susa said, pouring a healthy splash

of cream into her tea and adding a couple of sugar lumps. I took a tentative sip and decided cream and sugar were definitely the way to go.

Alice poured herself a cup of tea and took her seat between us. "All right. What is it you want to know?"

"Everything you can tell us about Emerson Pollack," I said.

Alice paused, her cup half raised. "Not someone with whom I've spent a great deal of time."

I took a sip of my doctored tea. "But someone you've heard of?"

"In passing. The kind of business he was involved in doesn't bear too much scrutiny," Alice said slowly as she raised her cup the rest of the way. "I haven't tried to learn much about what he did. Sometimes it pays to be discreet."

I glanced at Susa, who was staring wide-eyed at Alice. "Still, in this situation, I'd like to know what we're dealing with. In case the police make some wrong assumptions."

Alice shrugged. "All right, I'll tell you what I can. But let me say from the beginning, I never met Emerson Pollack, and, God knows, I never had any dealings with him. What I'm going to pass along is information I've heard second and third hand over a few years. I believe it's generally accurate, but I can't vouch for details."

I blew out a breath. This was sounding more and more ominous. "Understood."

"All right, then. Emerson Pollack served as a bank of last resort for people who needed money and couldn't find it on the legitimate market. He loaned money at high rates of interest, well above the going rate. And it was understood by any and all who took those loans that they needed to keep making payments regularly or they'd face dire consequences. Very dire consequences, as I understand it."

"He was a loan shark?" I'd guessed that already based on Thalia's experiences.

"Among his other activities." Alice sipped more tea, maybe deciding what direction she'd take us in next. "According to rumor, Pollack was also a financial advisor to several people who were in need of very specialized advice. People who had funds they not only wanted to increase, but also wanted to keep under the radar of those who are charged with keeping track of what money is where."

I must have looked as confused as I felt. Alice grimaced. "How much do you know about money laundering?"

"A little," I said. "It's when people make money through illegal stuff and then have to turn the illegal money into something that seems legal, right?"

Alice's grimace deepened. "That's a vastly oversimplified version, but yes. People like drug dealers or extortionists or officials who take bribes need to find a way to convert their ill-gotten gains into legitimate funds so that they can spend the money. Otherwise, the government—or several governments—may notice the suspicious amount of money they're tossing around and come knocking on their doors, asking to see their bank accounts."

"But if Pollack's money came from loans, wasn't that legit?" Susa asked. "I mean, even though he was charging really high interest?"

"Given that Pollack was careful to incorporate his business in a state that had very flexible usury laws, yes, he was legit. But as I said, he was also a financial advisor of a sort." Alice paused. "Let me repeat, this is all very much rumor, by the way. Pollack would never have allowed such speculation to become widely known if he'd heard about it. People were very careful not to cross him."

I nodded. "But he's in no position to hear it now."

Alice gave me the ghost of a smile. "True. Anyway, the speculation was that if you were generating money that you didn't want to account for, Pollack was the man to talk to. For a fee, he could guide you in the direction of a service company or an investment firm or somebody else that could convert those funds into something that would pass the sniff test. He supposedly specialized in individuals who needed to launder relatively minor amounts, mind you, hundreds of thousands rather than hundreds of millions. The big enterprises wouldn't have bothered with him."

Susa frowned. "What kind of business would they need to launder their ill-gotten gains?"

"Traditionally, businesses that generated a lot of cash have always been popular. Car washes were a big investment for a while. Massage parlors. Video arcades. Even restaurants and resorts. If a lot of cash is coming in, it becomes easier to conceal the dirty money within the relatively clean money." Alice shrugged. "Pollack may have controlled a lot of cash-heavy businesses through his loans. If so, he could have directed people who needed to launder their cash to businesses that might not ask many questions, given that Pollack controlled their finances."

My shoulders tightened as I thought about what she was saying. Thalia's business was one of those Pollack controlled or had a controlling interest in. But she didn't normally generate a lot of cash. At least I didn't think she did.

Pollack had paid Nate in cash. Had he paid anybody else that way? Marla, for example? Were there other features of the wedding and event planning business that he could have used for his clients? "What other ways could he have laundered their money?" I asked.

Alice stared at the ceiling as she ran through her mental list. "Off-shore banks, shell companies, invoice fraud."

"What kind of invoice fraud?" Susa sounded curious, as if she was getting into this whole idea.

"The easiest way is just to change the amount on the invoice so that it doesn't reflect the amount of money actually coming in or going out." Alice explained. "Art auctions are a good example. They're frequently secret, and the gallery is the only source of information about how much was spent for a given work of art. The crook could pay more or less than the invoice says, and the gallery could give him change in the form of clean money. But more importantly, the crook now has a clean source of funds in the form of a work of art valued at a particular level. He can sell it, or he can hold onto it, but chances are the government won't take it away."

I was beginning to feel dizzy. I've never been that great on financial stuff, and this was already way beyond my level. "But the point here is that Pollack was crooked. Which means lots of people might have wanted to get rid of him other than Thalia Rosenberg."

"Unquestionably." That ghost of a smile was back again. "But that's assuming everything I've just told you is accurate. As I said at the beginning of this conversation, this is entirely based on rumor. I've never talked to anyone who worked with Pollack directly, so we're into second- and third-hand information here as far as he's concerned. This information about money laundering is generic, and I have no idea whether Pollack used any of these methods or if he perhaps had developed methods of his own."

"Would an event planning business offer a way to launder funds?" I had no idea, but I figured Pollack had held onto Thalia's business for a reason.

Alice narrowed her eyes. "You're thinking of Rosenberg's company? I know squat about weddings. Do they involve a lot of cash?"

"I guess they can," I said slowly. "You're paying a lot of different people for different things—caterers, bakers, venue owners, clothing stores or rental shops, florists, musicians. I don't think Nate's been paid in cash much, but we've gotten cash tips. And Pollack did pay cash."

"Of course he did," Alice muttered. "Sounds like it has potential. Did Pollack refer clients to Rosenberg's business?"

"Thalia said he did, and it wouldn't be strange. After all, he owned an interest in her company."

"Exactly." Alice poured herself another cup of tea. "Anyone else want more?"

We both shook our heads. "But Pollack wouldn't push his daughter into getting married just so that he could launder some money," I said. "I mean, that sounds like overkill." And besides, Jennifer Pollack had seemed perfectly happy about the wedding although her fiancé getting drunk at the engagement party wasn't a plus.

"Maybe more like a target of opportunity," Susa

suggested. "As long as they were getting married, he could use the wedding to do a little business."

"The engagement party was more like a business get-together than family," I said. "And who knows what the groom's family was into?"

"Who's the groom?" Alice asked.

"Trent…" I paused, trying to remember the groom's last name. "Lukens, I think. Trent Lukens."

Alice looked like she'd tasted something sour. "Related to Hobart Lukens, no doubt."

"Who's Hobart Lukens?" Susa asked.

"Another individual whose business is on the shady side. A lot of the money behind the gambling proposition on the ballot last year came from Lukens. He owns resorts and sports bars that would have benefitted greatly from expanded gambling permits."

"So maybe a profitable alliance between the families?" The whole thing sounded more and more like some kind of medieval arranged marriage, although Jennifer Pollack hadn't appeared unwilling.

Alice took another sip of tea. "Probably one Pollack favored, at any rate."

That might well account for the speed in getting the wedding finalized. If Pollack was anticipating a business deal with Lukens, he might well prefer January to June.

"Do the cops know about Pollack?" Susa asked. "I mean, are they aware he was into all this sketchy stuff?"

"You'd have to ask Fowler about that, assuming he'd tell you, which he won't. I'd guess that they did, though. The rumors about Pollack have been floating around for a while. It's inevitable that someone must have brought them to the attention of the Feds if not the locals. Whether they could prove anything is another question. Given that Pollack never ended up in court so far as I know, I assume he was very good at covering his tracks. And now someone's made it much more difficult to ever find out what he was up to and with whom."

I paused. That honestly hadn't occurred to me—that someone might have killed Pollack to keep his business dealings secret. "Can't the cops access his business records as part of their investigation?"

"They can try," Alice said slowly. "But they won't succeed. Unless they can show very clearly that his finances and his business dealings were involved in his death, Pollack's lawyers and his estate will most likely fight very hard to keep his records private so that the government can't confiscate any of his assets."

This motive didn't help Thalia at all, given that she might well prefer her dealings with Pollack to stay private as well, particularly if he was sending her clients who wanted to launder their funds through a wedding or an anniversary party or some other high dollar event.

"Anything else?" Alice raised her eyebrows, waiting for whatever idiot questions we might still have.

I glanced at Susa. "No, I guess not. But thanks for the information. It makes some things a lot clearer."

Alice nodded. "Let me repeat, this is all very speculative, particularly when it's not clear who murdered Pollack and why. I'd be careful who I talked to about this. In fact, I'd keep quiet about it if I were you. If someone was willing to eliminate Pollack, he might well be willing to eliminate others as well."

That sent a quick shiver down my spine, but I couldn't argue with her. "I don't want to talk about it with a lot of people. In fact, telling Fowler was all I had in mind. Assuming he doesn't already know."

Alice shrugged. "He may or may not, depending on how chatty the Colorado Bureau of Investigation has been. And CBI may not know much themselves if the Feds are involved. Pollack may be dead, but the people who were involved in business dealings with him could still be around."

That was undoubtedly true, and enough to make me want to slink home in the shadows. We thanked Alice again and then walked out into the mountain twilight. It was still the time of year when the days were getting shorter, unfortunately.

"Well, that was enlightening," Susa said. "Also terrifying."

"You got that right." I blew out a long breath. "All of a sudden I don't want to talk to anybody about this, maybe not even Nate."

"Much as I like Nate, I agree with you. We should both keep this to ourselves."

"Right. Except for Fowler," I added.

Susa sighed. "You can tell Ethan if you want to. Personally, I'm going to forget I was ever here."

Very good advice, particularly for Susa. But I probably wouldn't take it myself.

Chapter 16

As it turned out, I didn't have a chance to talk to Fowler before Thanksgiving. On the Tuesday night before the big day, we got one of those snow dumps that happen in the mountains when you least expect or want it. It started to snow around dinnertime and by first light the next day, we'd gotten somewhere between six and twelve inches, depending on where you were in town. And it was still snowing.

This development threw the entire Thanksgiving celebration into chaos. Nobody knew how many people were likely to show up for dinner or how much snow was likely to be on the ground by Thanksgiving afternoon. Madge had already told everybody that the café would be closed on Thanksgiving Day so that Bobby and Nate could get to work on the turkey and ham and all the other goodies the café would provide for the dinner. Now there was a distinct possibility that not enough people would be able to make it through the snow-clogged streets to consume all that food. The café could always put turkey noodle soup or ham salad on the menu as daily specials, but would people want to eat Thanksgiving leftovers at the café when they were most likely already eating them at home?

At the farm, we were snowed in. The county plowed the highway at the entrance to our drive, but we were responsible for clearing the rest of the mile-and-a-half drive ourselves, which required heavy equipment. We had a deal with Terry Sylvester, who had an orchard down the road from us. Terry had a pickup with a snowplow attachment on the front, and he plowed our drive, along with a lot of other drives that ran down from the county highway. We paid him every time he ran his plow down our hillside, and that meant we didn't have to buy a plow attachment ourselves. This saved us a lot of trouble and expense, but it meant we had to wait until Terry got to us, maybe by mid-morning.

When he saw how much snow was stacked around the cabin, Nate promptly went back to bed. He had a point. It was cozy and warm in the bedroom, and we couldn't go anywhere until Terry showed up anyway. I crawled in beside him, determined to just nap for fifteen minutes or so. I woke up a couple of hours later when I heard Terry's pickup climbing up the hill to the county road.

"Time to get up," I mumbled, not moving.

Nate put his arms around me. "Any minute now."

We finally made it to vertical thirty minutes later and starting dressing for the arctic wilderness that waited just outside our front door—base layer, fleece-lined pants and shirt, parka, hat, and gloves.

I'd volunteered to come to the café and help with Thanksgiving prep although now it looked like we might not need as much food as we'd forecast. We took my pickup for its all-wheel drive and its high clearance, given that we might be driving through several inches of snow. It's still exciting to drive through a snowstorm, even though I no longer believe in my own invincibility the way I did when I was seventeen. We made it into town in slightly more time than we normally took to get there with only a few slides at snow-packed corners.

The snowplows had been through the city streets, clearing a couple of narrow lanes and leaving piles of snow at the sides which the locals would need to shovel through to clear their own driveways. This was an ongoing source of annoyance for people in town. By the end of the winter, the piles of icy snow at the edges of the streets could reach three or four feet in some places.

Nate pulled into the parking lot in front of the catering kitchen, which had been cleared by a commercial snowplowing company the café contracted with, and we tottered inside, trying not to slide on the packed snow. After we took off a couple of layers, we stepped into the café's kitchen. Marigold was taking a breather in a comfortable chair Bobby had found for her, propping her feet up on a crate of canned tomatoes, hands crossed on her pregnant belly. Bobby himself was behind the flattop, working on a couple of burgers. Coco sat next to Marigold, peeling apples.

"Slow day?" Nate peered into the café through the pass-through.

"Breakfast was decent," Marigold said.

"Maybe half as many people as usual." Bobby finished the burgers and dropped them into their plastic baskets along with scoops of fries. Marigold rolled her eyes, which I took to mean the breakfast crowd hadn't been off by that much.

"We'll start working on the Thanksgiving stuff over in the catering kitchen," Nate said.

"Don't make too much," Bobby said. "Chances are it's just going to be us. I doubt if anybody else will show up."

"Nonsense." Madge pushed through the door from

the dining room. "No one has called to cancel. The snow is supposed to stop this afternoon, and the streets will be clear by tomorrow morning. Everybody will be able to be up and around by the afternoon. It's going to be terrific." She gave Nate a determined smile. "Go ahead and make as much as you'd planned. I'm sure we'll have plenty of people to eat it."

Nate smiled back. "Yes, ma'am, we'll do our best."

Madge turned to Marigold, her forehead furrowing in concern. "Oh, dear, are you feeling tired? Why don't you go on home? Nate's here—he can help if there's a rush."

Bobby snorted, which I thought was his opinion on the possibility of a rush and not on Nate's helping.

"I'm fine, Madge. There isn't enough business right now for two of us to cook. I'll put my feet up for a while, and then I'll cook, and Bob can take it easy." Marigold raised her chin to a challenging angle.

Bobby narrowed his eyes at the idea of taking it easy, but he and Marigold could fight that particular battle. Nate nodded toward the catering kitchen, and the two of us took off. We spent the rest of the afternoon roasting the turkey and getting the dressing and sweet potatoes and cranberry sauce ready. The ham could be done tomorrow morning since it didn't take as much time as the turkey, and since the ham was Bobby's specialty.

As Madge had predicted, the snow stopped around three. I checked the café kitchen before we prepared to take off for the farm while it was still light. Bobby and Marigold had already gone home, but Coco was taking two pies out of the oven. The room smelled like my idea of heaven.

"Anybody call in to cancel for tomorrow?" I asked.

Coco shook her head. "Most of the people coming for dinner live downtown. If nothing else, they can hike over here tomorrow. I don't think we're going to have many no-shows, but I could be wrong. And even if we do, Thanksgiving's all about leftovers, right?"

"Right." And any leftover pie could come live at our house. "We got the turkey done and carved. It's in the refrigerator in the catering kitchen. Dressing and sweet potatoes and cranberries, too. Everything can just be reheated tomorrow."

"You taking off for the trackless wastes?" Coco asked.

"Yep. It's not too bad. The plows have been through." And I devoutly hoped Terry had come around a second time to clear out the snow that had fallen on the drive after his first pass. "Are you driving?"

"Nope. Marcus is going to pick me up when he gets his mom. He gave me a ride this morning." Marcus was Bianca's son, and a great guy. Fortunately, Coco thought so, too.

Driving home wasn't bad, but it also wasn't good. *Bad* when you're driving snowy roads in the mountains means you're in fear for your life most of the time you're moving. We had to put up with some deep snow here and there, but nothing that was going to send us into a ditch. And Terry had been by a second time, bless him.

It was, however, freakin' cold out there, so we broke out some stew and beer for dinner, then watched TV while checking the weather service every fifteen minutes.

****

Thanksgiving dawned very cold and very bright, sunlight sparkling on the new-fallen snow. It was

181

gorgeous and slightly threatening, given that you could freeze to death on a sunny day just as easily as a snowy one when the temperature was this low. Uncle Mike came down for breakfast and to grab a ride to the café. He was going to stay over at Madge's place or maybe use her car to drive to the farm. We were all still in the "don't ask, don't tell" stage of their relationship, but it was also the "don't care" stage, so nobody was concerned.

The hairiest part of the ride was our drive, which has a steep patch near the end. But we were in Nate's SUV, and it had very good tires, so we made it to the top with only minor panic. At the café, all the various ovens were already in use, and Coco had put out a tray of her pastries for all of us kitchen types so we wouldn't be malnourished. Guests started showing up around ten, all of them bearing food, which in some cases needed to be warmed up. That meant a lot of people milling around in a small space that was dominated by Bobby, who hated having strangers hanging out in his kitchen.

Nate herded the people he knew into the catering kitchen and let them prep to their heart's content. Susa showed up around noon, and I brought her back to hang out. There was a small dining space beside the catering kitchen, the space Nate wanted to make into a bistro someday. Right now, we'd managed to fit in four tables, although one of them had a wall of boxes behind it since the dining space was usually used for storage.

The café dining room was already filling up with Madge's friends and some of Uncle Mike's buddies from his favorite coffee shop, along with a few farmers. Madge was on the money when she said we wouldn't have any cancellations. I was just hoping we'd have enough chairs so that everybody could eat sitting down.

It was chaotic and frenzied and joyful, just the kind of Thanksgiving I like. The food was served on the counter in the dining room, the number of dishes constantly changing as one chef's offering was finished off and another chef's dish took its place. This led to a lot of people cycling through the line multiple times just to see what was new and tasty, which also led to a lot of people standing around talking and chewing. By mid-afternoon, Susa and Coco were sitting together with Bianca and her son, Marcus, who'd brought a gorgeous charcuterie platter along with his mom's rolls, both of which disappeared very quickly.

Lots of people I vaguely recognized circulated through the dining room and kitchen and catering space, with more sliding in and out the door. Annabelle Dorsey wandered through with her daughter, Dorothy, who looked alternately bored and fascinated. Ted Sylvano, who ran an upscale grocery in Geary that stocked my jam, stood talking to Donnie McCray, Uncle Mike's second in command at the farm and Dolce's father. At one point I saw Thalia and Beverly, her assistant, loading their plates with some of Coco's Dutch apple pie. Several other people I vaguely recognized circulated through the food lines, cooks or people who worked at the farmers market. It occurred to me then that I had no idea who all these people were and who'd invited them, and I'd probably never see them all, given the crush of people in the dining room.

Around two, I saw Fowler, in uniform, filling a plate from the current array of goodies. Several of his cops had already circulated through, so maybe he'd waited until all of them had been fed before he came over himself.

I'd been thinking about what I'd say to him about what Alice had told me, if anything. I felt like I needed to pass on what she'd said, but I knew he'd snarl at me. Fowler was very strict about amateurs getting in his way. We'd batted heads before over my asking questions about his cases. Still, my talking to Alice was about as far as I was going to go on this one, and I felt like Fowler needed to know what I'd found out, just in case he didn't know already.

Once he'd finished getting his food, he paused, searching for a place to sit down. I sidled up to him then. "Come on. I'll find you a table."

Fowler looked mildly surprised, but he was willing to follow me into the catering area. Nate and some of his chef friends were in the kitchen talking about food prices, so I directed Fowler into the small dining area where I'd been sitting with Susa earlier. There were a few people at the other tables, but they were busy talking to each other, so they probably wouldn't pay much attention to us. The dining area was like a maze, with stacks of cartons forming walls between the tables, which at least gave the illusion of privacy.

I could hear Nate's friend Spence raising his voice in the catering kitchen, followed by raucous laughter. At one of the other tables, a guy was holding forth about cryptocurrency in one of those voices that tends to pierce through every other sound.

Fowler put down his plate and narrowed his eyes at me as I dropped into a chair opposite him. "You're not eating?"

"I've already had seconds. I'm letting everything settle before I have any more. Besides, I need to talk to you."

Fowler grimaced as he cut off a bite of turkey and gravy. "Are you going to tell me something that will ruin my appetite?"

"Absolutely not." I pulled myself up straight. The cryptocurrency guy was getting to his point, but his dinner companion was disagreeing. Loudly. Seemed like a good time to talk about things I didn't want other people to hear. "I talked to Alice Hoover the other day." I wasn't going to tell him Susa had also been there since I wasn't sure how he'd take the news.

"About what?'

"Emerson Pollack."

Fowler slowed as he stabbed a green bean. "Why did the subject of Emerson Pollack come up?"

"Because I brought it up." Fowler gave me a sour look, but I raised a hand. "Just let me tell you what she said, okay? I haven't done anything else." Well, besides talking to Thalia, but Fowler would have talked to her, too. He might not have thought to talk to Alice.

"What did Alice have to say about Pollack?" Fowler asked reluctantly.

"She said she didn't know anything specific, just rumors. First off, she said he was a loan shark, which I guess was common knowledge." And which wasn't necessarily illegal. At least Alice had implied it wasn't. "But along with his loan sharking, he was also a financial advisor to a lot of sketchy people." The cryptocurrency duo had subsided a bit, so I lowered my voice.

Fowler nodded as he chewed. "He may have been. That's not illegal unless he gave them illegal advice."

I sighed. "Well, that's the point, sort of. Some of his advice might have been as sketchy as his clients."

As more laughter boomed from the kitchen, Fowler

stabbed another green bean, maybe a little more aggressively than necessary. "Go on."

I took a moment to glance around the room, making sure the people at the other tables weren't listening. The cryptocurrency guys were getting up from their table, still muttering. Nobody else seemed interested, but I had an uncomfortable feeling between my shoulder blades, as if we might have an audience I wasn't aware of.

Imagination. I took a deep breath. "According to the rumors, he was the go-to guy for money laundering. For small time money laundering, that is. If people had a few hundred thousand they needed to make legit, he could find them places to stash it. And some of those places may have been with companies where he'd loaned money and had a part ownership. Places that were otherwise legit, but where he could lean on the business owners to do what he wanted them to do. In fact, he was a go-to guy for people like Thalia and other small businesses. He'd loan them money when nobody else would. Thalia isn't the only one who wanted his money, and some of those people may have been at that engagement party. Maybe people who took money from Pollack could be suspects."

Fowler stirred a little gravy into his mashed potatoes. "Yeah. That had occurred to us already. Anything else?"

"The groom's family is sort of dicey," I said. "He's related to Hobart Lukens, who's got some gambling connections. That might have been why Pollack had the wedding on the fast track—so that he and Lukens could do some business together."

Fowler sighed. "I know Lukens. Didn't realize he was connected to the groom, though." He took a moment to study me. "These are all rumors. No proof, I take it."

I shook my head. "According to Alice, people were nervous about Pollack. He didn't like anyone poking around in his business. So most of this was just general speculation." I leaned a little closer, keeping my voice down. "In fact, Alice warned me to keep quiet about Pollack except for passing the information on to you."

Fowler looked down at his plate again, cutting off a little more turkey. "Have you told anyone else?"

"Nobody. Alice knows what she's talking about."

"Yeah, Alice has good sources. And I'd go double on what she told you." He checked around the room before he took another bite of dressing. "This isn't a topic for general conversation."

He gave me a long look that made me want to duck. "Did you know this already?" I asked.

He spread a little cranberry sauce over his turkey. "A lot of it. Mr. Pollack has aroused some interest from law enforcement over the years."

"So the person who attacked him might be someone who was trying to set something up with him. Maybe someone who wasn't happy with what Pollack was willing to offer." Not including Thalia, who didn't have any particular axe to grind with Pollack.

Fowler paused then cut off another piece of turkey. "Possible."

"And you're considering people who had business with Pollack? Or wanted to have?"

Fowler gave me an annoyed look. "We're talking to a lot of people who dealt with him."

That was probably the end of this conversation. I pushed away from the table. "Okay, I guess that's all I had to tell you. Hope it didn't affect your appetite." It hadn't, so far as I could tell.

"Nope, I'm good."

"There you are." Susa stepped around a stack of boxes along the edge of the room. "I thought I saw you come in. Lots of people coming and going around here."

Fowler gave her a slow smile. "I would have stopped by, but I thought you were busy with the Jordans. Plus, Roxy dragged me in here."

I started to protest, but Susa shrugged. "She made a good choice. If she was talking about what I think she was talking about, it wasn't for general consumption."

Fowler put his fork down and gave me what I thought of as his turn-to-stone stare. "You said you didn't tell anyone." He gestured toward Susa. "She counts as someone."

"You didn't tell him?" Susa raised her eyebrows as I shook my head. "Noble of you, but unnecessary." She turned to Fowler again. "I was there with her. Alice is my friend—or my contact, anyway. If you've got questions, I can give you some details. I took notes."

I blinked at her. Had she put her notes into our online sharing app? Was that safe?

Fowler closed his eyes, and I had the feeling he was fighting hard not to yell. "You took notes. And you no doubt put them online. About stuff Alice told you not to share?"

"I'm not sharing my notes with anyone but you and Roxy. And they're so well protected it would take the electronic equivalent of a bulldozer to break in. Trust me on this." Susa dropped into the chair I'd just vacated. "So if you have any comments, I'm ready to listen."

"I'll just revisit the dining room. There's probably something I haven't tasted," I said. But of course, neither of them was paying attention to me.

Just as well. Right then it was best to just disappear.

Chapter 17

The meal went on for most of the day, with volunteers loading the dishwasher when it needed to be done. Bobby took Marigold home around four, although I thought Marigold herself could have hung in there a lot longer. Marcus disappeared with Coco and his mom a little later, and other people began to wander off as things wound down.

Madge sat in the dining room with Uncle Mike and some other friends, sipping coffee and having one more piece of pie for the road.

As the hordes began to depart, I helped Nate straighten up the kitchen. Coco had already cleaned up her station and encased the leftover pie in plastic wrap before putting it in the refrigerator. Wrapped or not, it was going home with us—I'd already decided that. We could leave whatever pots and pans needed to be cleaned up for Tres, the café's dishwasher/janitor, to take care of on Friday. Most of the plates that weren't disposables had gone home with the cooks who brought them. I figured the orphans could be claimed during the next week when people remembered that they'd brought their food in a bowl that wasn't currently in their kitchens.

Nate wiped down the counters, and I did a quick sweep around the floor with a push broom to get any major debris although, again, Tres would do a much better job on the deep cleaning tomorrow.

I glanced up as Nate came into the dining room. "It's snowing," he said.

"Again? Do we need to start home?" If the roads got too snowy, we might be stuck in Nate's old apartment in town, which wouldn't be nearly as cozy as the cabin.

Nate shook his head. "It's not heavy yet. You want to go for a walk before we drive back?"

We'd been inside the café all day, which had been fun but also sort of stuffy. The idea of a walk through the cold winter air sounded lovely. "Yeah," I said. "That would be nice."

We bundled up because the temperature was still in the single digits, but there was no wind for once. The snowflakes were falling in a lacy drift through the twilight, and the snow seemed to sort of muffle the sound. Everything was quiet, except for the noise of an occasional car or a barking dog a few blocks over. Nate turned toward a street behind the café where the drifts at the sides created by the snowplow were a couple of feet high.

"Let's go to the park," he said.

We walked down the middle of the empty street because the sidewalks hadn't been cleared yet. No traffic to speak of, and it felt oddly isolated as if the two of us were the only ones around Shavano on this Thanksgiving night. The new snow crunched under our boots as we stepped through the the pools of light created by the streetlights. I leaned closer to Nate in the gathering darkness, and he put his arm around my shoulders. "Pretty night."

I grinned up at him. "If you don't count the fact that it's freezing, yeah."

Freezing or not, it was still pleasant to be out

walking with him, feeling the icy flick of snowflakes on my cheeks. Mountain magic for those who get out and look for it. We didn't do this as often as we should have, but tonight was a rare opportunity to enjoy it.

After a few minutes, I heard the noise of a car rolling along the snowy street some ways behind us. It sounded like it was coming faster than was wise, given how slippery the streets still were. Nate moved over to the side to let it pass, but we couldn't get all the way out of the street because of the drifts left by the plow.

And the car was speeding up.

"What the hell?" I glanced over my shoulder, and discovered it wasn't a car but a pickup with a snowplow attachment on the front. And it wasn't pulling over to get around us. In fact, it was driving straight for us, although the packed snow on the street was slowing it down some.

Nate grabbed my hand. "Come on, we need to run."

Both of us were wearing snow boots with tough soles. They weren't ideal for running, though. I thought about jumping over the drifts at the side, but they were almost three feet high, and if either of us slipped, we might roll into the path of the truck. Nate was pulling hard on my arm as we heard the truck's wheels spinning against the snow.

The truck's headlights were full on, blinding me when I looked backward. My feet kept sliding in the snowy tracks even as I tried to increase my speed. Nate's hold on my arm slipped, so that he was holding onto the cuff of my sleeve even as I dug in my toes to try to get purchase on the packed snow.

Then I saw a break in the snow drift ahead of us. "There," I panted. "Go there."

Nate grabbed hold of me again, dragging me toward

the open space. Then he turned sharply and jumped, pulling me along with him. The break in the snow wasn't much, maybe a foot or so, but it was enough to get us through and out of the street. I fell to my knees as Nate landed next to me on his back. The truck swerved toward us, and for a moment I was terrified that it would keep coming up onto the sidewalk and crush us before we could get out of the way. But then it hit the snowbank and bounced away.

He grabbed a chunk of ice from the ground beside him, throwing it at the side of the truck as it pulled away. I heard a dull *thunk* and hoped mightily that he'd dented the door. Then we both lay panting on the snow-covered sidewalk, listening to the truck roar down the street away from us.

"Are you okay?" Nate asked finally, groping for my hand.

"I think so. What about you?" We were both covered with loose snow, but I couldn't see any blood.

Nate pulled himself to his feet, staring after the truck's retreating taillights. "I'm okay. What the hell was that all about?"

"I think somebody tried to run us down." That was stating the obvious. The initial rush of adrenaline I'd felt was beginning to wear off, and I realized that no matter how soft the snow might have appeared, landing on it had been a painful experience.

"No shit. Have you got your phone?"

I patted my jacket pocket and found my phone, which was unscathed. "911?"

Nate nodded. "We need to let somebody know about this."

I described what had happened to the police

dispatcher, who promised to send someone right away. I figured not much stuff happened on Thanksgiving night, so lots of cops might be available.

"Tell them we'll meet them at the café," Nate said. "It's too cold to wait around here."

I endorsed that idea. I told the dispatcher where we'd be, then we started walking again, staying on the snowy sidewalks, and keeping an eye out for pickup plows. I was surprised at how close we'd been to the café—it had seemed like we'd walked a lot farther. And the distance we'd run had felt like miles at the time.

"Who the hell would do that?" Nate said as we trudged up the walk to the café's back door.

"Kids?" I didn't believe it, but maybe.

Nate shook his head. "Kids wouldn't have a pickup with a snowplow. At least none of the kids I know would have one."

I took a deep breath, debating whether to say anything or not. But someone had tried to kill Nate, who was an innocent bystander. And I had information that he might need to know. "It might have to do with what Alice told me about Pollack."

Nate stopped, staring down at me. "And that would be?"

"She said there were a lot of rumors around Pollack, that he was a loan shark who might also have laundered money for his clients. She also told me not to talk about Pollack to anybody, that it was dangerous to have too much information about someone like him, and that even asking questions could get me in trouble."

Nate stood blinking in the snow. "And did you talk about Pollack to anybody after that?"

"Just Fowler. This afternoon. He needed to know the

information I got from Alice if he didn't know it already." I bit my lip. It had all made sense at the time.

"Where were you when you told him this?"

"Back in the seating area beside the catering kitchen. There were a few other people there, but not many. And nobody was listening." And yes, I had felt uncomfortably as if someone might have heard us, but I'd decided that was imagination, brought on by Alice's warnings.

"Still, somebody might have heard," Nate said slowly.

"Yeah." I closed my eyes. "I guess. But why would they try to kill us over it? I mean, I'd already told Fowler."

"Maybe they were afraid you'd be telling other people, too, and one of the ones you told might figure out who killed Pollack. Or maybe you hadn't found out everything yet, and they wanted to stop you before you did. Running us down with a snowplow doesn't strike me as an idea that took a lot of advance planning." Nate put a hand on my back, pushing me gently through the rear entry of the café.

"I'm sorry," I mumbled.

"What for?"

"For not telling you. I just…didn't want to get you involved. Alice made the whole thing sound scary."

"Which meant it was scary for you, too." Nate looked away as he relocked the back door.

"Yeah. If I'd known in advance what I was getting into, I might have backed off." Which was what Nate had wanted me to do in the first place.

We stepped into the darkened kitchen, and Nate paused. After a moment, he put his arms around me, pulling me close. "Don't keep things from me," he said.

"If you're in danger, I need to know about it."

"I didn't mean to." I felt tears threatening, which I didn't need right then. I snuggled closer to him, wrapping my arms around his waist and pressing my face to his chest. "And I didn't think I was in danger. I never dreamed something like this could happen."

Someone pounded on the front door, and we jumped apart, startled. "Probably the cops," Nate said, turning toward the door.

I wasn't surprised to see Fowler waiting for us. After all, he was on duty and Thanksgiving was probably a very slow crime day. "Evening," he said as he stepped inside, followed by a police officer in uniform. "Everybody gone home?"

"Yeah," Nate said. "We were ready to leave ourselves, but we decided to take a walk first. To clear out the cobwebs."

"Probably a good idea. Normally. So tell me what happened."

"We walked toward the park," Nate said. "Down Fifth Street. Nobody was around, and the sidewalks hadn't been shoveled yet, so we walked in the street. A truck with a snowplow attachment came up behind us and tried to run us down. We jumped a snowdrift and got onto the sidewalk before it got to us."

"You're sure he was trying to run you down, that it wasn't just that he didn't see you?"

"I'm sure. He tried to jump the curb and keep going at the end, but he couldn't get through the drift."

"Can you show me where all this happened?" Fowler asked. "We've got a patrol car so we can drive over."

"Easier to walk," Nate said. "It's not far."

The four of us hiked through the snow again to the street where we'd been walking. Fortunately, the snow hadn't yet filled in the tracks of the truck or our footprints as we ran away from it.

It was dark by now, illuminated by the streetlights. Fowler aimed his flashlight along the street, then handed it to the other cop so that he could pull out his cell phone. They took a series of shots, including close-ups of the tire tracks. I wasn't sure how well they'd come out, given the darkness and difficulty of getting clear shots of the marks in the snow.

"We'll come tomorrow when it's light," Fowler said. "Maybe get some better shots." Of course, by tomorrow, the snow would have filled in the tire tracks and made the marks of our struggle indistinct, assuming somebody hadn't driven over them by then.

Fowler studied us again. "You notice what kind of truck it was? Make and model maybe?"

I shook my head. "The front was covered by the snowplow attachment. I couldn't see much of the truck."

"It was a heavy-duty pickup, but I didn't see it clearly," Nate said. "But I hit it on the passenger's side door with a chunk of ice. With any luck it left a mark."

Fowler grimaced. "Let's hope for that luck."

Finally, we walked to the café. By then I was thoroughly chilled, plus my knees had begun to throb from my hard landing on the snow. Nate unlocked the back door of the café as Fowler turned to his police officer assistant. "You can go on back. Take the car. I'll hike over when I've finished talking to these folks."

The police officer was delighted to be returning to the warmth of the police station. Fowler followed us inside.

I peeled off my coat and hat, while Nate stepped into the pantry and emerged with a bottle of the brandy Coco used to make brandy-snap cookies. "Not exactly SOP, but it's enough to warm you up."

"Right." I grabbed three juice glasses from the cabinet, then gave Fowler a questioning look.

He nodded. "A small one. Enough to thaw me out."

Nate took off his own coat and gloves, then poured three small brandies. We pulled up some chairs and sipped. I don't drink a lot of hard liquor—I'm more a beer and wine type—but the brandy warmed me all the way to my toes. I blew out a long breath and relaxed in my chair.

"So," Fowler said.

"So?"

"So what's your take on the truck that tried to run you down? Somebody joyriding? Or something else?"

I sighed, rubbing my eyes. "Joyriding in a snowplow seems a little hard to buy."

Fowler shrugged. "Most likely stolen. I'll check the reports when I get back to the station, but the owner may not even realize it's gone yet. If he's celebrating Thanksgiving, that is."

"Does that make joyriding more likely?" If a bored teenager stole a snowplow, would he be likely to try to run down a couple of random walkers rather than plowing a trench through the park? Maybe.

"It's a clear possibility," Fowler said. "In which case, we'll never catch him unless he's dumb enough to do it again. Or unless we find some evidence left behind in the snowplow."

"Could it have been related to what Roxy heard from Alice Hoover?" Nate's face had no expression beyond polite curiosity.

Fowler studied him for a moment. "It's possible," he said finally. "Anything's possible." He turned to me. "Who all have you told about what Alice said?"

"You," I said. "And Nate. I told Nate tonight, after the truck tried to run us down."

Fowler nodded slowly. "So if the driver knew what Alice told you, he'd have had to hear it when you told me about it this afternoon."

"Pretty much." I supposed it was possible Susa had told somebody, but I didn't think it was likely. She'd been as spooked as I was when we left Alice's place. And the only person she might tell would be Fowler.

Fowler stared down at his brandy. "Did you notice anybody around while we were talking? Anyone who might have been listening?"

"There were people at the other tables, but they weren't close, and they weren't interested in us. The guys talking about cryptocurrency two tables over were loud." I'd told myself that at the time. Now I wondered if they'd been as effective at covering up what we'd been saying as I'd assumed at the time.

"I didn't notice anybody, but I was concentrating on my dinner," Fowler said and gave Nate a half smile. "Great turkey."

"Thanks. We've got some leftovers if you're interested." Nate wasn't smiling, but he seemed a little less tense.

"I might be." Fowler turned to me. "Susa wasn't as quiet as you were."

"True." I blew out a breath. "But she also wasn't talking about specifics, or at least I don't think she was. Anyone listening would have a tough time figuring stuff out based on what she was saying."

Fowler leaned back in his chair. "So here's the thing. If this was related to what Alice told you, and that's a very big *if* by the way, then the driver might have meant to scare you into staying quiet. And I'd say that's a good idea."

My jaw tightened. "You think scaring me was good?" If so, then the driver had more than accomplished Fowler's goal.

"No. I think you staying quiet is good. And I think you staying out of the Pollack case is even better. I don't even know why you were involved in the first place."

"Because Madge was worried about Thalia and her business," I said. It was late, and I was a little lightheaded from the brandy. Otherwise, I wouldn't have brought up Madge's name. Time for honesty. "And I was curious."

"I wasn't going after Ms. Rosenberg any more than anyone else. You should know by now that there are a lot of people who'd like to see Emerson Pollack out of commission." Fowler sipped his brandy again. "I can try to track down whoever killed Pollack, or I can try to keep track of you and your investigations. Doing both is tough."

I gritted my teeth, ready to let him know just what I thought of that, and just how little I needed him keeping track of me. But Nate reached over and took my hand. "Keeping track of Roxy is my job. So is protecting her. Consider yourself off duty where she's concerned." He gave Fowler a flat look.

Fowler pushed his chair away from the table. "Glad to hear it. I'll let you know if we find out anything about the truck."

Nate nodded. "Thanks. I appreciate it."

Fowler pulled on his parka and his hat. "Guess I'll get back. Thanks for the brandy."

"Anytime," Nate said. But that was mostly a formality.

I sat at the table, steaming. It's annoying to have someone talk about you as if you aren't in the room, and as if you have no part in decisions that affect your life. I'm used to Fowler telling me to butt out of his investigations although in this case, I'd argue that I hadn't really butted into those investigations in any serious way. But I wasn't used to Nate talking about me as if I was some fragile flower. I'm a big girl—*very big,* some people might say—and I can take care of myself.

I gave Nate a burning look, but he shook his head. "I know you're pissed, but, Jesus, Rox, where does Fowler get off talking like he's in charge of taking care of you? Hell, you do a good job of taking care of yourself most of the time. And if you need protecting, that's my job, dammit, not his."

I took a deep breath, telling myself to cool it. I'd never heard Nate spell that out before. And it didn't piss me off, now that I thought about it. It almost brought tears to my eyes for some reason I couldn't define. "I'd say we take care of each other, as much as we can. I've got your back like you've got mine. I love you, Nathan."

Nate stared at me across the darkened kitchen. "I know. I love you, too."

I rubbed a hand across the back of my neck. It had been a very long day.

Nate extended his hand to me. "Let's get out of here, okay?"

"Let's," I said. And we did.

Chapter 18

In spite of my determination not to let Fowler dictate what I did with my time, I did no more investigating of Emerson Pollack for the next couple of weeks. After all, it wasn't like I had nothing else going on in my life. I still had to finish getting the wine jelly ready for The Wedding, as well as running the occasional errand for Thalia in her wedding planning since she'd given both Beverly and Danielle the rest of the month off.

And I still had jam to make. My mail orders had picked up with people buying stuff for gifts, and Dolce and I were cooking full time to keep up with the demand. Bianca and the Made in Colorado store both ran low and wanted more supplies. So did Sylvano's in Geary. I was dividing all my time between cooking jam and making deliveries, but that was a good problem to have.

Fowler turned out to be right about the truck that had tried to run us down being stolen. The owner didn't even realize it was gone until he went outside his mother-in-law's house after Thanksgiving dinner and found a blank space where his truck ought to have been. The truck itself was found later on another side street. It had a big dent in the passenger's side door where Nate had heaved the chunk of ice, so we could be pretty sure it was the same truck that had come after us on the snowy street. Fowler's cops had gone over the inside carefully, but the driver, whoever it had been, had left nothing behind.

Given the number of people who used the truck regularly, DNA wasn't even a possibility. And nobody had seen anything.

That put an end to that line of inquiry, and I had other stuff to think about.

In spite of all the last-minute jam making, I was pretty much on top of things as far as Luscious Delights went. I'd had very good sales at the Winter Market a few weeks before Thanksgiving, and thanks to the work Dolce and I were putting in, I had a good supply of my perennials ready for Christmas sales. Bridget had designed a couple of gift boxes for those who wanted to send jam to people on their gift list, and she spent a lot of her afternoons assembling boxes and getting them ready for pickup.

I'd finally gotten a storage shed installed beside my cabin, so I no longer had to stack the cases of jam in random areas around the house. That also meant I could make lots of jam when I had the time and the fruit without worrying about having the space to keep it. I made a few cases of my December jam of the month, which was a spiced apple jelly I could have made in my sleep. After that it was wine jelly all day for me.

Dolce was a gem in all of this, making strawberry and peach and raspberry jam with a lot of professionalism. Every time I thought about losing her when she left for college, it made my heart ache. But I also knew I needed to think about taking the next step and hiring some full-time help. Bridget was in charge of order fulfillment for my web site and was now working three-quarters time for me, having cut back her hours waiting tables at High Country. If my sales kept increasing, I could probably hire her on full time within the next year. But I needed someone to help with the cooking, too. Right now, I was running at capacity for the slow season, which had given me enough time to do the favors for The Wedding. But as farmers market season approached, I'd need to produce a lot more jam than I could do on my own. My web-site sales were increasing steadily, and the farmers market sales kept pace.

Beck, my summer sales assistant, was a sweetie, but she didn't have any interest in becoming a jam cook. Besides, I needed more help than I could get from someone who could only work after school. Once Dolce was gone, I'd need to find someone with more hours available.

Nate had his own hands full with the Christmas party season in full swing. In a way, the postponement of the Pollack wedding had been a big help. Now Nate and Dex could concentrate on the office parties they had scheduled, along with some engagement parties and one big society blowout on December twenty-third, involving both apps and a buffet for a hundred or so. It was being held in the Blankenship House, a local historic house that belonged to the Shavano County Historical Association. I'd had some unpleasant interactions with the previous owner of the house, but he was now a resident of the state prison system, and his soon-to-be-ex-wife had been very happy to sell it to the association for a reasonable price and a steep tax write-off.

The Christmas party was to be a fundraiser for the association and for a new Shavano historical museum since the old one was housed in a distinctly unlovely strip mall. After a lot of consultation between the association, Nate, and Madge—who was, of course, on the association board—they'd decided on a menu of spaghetti Bolognese, salmon rillettes, and vegan fried rice. The idea was to create food that was elegant, but not terribly expensive so the association could keep some of the proceeds from the tickets for the new building. All the entrees also had the distinct advantage of being dishes that could be made in advance; in fact, the Bolognese actually improved if it sat in the refrigerator for a few days. Dessert would be a cake from no less than Marla Purdue, who was donating her time to the cause.

But that was for the twenty-third, and meanwhile there were a lot of different parties to get through. Since I had a little free time if you didn't count the wine jelly and the deliveries, I spent a few hours in the catering kitchen making Asian meatballs, which could be frozen after cooking and then reheated in a hot skillet. They were a popular choice, which meant they showed up at multiple parties. That in turn meant that I was cooking literally hundreds of the things. There is a certain Zen involved in making a couple hundred meatballs. I listened to audio books over my headphones as I worked, waving at Nate when he passed through the kitchen. Slowly bags full of frozen meatballs began to accumulate in the back of the freezer, to be pulled out and carried off to whatever office party we were doing each evening.

I also helped in the kitchen at some of these parties. Dex had a family, and he liked to spend time with them occasionally. I didn't have any comparable excuse; plus working the office parties meant I got to spend time with Nate. So I stayed in the kitchens at the various venues, warming up the apps that needed warming and laying out the others in appropriate patterns on the big party trays. It wasn't particularly demanding work although I did spend a lot of time on my feet.

Nate spent a lot more, since he was continually checking to make sure we had adequate food for the starving masses, as well as taking away empty trays and returning with the ones I'd filled. He'd learned by now to hire a busser for any party with more than twenty people in attendance. The number of plates and glasses thirty or more people could dirty in a couple of hours would be stunning to anybody who didn't spend much time around party hearty types. Along with preparing the food, I also loaded the dishwasher when I had a spare moment.

I liked working with Nate—we made a good team. I couldn't do it all the time, and the closer we got to farmers market season, the less time I'd have to do anything with the catering business. But for now, the parties meant we got to spend a little more time together, even if a lot of that time was taken up with running back and forth between the kitchen and the dining room of whatever venue we were currently using.

On a Friday night a little over a week before Christmas, we were in the weird modern building where we'd served the fatal Pollack engagement dinner. I have to admit that it gave me the creeps. Or rather, it gave me the creeps when we walked in. By the time we were serving the food to the cocktail party taking place in the smaller dining room, I was way too busy to consider anything like bad karma.

I wasn't sure who was throwing the party we were feeding. Most of the parties we'd done over the past week or so had been office parties, but there had also been a few club Christmas parties and even one party for a family that couldn't get together on Christmas for some reason. The first hint I got that the party at the event center was for a different kind of group came when I realized we hadn't brought along any of my bags of frozen meatballs. I took a good look at the menu then. Apparently, we weren't serving them any meat at all. We had our vegan filo veggie packets, which were delicious, although it often took people a while to try them. We also had a sizeable crudité tray with one of Nate's signature avocado dips, some caprese skewers with a balsamic drizzle, and some cheese taquitos with salsa. The closest thing to meat was a platter of devils on horseback, which were dates stuffed with cheese and wrapped in prosciutto. And, somewhat shockingly, there was a big platter of deviled eggs with capers.

"Who are we feeding tonight?" I asked when Nate came in to grab another platter of crudités.

He rolled his eyes. "A sorority, and don't ask me the name. Kappa or Delta or Gamma or something. It's a cocktail party with the state officers and a bunch of students from Beardsley."

Beardsley College was located in Geary. It was all female and very exclusive, like a lot of things in Geary. Shavano made do with Shavano County Community College, thank you very much.

"They didn't even want chicken satay?" We did a lot of chicken apps, and chicken satay was popular with many women's groups.

Nate shook his head. "Apparently, they've got a lot of vegetarians and vegans. From what I've seen, they also have a lot of girls who aren't into eating at all. The cheese and prosciutto and deviled eggs are for the keto followers."

I cast a guilty look at the desserts we had ready to

serve when the party began to wind down a bit. The two trays held Coco's pecan tassies, little pecan pies with dollops of whipped cream so delicious they could reduce a dieter to tears. I hoped we wouldn't have a lot of sobbing girls to deal with after we put them out.

Nate understood what I was thinking. "I'll put them out. You never know—one or two of them might break down and try a tassie. Once they've tried one, they're doomed."

"Definitely." Nobody who ate one of Coco's treats could stop herself from a second and even a third.

Nate balanced the crudités on his hand. "Let me finish up with these, and then we can see what happens with the desserts." He grabbed another tray with the final servings of the caprese skewers and the taquitos and headed for the dining room.

I had a certain amount of sympathy for the sorority sisters. My few attempts at dieting had all foundered on the shoals of holiday eating. And we'd provided them with some apps that had a lot of protein and a lot of flavor. But it was Christmastime, and nobody got away from a holiday party without a cookie or two.

I started loading dishes into the industrial-size dishwasher. Clean-up was the responsibility of the management, as we knew only too well. I found myself wondering if the same Zamboni operator was still around to sweep the dining room, and if I could take advantage of his presence to ask him a few questions.

Knock it off. You're retired from this investigation, remember?

I was indeed. The Zamboni guy was safe from me.

A few minutes later, the door to the dining room swung open and I glanced up, expecting to see Nate.

Instead, I saw one of the sorority girls, or so I thought. She seemed vaguely familiar, but I couldn't place her. She stood in the doorway, glancing around the kitchen as if she was searching for something and not finding it.

"Can I help you?" I asked.

"I'm looking for Mr. Robicheaux." She paused, giving me a long once-over. "You're his assistant, aren't you? I'm sorry, I don't remember your name."

But I remembered hers. Jennifer Pollack. She was different somehow, although I couldn't put my finger on it. She was wearing designer jeans that were artfully aged, but the sweater wasn't cashmere this time. In fact, it looked like someone had knitted it for her. Her hair was pulled back in a ponytail, and she was wearing, so help me God, combat boots with two-inch lug soles. I wasn't sure whether the changes were due to this being a sorority party, but she was more like a college student and less like a bride.

"I'm Roxanne Constantine, Ms. Pollack. Can I help?"

Jennifer looked a little confused, as if she wasn't sure how helpful I could be. "I…need to explain about the wedding. My wedding, that is."

We hadn't ever gotten the final details about whether the wedding had been postponed until a later date, and if so, what that later date was. Thalia had said she'd find out, but she'd never mentioned it. "Mr. Robicheaux is out in the dining room. He should be here in a few minutes if you don't mind waiting." Although I didn't know how eager Nate would be to have a conference while he was supposed to be keeping an eye on the food situation.

"Oh. Okay. No, I don't mind." She pulled up one of

the stools from the prep area and sat down opposite where I was loading the dishwasher. I don't normally work with an audience, but I decided I could put up with it this time around.

"Are you a member of the sorority?" I asked.

Jennifer nodded. "I joined when I was a freshman. I'm a senior now."

She was a senior at an exclusive college and a sorority member? That didn't seem to go along with her sudden marriage. For some reason, I'd assumed she was older than that.

"Do you like it at Beardsley?" I tried to remember if I'd ever met one of their students before.

"It's been a good experience. I'm a finance major. With a marketing minor."

I wondered if her father had demanded the major. But maybe she had an interest in business herself. Maybe she'd inherited her dad's business, in fact. That was enough to give me a quick shiver.

Nate pushed through the kitchen door again, carrying a tray with a couple of empty platters. He paused when he saw Jennifer sitting on her stool. "Hello?"

"Ms. Pollack wanted to talk to you about her wedding," I said quickly. He probably didn't recognize Jennifer either.

"Oh." Nate put the tray on the kitchen counter. "Let's do a last pass with what we've got left, then I'll take the desserts up."

I took the hint and started laying out what we had left of the apps. The crudités and devils on horseback were finished, and the deviled eggs had disappeared early on.

Nate turned to Jennifer. "What can I do for you, Ms. Pollack?"

"Well, I just wanted to let you know the wedding's been postponed indefinitely." She raised her chin. "I know the deposit is non-refundable and we still owe you a partial payment."

Nate nodded. "It's all in the contract. You can give me a call if anything's unclear. I'm sorry the wedding's been postponed."

"I'm not," Jennifer said flatly.

Nate and I both paused, blinking, and Jennifer flushed.

"I shouldn't have said that. But this January wedding was really my father's idea. I felt like we should wait until after graduation. We'd just gotten engaged in the fall. I wanted some time to enjoy it." Jennifer bit her lip. "I don't know why Daddy and Mr. Lukens were so set on it. But they were. After what happened, I don't want to go on with it. At least not for several months."

The idea that the wedding was the two crime bosses' doing opened several interesting avenues, including the obvious—what would they have gotten out of it? Did their determination have anything to do with the money laundering? Still, Jennifer was a bride who'd just lost her father. It was not the right time to question her about her father's business.

"I did buy beef tenderloin and salmon for the wedding," Nate said slowly. "It's in the freezer at the café. Technically, it's all yours if you want it."

I couldn't imagine what Jennifer would do with a hundred pounds of beef tenderloin and another hundred or so of salmon, but Nate was nothing if not conscientious.

Jennifer frowned. "I don't have any use for it. Is there somewhere we could donate it?"

Nate narrowed his eyes, thinking. "There's the homeless shelter on Second Street, and the United Shavano Churches group. And the Community Table people might be able to use it."

I wished Madge was there. She organized lots of food drives and other charitable ventures. She might know a group that needed something special for Christmas dinner. And suddenly, so did I.

"The women's shelter," I said.

Nate looked my way. "They could use the meat?"

"Absolutely. They've got women and children living there, and they need something special for Christmas. Maybe they could share it with one of the other groups. Mrs. Robicheaux would know."

Jennifer nodded vigorously. "The women's shelter. That's a wonderful idea. Give it to them, and if they can't use it all, they can find someone to share it with. Donate it to people who need a good meal."

"Okay, we'll do that." Nate picked up the tray that had the last of the apps laid out. "Let us know if we can do anything else." That was a very polite way of telling her we'd be willing to work with her again if and when she decided to reschedule her wedding.

"Thank you. I'll do that." Jennifer watched him step through the door to the dining room carrying the tray on his shoulder. "He's very handsome," she said, turning to me.

"I agree." I didn't know if she realized we were together, but Nate's yumminess was something I could endorse.

"Oh, what are those?" Jennifer's gaze had fastened

on the tray with Coco's pecan tassies.

"Dessert. Pecan tassies. They're delicious. Coco Robicheaux makes them." On an impulse, I grabbed the bowl of whipped cream and put a dollop on two of them. "Try some."

Jennifer stared at the platter for a moment as if it were a coiled rattlesnake. Then she reached out and took one of the tassies with whipped cream. She bit in cautiously, then chewed a bit as she stared into space. Her expression reminded me of a mathematician who has suddenly seen the path to a solution she'd never considered before. "Oh my God."

"I know, right?"

Nate reappeared in the kitchen with his empty tray. He watched as Jennifer took a second tassie. This one she consumed in a single bite. Then she closed her eyes in bliss.

He grinned in my direction. "Guess I'd better get those out there on the table."

"Guess you better."

Nate picked up the tray with the tassies and the bowl of whipped cream and started toward the door. Jennifer dropped to her feet and stepped after him. She turned as she got to the doorway. "Thanks. For everything."

"You're more than welcome."

After she disappeared through the door, I went back to loading the dishwasher, resisting all temptation to sneak into the dining room and see who ate dessert. I had no idea if the iron-disciplined sisters would break down and eat the tassies. But I thought they'd have a fight on their hands if they got between Jennifer and the dessert table.

Chapter 19

The closer we got to Christmas, the fewer parties we had left to do. Finally, only one remained—the Robicheaux Café staff party. Theoretically, this was an event for the kitchen and wait staff, along with a few miscellaneous people like the café's suppliers and the various significant others attached to the employees. But Madge being Madge, there were always a few other people she'd invited to just "drop by for a glass of wine and a cookie." The number of guests wasn't as large as the Thanksgiving blowout, but it was also more than just the people immediately associated with the café.

I wasn't surprised to see Thalia there. She'd been getting the finishing touches done on The Wedding, now less than two weeks away, and she'd earned not only my undying gratitude, but also Nate's, Coco's, Uncle Mike's, and, of course, Madge's. I no longer found it hard to drop off to sleep, consumed by the possibility that I'd forgotten to do something vital in the preparations. Nobody was allowed to forget anything when Thalia was around, which was all to the good.

Marcus was at the party because Coco had brought him, and Bianca was there because she was technically one of our suppliers. The café couldn't afford to buy her bread, but Robicheaux Catering depended on her baguettes. She planted herself at a table near the door where people coming and going could stop and gossip. I found a chair beside her, and sat down, nibbling on a slice of Coco's flourless chocolate cake.

Bianca had a slice of her own. "This is really good," she said, chewing a bite with a critical expression. From her, that was high praise, particularly when it was directed toward another baker.

I nodded. "Really, really good." In truth, the cake was outstanding, like most of Coco's stuff. It was a good thing she and Bianca did very different kinds of baking. Otherwise, the rivalry might have wiped out any chance for a serious relationship between Marcus and Coco.

"You doing any more of that wine jelly?" Bianca cut another bite. "I sold what you gave me, and people enjoyed it on brioche bread."

I'd made a few extra jars of the wine jelly, which I'd given to Bianca just to see if it would sell. I'd priced it a little above my usual, given that the ingredients themselves were pricey, wine costing considerably more than the raspberries and peaches I got from the farm. "I'll see what happens after The Wedding," I said. "I'm giving out mini jars as wedding favors, and I don't know if the guests will want to buy more. Plus it may be more of a holiday thing."

By then, after making over a hundred jars of the stuff, I was thoroughly sick of wine jelly. The thought of making more, even to sell at Bianca's bakery, was more than I could face. But I was enough of a businesswoman to know I'd make it if I had a good chance of selling it.

Bianca chewed her bite of cake. "It does go along with Christmas and New Year's. People drink a lot more mulled wine when they're feeling festive."

I glanced down at my own cup of mulled wine, which Madge served every year for Christmas. The wine jelly did taste a little like it. Maybe that was why I wasn't slurping my wine down with enthusiasm.

"If you don't want to make it now, maybe you could make it next year. Use it for your jam of the month and sell it at my place around Christmas time."

I nodded. "That sounds good. I'll try putting it on my calendar, so I won't forget next year." At the moment, the idea of forgetting all about wine jelly was really appealing. I hoped that idea would pass by next Christmas.

I poured out my mulled wine when no one was looking and grabbed some coffee instead. It tasted better with the array of Coco's desserts anyway. Thalia beckoned me from the table where she was sitting with several piles of papers in front of her. When I got closer, I recognized her ubiquitous checklists. Maybe they were for some other wedding, but I doubted it.

I did a quick inspection of the checklist form one more time. I'd thought it might be possible that the scrap of paper Fowler had found under Pollack's body was from one of Thalia's checklists, since there'd been several of them for the Pollack wedding. But now that I considered the checklists I'd been working with for a couple of weeks, the scrap clearly wasn't from Thalia. The font Thalia used was nowhere near the ornate font on the scrap of paper. On the other hand, it was probably a good thing that the scrap wasn't from Thalia. That was one less thing to tie her to Pollack.

"I got the flowers worked out." Thalia glanced up as I pulled up a chair. "Hollingsworth, the wholesale florist, has poinsettias they've been renting out for decorations at various events during the season. They usually get rid of them after Christmas, but they'll let us have them for a greatly reduced price. Ditto for the greenery. We'll have to install them ourselves since Hollingsworth isn't one of our regular floral designers, but that shouldn't be a problem."

She gave me a gleaming smile, and I knew only too well who was going to be installing those poinsettias and evergreen boughs, probably the day before the wedding.

Groovy.

"Nate said he's ready to go with the wedding dinner, so that's covered, too."

It was indeed. Nate and Bobby had decided to make their dad's chili recipe for the wedding since everybody had heard the story about Madge's father requiring it for the reception when she'd married Robert, senior. I wondered if that wouldn't put a damper on Madge's enjoyment of the wedding, but Nate was sure it wouldn't.

"Bobby and Coco and I talked about it, and we all thought she'd love it. That it would be sort of like getting my dad's blessing on the whole evening."

The Robicheaux kids knew their mom better than I did, and serving chili and cornbread, with sides including coleslaw and quesadillas, would be a lot easier than fancier entrees. The more I considered it, the more I thought it was a great idea, given that most people would be thoroughly sick of holiday food by then. I wasn't sure how we were going to work champagne into this—and Nate was already talking about washtubs full of beers—but maybe we could save the champagne to go with Marla's cake.

"Now," Thalia said, "about music."

This was an ongoing argument between us. Several of Shavano's chefs had formed a roots rock band called The Flamin' Cooks. Madge wanted them to perform at the reception, even though they weren't exactly pros. Thalia was arguing for a DJ and recorded music, which was marginally classier, but not as much fun. I'd been trying to broker a compromise by which the DJ could start the evening, and the Flamers could finish it. Most of the guests would probably be somewhat toasted by the end of the evening anyway, and they'd be a lot more likely to treat the Flamers with enthusiasm if they were getting them after an evening of carbs and tearful toasts.

Thalia didn't see it that way. "Weddings are once in a lifetime occasions," she said now. "They're not an opportunity for amateurs to take the stage."

"The band members are Madge's friends. She really wants them to play." And yes, they were amateurs, but they weren't that bad.

Thalia snorted. "Then we'll need to convince her that this isn't the right time. She can have them play at some other party."

I thought of all the responses I could make, including the fact that this *once in a lifetime occasion* had actually occurred before for both Madge and Uncle Mike during their first marriages, but the argument was pointless. It was Madge's wedding, and Madge wanted her friends to play. She'd already asked them, in fact, and I for one had no intention of telling them she'd changed her mind.

It took another half hour or so, but eventually Thalia accepted that the Flamers were going to be onstage for at least a short set. Not that she was happy about it, but she accepted it.

"So," I said, "to sum up, we've got the flowers. We've got the food. We've got the entertainment. Madge already had the officiant confirmed. What does that leave?" I was hoping the answer was *not much.*

Thalia frowned. "I need to get the photographer to commit."

"I've already talked to him, and he's solid. If he backs out for some reason, Dolce could take over. She's done photography classes at school, and she's got the equipment."

Thalia wasn't too impressed at the idea of a high school student filling in as a photographer, but if we needed a fallback, Dolce was available. She took a deep breath. "There's the problem of the dresses. Madge still hasn't decided on a dress, and I don't know what to do about her attendants."

Oh, for Pete's sake. I was one of those attendants. So was Coco. So was Marigold, assuming she was still on her feet when it was time for the wedding. Given our wildly different sizes, there was no way we could all wear the same dress. "We'll coordinate on color," I said, "but that's probably the best we can do. And Madge will decide on her dress when she's ready to decide."

Thalia raised her eyebrows but decided to let it go. Just as well. We weren't going to get any further on that issue. Madge was adamant on her right to choose her own dress without interference from friends or family members.

I wandered off to find Nate and pass along the news about the floral design work we were probably going to be saddled with the day before the wedding. "No problem," he said. "We can drag a few poinsettias around, and by now I'm used to hanging greenery." He gestured toward the bountiful displays of artificial pine boughs that decorated the café's dining room.

Decorating the barn for The Wedding would be a lot

tougher than getting the café ready for Christmas, particularly when you considered that Thalia would be there and serving as design field marshal. But sufficient to the day, as they say. I headed home in Nate's SUV, more relaxed than I'd felt in a while.

We had one more catering job to worry about before Christmas—the historical society shindig at the Blankenship House. Nate and Dex did most of the meal prep although I did my bit by making a couple hundred more Asian meatballs. The society had hired wait staff and a bartender for the event, so we didn't have to worry about being in too many places at once. It would mainly be a matter of getting the food ready and served on time. The entrees had all been taken care of, but they'd need to be rewarmed when we got there. The apps were taking most of the remaining prep time.

We were all pressed into service to get the crudités done. For once, I wished we could have gone with pre-prepped baby carrots, but that wouldn't have been the Robicheaux Catering way. We sliced up bags of carrots and celery sticks, cut broccoli florets and radish flowers, made sturdy cucumber slices on the mandolin, blanched green beans and asparagus spears, carved sweet red pepper chunks, and added a sprinkling of cherry tomatoes to lend the tray some punch. Unlike the sorority girls, the society wanted creamy dips, so we obliged with a gorgeous herbed-cheese dip and a more traditional chipotle ranch, along with some fresh hummus for the non-dairy crowd.

We did the same caprese skewers we'd done for the sorority sisters, but a whole lot more of them. The vegan filo packets made another appearance, along with endive leaves stuffed with goat cheese and walnuts. And along with the meatballs, we did the chicken satay the sorority sisters had chosen not to serve. Their loss, believe me.

By the night of the twenty-third, we were absolutely ready to go. Nate, Dex, and I were all in the kitchen, and we were all wearing our chef's coats. Nate had sprung for some black ball caps with Robicheaux Catering embroidered across the front in scarlet, and we all had them on, too. We looked like pros. Hell, we *were* pros.

I'd never been inside the Blankenship House before, so I took a few minutes to poke around after we got there. It was large and faintly cold, both in terms of temperature and ambiance. I wondered if the previous owner's larcenous tendencies had somehow rubbed off on the house, but that made no sense. Still, I thought Alice Hoover's house was more impressive as a restored historic home, even though it was considerably smaller.

Nate took dining room duty during the cocktail hour, when our biggest responsibility was keeping the appetizers coming. Dex and I warmed what needed to be warmed and took the cool things out of the refrigerator. We arranged the trays of crudités and skewers and endive leaves. We warmed up the chicken satay and meatballs and arranged them around bowls of the appropriate sauces.

We worked our fannies off, in other words.

Nate came and went regularly, dropping off empty trays and picking up full ones. We'd already decided to get everything out on the serving tables early so that we could switch over to getting the buffet set up before people started moving into the dining room. My last pass at setting up a crudité tray was a thing of beauty, with artful piles of veggies around the bowls of dip. Those piles represented the last of the veggies, and once I had them set up, I grabbed a bag of Coco's salad and made for the buffet line.

We'd already decided to have a big bin of salad alongside the three entrees, but not to bother with any other sides. The salmon rillettes needed a basket of crostini as a go-with, but that was as close as we were going to get. I dumped the salad into a large stainless-steel bowl and then filled the containers of dressing that went along the side. Coco had also provided a large bag of croutons, and I sprinkled them over the lettuce as artfully as I could.

Nate and Dex were filling the entrée hot trays. They'd stay in the dining room to watch over the buffet table but not to serve since the society trusted its members to take fair portions for themselves. I thought that attitude was a bit naïve but not my problem, fortunately.

As I turned to go back to the kitchen, I decided to take a quick detour through the dessert room. There were three tables set up at the front with goodies—Christmas cookies, an array of lemon and blueberry tarts, along with some delectable-looking cannoli studded with chocolate chips.

But Marla's cake was the centerpiece, an amazing construction of buttercream and fondant, with a tumble of colorful flowers that seemed to come out of the cake's interior. The layers resembled terraces on a hillside, with a suggestion of a turret at the top.

A placard, placed at a corner of the table, read,
Yellow cake with raspberry filling
Ganache frosting
Fondant ornaments
Marla Purdue Cakes

I stepped back to take another look at the cake. Something about it tickled at my memory, but I wasn't sure what. I dug around in the pocket of my chef's pants and pulled out my cell phone. The light in the dessert room was a little dim—the society honchos wanted to keep it dark until it was time for the crowd to move in—but I got a couple of shots of the table and one of the placard.

"We don't usually allow photographs," someone said behind me.

Naturally, I jumped, although I was pretty sure I wasn't doing anything wrong. Beverly, Thalia's assistant, stepped up beside me. "I don't know that it's a problem with you, though. Mom's concerned about other cake designers stealing her ideas."

I blinked at her. "Mom?"

Beverly narrowed her eyes. "Marla Purdue, my mom. That's her cake."

"I didn't know you were related. Do you work with her, too?"

Beverly shrugged. "Not really. I can help out in a pinch, but baking was never my thing. I'm more interested in what Thalia's doing, the event planning."

"But you knew about the wedding business through your mom. That must have helped when you went to work with Thalia." Actually, I had no idea how involved in the wedding business Marla was. She came across as someone who regarded everyone else with a certain lofty indifference.

"Mom introduced me to Thalia, but I got the job on my own. I have a degree in hospitality management." Beverly sounded miffed, but I hadn't meant to imply she'd gotten her job through nepotism.

"Thalia's the best," I said quickly. "The two of you do great work."

Beverly raised an eyebrow. "Thanks. We didn't have much to do with this one, but we did donate some time. Good for community relations."

I nodded. "I thought you were off this month?"

"Pretty much. Thalia's working on Madge's wedding, but it's informal. It doesn't take a great deal of her time."

I decided not to be annoyed about that judgment. Maybe it did look easy from the outside, but from the inside, The Wedding had often felt like a massive pain. Still, for someone like Thalia, it might be a simple gig.

"I guess the Pollack murder left a big hole in your schedule."

"Sort of. He paid a lot of it in advance, though. We didn't get hurt too much."

If either of us had had any kind of affection for Emerson Pollack, that statement would have sounded callous. As it was, it sounded about right.

"I guess I'd better get back to the kitchen," I said. "We need to keep the buffet going."

Beverly returned to studying the cake. "Go to it."

By the time I was in the kitchen, I'd filed Marla's cake under *to be continued.* There'd been something about it that had pinched at my memory, but I didn't have time to mess around with it now. I spent the next two hours warming pots of Bolognese sauce and spaghetti, pulling containers of salmon rillettes out of the refrigerator, and running hotel pans of vegan fried rice through the oven. I toasted more crostini to go with the rillettes. I carted up bags of salad and croutons to refill the salad bowl. Dex and Nate would occasionally appear to carry up the hotel pans for the buffet.

Feeding over a hundred people was more work than the parties of fifty or sixty we'd been doing earlier in the week, but we must have been doing it the right way. Nate said they'd gotten compliments on both the apps and the buffet. Even the salmon rillettes, which had been a bit off the beaten track, had won some new fans. "We're gold, babe," Nate said when he came down to grab the last refill of Bolognese sauce. "And we're almost done. They're going to do a few speeches and then let everybody go to the dessert room."

"Just in time," I said.

The Bolognese was pretty much done, although I had more spaghetti that might stretch it a bit. The salmon and the fried rice were holding out, but that was because they had a smaller following. Bianca's baguettes were gone, except for the one I was reserving for crostini. The society types weren't eating like flocks of locusts, but they were close.

"Have you seen the dessert room yet?" I asked him.

He shook his head. "Haven't had time."

"I'll grab the rest of the fried rice and join you. It's worth checking out."

The dining room buzzed with the sounds of satisfied diners. In my experience, people who haven't had an enjoyable meal have a different tone to their conversation. Nate switched out the empty Bolognese pan for the mostly full one, and I did the same for the rice. A few people were already gathering with clean plates as we walked away with our dirty pans, taking a quick detour through the dessert room.

Nate stopped in front of Marla's cake, narrowing his eyes. "What do you think?" I asked.

"It's gorgeous, but how do you cut it?" He frowned. "Tell me they've got someone here who'll do the slicing."

Considering our experiences the last time we'd gotten roped into slicing one of Marla's cakes, I hoped they did. "Beverly's here. She can take over."

"Beverly? You mean Thalia's assistant?"

"She's Marla's daughter."

Nate stared at the cake again. "If Beverly is Marla's daughter, why the hell did we get stuck slicing her cake at the engagement party?"

Good question. "Was she there? I don't remember."

"I don't either." Nate sighed. "Water under the bridge. Let's get these pans down to the kitchen and start cleanup."

That sounded like a very good idea, but I still found myself a little curious about the cake question. Maybe I'd ask Thalia. Assuming I remembered.

Chapter 20

The museum society party was a big success, according to Madge. She said people complimented the food all evening long. She'd even handed out most of the business cards she'd brought. I found myself wondering just what the museum society officers thought about Madge handing out business cards for her own catering business, but I was pretty sure nobody was going to call her on it. Everybody loved Madge, and everybody wanted her on their committees.

"Speaking of which," she said, "we need better business cards than these. The font's not great—too fancy. I'm sorry I let Coco talk me into them."

She perched on a chair at the side of the Blankenship House kitchen, watching us pack up. The society had hired a cleaning service to come in the next day and put the house to rights, so for once we didn't have to do the dishes.

"Let me see," Nate said. "I haven't checked those cards in a while." He took the card from her hand, squinting. "You're right. We can do better than this."

Madge gave him a brilliant smile. "Great. I ran out of cards tonight, which means we need to order more anyway."

Dex loaded the last hotel pan into the carrier. We'd rinsed them out, but we'd have to take them to the café for washing. "Let me help you load up," he said. "Then

227

I can go home." It was a very polite nudge to Madge that we all needed to get going.

"Oh, absolutely, let's move along," Madge said. "We'll all sleep late tomorrow."

I planned on doing that, although Thalia would probably be on my case by nine, which would limit my lateness.

Unloading didn't take much time, and then Nate and I were off to the cabin. We'd put together a quick meal from the dinner apps, along with some leftover salmon rillettes. It wouldn't be particularly nourishing, but it would save us having to rustle anything up at home.

When we were seated at the kitchen table, a basket of crostini and a deli container of salmon rillettes in front of us, Nate pulled out the business card again. "Mom's right. This absolutely doesn't work. I don't remember even seeing this before she ordered them."

I took the business card as he helped himself to a couple of vegan filo packets. "Let me see."

"It's the font," Nate said. "It's too ornate. It doesn't fit with the business."

I stared down at the card, not really reading it as a series of things clicked together in my brain. "The font," I said slowly. "My God, the font."

Nate frowned. "It's not that bad. Just inappropriate."

I shook my head. "Not that font. This one." I fumbled in my pants pocket and pulled out my phone, flipping quickly through the photos. "Look."

Nate squinted, studying the picture of Marla's cake. "Yeah, nice cake. I guess. What did you say about the font? What font? Is there writing on the cake I can't see?"

"No." I grabbed the phone and pulled up the picture of the placard at the corner of Marla's table, zooming in as much as I could. "That font. Does is seem familiar?"

Nate stared at the picture, eyes narrowing. "I don't know. Maybe…"

I zoomed in closer. "Check the word *Ganache*."

Nate stared a moment longer. "Oh, hell no, it can't be."

"It is. And that's Marla's font. She uses it on all her stuff—business cards, advertising, everything. I just didn't recognize it until now." I took a breath to try to slow down my racing heart. "Look here, at *Ganache*. That's the *Gan* on the slip of torn paper Fowler found beneath Pollack's body. I'd bet you anything."

Nate blew out a long breath. "I don't remember that piece of paper well enough to say one way or the other. But the font looks familiar. That's the best I can do."

"Fowler would know," I said slowly.

"We're not going to town," Nate said. "Not tonight. We're both too exhausted to do anything more. Tomorrow's time enough."

I rotated my shoulders, trying to shake loose the tension. "I need to pass this information on now. I want more people to know about it than just us."

"You think you're in danger?"

"I think somebody tried to run us down for reasons we still don't understand. I want Fowler to know."

Nate sighed. "Do you have his number?"

The only number I had for Fowler was his office downtown, and even he wouldn't be there this late on a Friday night. "I've got Susa's number. I can call her and ask her to get in touch with him, tell him to call."

"Susa's going to love getting a phone call after ten on a Friday night."

"Can't be helped." I punched in her number and

waited while it rang a few times.

Finally, Susa picked up and said, "What's up?" She sounded annoyed but not seriously.

"I need to leave a message for Fowler. It's serious. Let me tell you what it is, and maybe you can text it to him."

"Oh, hang on, I can do better than that."

There was a momentary pause with the sound of muttered voices, then Fowler came on the line. "What?" He sounded more annoyed than Susa, but then he hadn't been my best friend since second grade.

"I'm going to email an image to Susa. Take a look and see if you recognize it." I sent the photo of the placard and held my breath.

A moment later Fowler was back, still annoyed. "What am I supposed to be seeing here?"

"Check the word *Ganache* and see if you recognize the font."

This time he was gone longer, then, "Shit," he muttered. "Where did you get this? And when?"

"I got it tonight. At the museum society gala we catered. Marla Purdue did the cake. That's the font she uses on all her stuff. I recognized it when I saw the placard. So did Nate."

Nate scowled at me, but he'd said he recognized the font, even if he wasn't sure about the connection to Fowler's scrap of paper, so I wasn't lying.

I heard more muttering on the other end, and then Susa was back on the line. I had a feeling she'd wrenched the phone from Fowler's hand. "Do you need us to come out now? We can."

Fowler said something sharp in the background. I didn't blame him. "No, that's all right. I just wanted to pass this along while I could."

"You're sure? Ethan will have questions—you know that."

Suddenly I felt too tired to talk more. "Not tonight. You could come out for brunch tomorrow if Fowler's free."

"He will be," Susa's voice sounded like a cross between a promise and a threat.

"Okay, see you around eleven." I disconnected and then turned to Nate. "I'm sorry. You don't have to do this if you don't want to. But I want to pass on the details before I think about this too much. I don't want to lose my nerve."

Nate shook his head. "I can't imagine you losing your nerve, Roxanne. Ever. But it's okay. We've got some of Coco's cinnamon rolls in the freezer. If we need something for brunch, they'll work."

I nodded, as another wave of exhaustion washed over me. "Good."

Nate extended his hand. "It's been a long day. Want to go to bed?"

"Yes," I said. "Yes, I really do."

And so we did.

****

The next day, I found myself wondering if I'd been a little too confident about that font. It had certainly looked like the same one when I'd seen it at the gala, but the light in the dessert room had been turned low. Maybe I'd made more of it than I should have.

"Do we have anything printed from Marla?" I asked Nate. "Anything where we could see the font close up?"

"Let me go through the wedding stuff. Maybe I got one of her brochures or something."

Nate headed to the spare bedroom that served as our mutual office, leaving me to figure out what we could have for brunch. I had eggs and bacon, and I could always make pancakes, but that seemed a little mundane, even with Coco's cinnamon rolls thrown in. I was considering the waffle maker when Nate reappeared a few minutes later. "What's up?"

"I was thinking maybe I could do waffles."

He grimaced. "Nope. That waffle maker is a disaster. It never gets hot enough."

"Pancakes?" They might have been a pedestrian brunch dish, but my pancakes were still more than decent.

Nate took hold of my shoulders and lifted me out of the way, quite a feat, given my size. "I'm the brunch guy. And I don't have to make omelets at the café this week since we'll be closed for Christmas."

By the time Fowler pulled up, Nate had whipped up a couple of lovely omelets, along with bacon and sausage from the freezer. Coco's cinnamon rolls fit right in, and I could always make toast if anyone was so unwise as to refuse a cinnamon roll.

I wasn't surprised to see Susa sitting in the passenger seat in Fowler's SUV. He would no doubt have been happier if she'd stayed home, but Susa wasn't going to do that. Not when she'd already heard Alice's assessment of Emerson Pollack.

I got everybody set up with omelets and coffee and go-withs, along with a plate of Coco's cinnamon rolls warm from the oven and smelling divine. Susa was full of chatter about Christmas; it was Christmas Eve, after all. She was joining us at Madge's house on Christmas day, then traveling down to spend time with her parents at their house in Phoenix after The Wedding on New Year's Eve.

"Are you sticking around for Christmas?" I asked Fowler.

He shrugged. "Yeah. It's another one of those holidays where the single people work the station while the people with families take the day off."

I wondered if some of the singles would prefer to take off and spend the day with family, too, since a lot of his personnel were young enough to have folks who wanted them around the Christmas tree. Maybe Christmas crime was light enough to let most of the people off, but Fowler would stick around.

Nate gave him a long look. "You could drop by my mom's house and grab some dinner in the afternoon. She'd be glad to have you, and there's always a lot of food." And, of course, Susa would be there, too.

That invitation required a great surge of holiday spirit. Nate and Fowler didn't get along all that well, and they'd had that exchange of words on Thanksgiving night, but Christmas is Christmas. And Nate's a fundamentally nice guy.

"Thanks," Fowler said. "I'll keep that in mind."

After we'd eaten everything I'd fixed, Fowler leaned back in his chair. "Okay, tell me what you know. I've got to get to my office soon." Susa grimaced but held her peace.

"Okay." I gathered my thoughts together so that I could make something close to a reasonable presentation. "You've already seen the picture. I took it last night at the gala. I didn't recognize it right away, but after a while I was pretty sure it was the same font. Is it?"

Fowler picked up his phone. "The original is in

evidence, but here's a shot of it."

It was a clear enough picture, although as I'd remembered, the paper was seriously blood-stained. Susa leaned close to take a look, then narrowed her eyes. "Similar."

"Hang on." Nate stepped away from the table, then returned with a sheet of paper. "This is one of Marla's ingredients lists. It uses the same font. In fact, I'd guess that fragment came from a list like this one."

Fowler stared at the sheet for a long moment, particularly at the entry for ganache frosting. "I suppose it's possible somebody else in town uses the same font."

"Possible, but not likely," I said. "Marla's strictly first class. She wouldn't be happy if her font showed up in a lot of other businesses."

Fowler nodded slowly. "Well, here's the problem. Marla Purdue has an air-tight alibi. We checked her like we checked everyone else, and she was in her shop working on a cake with her assistant. She went straight from the event center to her shop and stayed there. She couldn't have stabbed Pollack."

"I don't know that I ever thought Marla did it," I mused. "But someone gave Pollack one of her ingredients lists, maybe as part of the informational packet she hands out to potential customers."

Fowler frowned. "Who had copies of her lists? And why would they be giving him one at that dinner?"

"Anyone who was connected to either Thalia or Marla would probably have access to those informational packets. That would include the two of them, along with Thalia's assistant Beverly Freedman, who's also Marla's daughter. And it would include Marla's staff and Thalia's staff, such as it is. I guess it's conceivable that one of the wedding guests asked for information about Marla's cakes after they had a piece of the engagement party cake, and they might have gotten a copy. The real question would be whether there were copies of Marla's information packets at the dinner and who might have picked one up."

Although frankly I found it hard to believe that most of the guests at the dinner would have been impressed enough by the cake to seek out more information about the baker.

"Any idea who would know about that?" Fowler raised his eyebrows.

I sighed. "Thalia or Marla, most likely. But you might also want to see if Pollack loaned Marla start-up money the way he did Thalia. Maybe he was pressuring her for something. Or maybe he'd decided her business would be a great front for some money laundering." But even as I said it, I realized it sounded thin. Marla would be the most likely candidate to kill Pollack if he was blackmailing her, and Marla couldn't have done it. "I don't know. Maybe Marla gave Pollack her packet of information when he ordered the cake from her. Maybe Beverly or Thalia passed it on to him that night. I don't know anything for sure. Just that that fragment of paper comes from one of Marla Purdue's lists."

"Yeah, at least we know that much." Fowler rubbed a hand across his chin, staring down at the two font examples. "Maybe I'll go have another conversation with Ms. Purdue. CBI has Pollack's financial records, but I hear they're tough to interpret—there may be another set of books somewhere. Still, you'd expect him to have a list of clients in his own office."

"He'll have kept track of anyone he loaned money

to and what they still owed," Susa said. "Even crooks have to keep accounts, although they may be disguised as something else."

Fowler gave her a look that mixed exasperation with something like affection. "I've got to get down to the office," he said. "I doubt there'll be much going on, but I need to be there just the same." He glanced at me and Nate. "Thanks for the brunch. Should carry me through most of the day, and it's a lot better food than what I normally get."

I started to say *any time* but then decided that wasn't an invitation Nate would be happy about. "Glad to have you" was a little less specific.

Nate watched as Fowler's car rolled up the drive to the highway. "You think there's a chance Beverly's the one who killed Pollack?"

"I don't have much reason to think so," I said slowly. "When you consider it, the evidence is flimsy. The piece of paper under Pollack's body most likely came from something in Marla's information packet. But according to Fowler, Marla's not a suspect. I think Beverly was there, but so were we. So was Thalia. Hell, so were a roomful of people, many of whom may have been in the same line of business as Pollack and may well have had a good reason to hate him. I was surprised to find out Beverly was Marla's daughter. But that doesn't necessarily mean she's a suspect. She works for Thalia, not Marla, and I wouldn't expect her to be passing out her mother's promotional stuff at a rehearsal dinner. For all we know that list may have nothing to do with Pollack's killer."

"It may not. But it's information we didn't know before. And neither did Fowler. If Marla's bakery is involved more than he realized, it's logical to consider her again. Both the paper and the murder weapon came from her. And maybe he'll consider other people associated with her, too." He shrugged. "You gave Fowler information he didn't have. Now it's up to him to decide what to do with it."

I put my arm around his waist, resting my head against his shoulder. "Thanks. And now I'm done with it, so help me. We've got a ton of work to do to get the barn ready for The Wedding."

"To say nothing of Christmas being tomorrow," Nate added dryly.

"Oh, Lord," I moaned. "I've still got wrapping to do. And I was going to bake some cookies. And maybe make some buckeyes."

"Coco will make enough cookies to take care of everybody in Shavano. And Mom will have the fudge part of things covered. Buckeyes, on the other hand…"

"Okay," I said. "Let me finish wrapping a couple of presents, and then I'll make some buckeyes."

And I wouldn't think about Emerson Pollack or Marla Purdue or Beverly Freedman. Or I'd do my very best not to.

Chapter 21

Christmas was great. The day after Christmas—not so much.

We had six days to get things whipped into shape with Thalia assuming her field marshal position. We all assembled in the barn on the twenty-sixth, slightly sleepy, slightly logy with over-indulgence. Slugs, in other words. Thalia regarded us with something like contempt. "All right," she called out from her perch in the loft. "Cleaning first. Then we arrange the room. Then we decorate."

Uncle Mike had already started on the barn renovation before Madge said yes to his marriage proposal—it was something he'd been planning for years. But it was one of those projects that sort of limp along behind the scenes, getting a little more done whenever any of us had a spare week or two. However, when the two of them decided to have the wedding in the barn, things got going at a much more accelerated pace.

Now the structure was done—floors sanded and stained; insulation and sheetrock walls added around the great room at the center; electricity, plumbing, and heating installed. There were two full baths on the first floor and a half bath in the loft that extended halfway across the barn upstairs. But there was no furniture to speak of since it was being kept empty until the wedding seating could be put in place. A feeling of emptiness still lingered around the structure even though it was pretty much finished. When Thalia gave us our marching orders, I thought I could hear an echo.

We were going to fill that emptiness, but first we needed to give the place a good going-over from top to bottom. Nate and Madge were both excused from all of these duties because they had a café and catering business to run, but Uncle Mike and I, along with Donnie, Carmen, Dolce, and several of our farming neighbors who were less occupied during the winter months all got to work under Thalia's direction.

We swept, we polished, we dusted, we carried out the end of the construction trash, and by the end of the day, I could only hope Nate had something in mind for dinner because I was pretty sure I wouldn't be able to raise a hand for the rest of the evening except to take a very hot shower.

The next day the rented wedding furniture arrived, and we began to put it in place. Thalia had a very definite arrangement in mind. Tables for six, around twenty of them, arranged across the middle of the great room. A raised dais at the end of the room where Uncle Mike and Madge would say their vows. A long table for the wedding party that would be put in place after the vows part of the evening was completed. This should have been easy to set up, but the field marshal had other ideas. She insisted the tables be an exact number of inches apart, and she checked each one with her yardstick. The chairs were arranged in an equidistant hexagon—the yardstick came into use again.

The whole thing reminded me of a show I'd seen once about Buckingham Palace in which the footmen were shown arranging the plates so that they were all precisely the same distance from the table's edge. They, too, used a ruler.

By the end of the day, I was visualizing all sorts of creative ways to kill Thalia, many of them involving a yardstick. But even I had to admit that the room was lovely. Or it would be when we got the decorations up, which would happen tomorrow.

Uncle Mike came down to have dinner with us. Madge had gone to town to check on Marigold, who'd been having Braxton Hicks contractions. I wondered what would happen if Marigold went into labor on the day of The Wedding. But then I decided not to worry about it. Her official due date was still a few weeks away, and Thalia would never allow a birth to upstage one of her weddings. She'd undoubtedly forbid the infant from making her arrival until the ceremony was completed. And the infant would no doubt obey.

Good luck, Marigold.

Nate was still doing most of the cooking in the evening since I still felt that lifting my arms took more strength than I could generate after a day with Thalia. He warmed up a dish of scalloped potatoes to go with cold ham, both leftovers from Christmas dinner. Nate hadn't been kidding when he'd told Fowler there'd be lots of food. And fortunately, a lot of that food was still available.

"So what do you think?" Uncle Mike asked when he was sitting down with a beer. "Does the barn look okay? Is it going to work?"

"It looks great," I said loyally. I would have said that even if it looked crappy, but it really did look great. Thalia might be a pain in the ass in some respects, but she knew her stuff.

"I guess tomorrow we put on the tablecloths and stuff. I'm not sure what decorating Thalia wants done."

"Tablecloths are part of it," I agreed. "And she's got poinsettias and greenery to hang around the support posts." The barn didn't exactly have pillars, but there were support posts for the loft overhead.

"And candles and the jam and whatever stuff Thalia came up with for table decorations," Uncle Mike said a little gloomily. "At least we'll be able to take a couple of days off after we finish up tomorrow."

I had my doubts about that. Thalia obviously had more in mind than just the basic decorating we were doing tomorrow. And then we had the rehearsal dinner on Friday night, although that would happen at Uncle Mike's place, and Madge had kept to her pledge to order Moretti's pizza.

I figured I'd get a bye from any more work Thalia had planned for the rest of the week, though, since Nate and I had to get going on the wedding dinner. Originally, Bobby and Nate were going to work together, but Bobby was staying close to Marigold. I didn't mind—it gave me an excuse to avoid the barn. Chili didn't make itself, but it was one of those meals that improved the longer is sat in the refrigerator. We were also making a pot of vegetarian chili for the non-meat eaters in the crowd. And cornbread and slaw and quesadillas. And whatever we were going to do for apps. If we worked at it, we could stretch meal prep to take up most of Thursday and Friday.

But before that, I had to get through Wednesday. Nate sent me off to the barn that morning as if he was sending me off to battle, and in a way he was. Our volunteers had diminished after two days of hard work, but Donnie, Carmen, Dolce, and Uncle Mike were still there, doggedly pursuing the perfect wedding layout.

We all helped Thalia carry in the poinsettias and greenery she'd gotten from the wholesale florist's showroom. The poinsettias were a little shopworn from having been used repeatedly to decorate Christmas parties, but they'd be fine with the lights dimmed down as they would be at the wedding. Donnie and Uncle Mike found ladders that would allow them to hang the evergreen garlands around the sides of the loft, and Carmen, Dolce, and I set about placing the poinsettias where Thalia wanted them.

Thalia, it should be noted, was in fine fettle. Even if the rest of us were beginning to flag, Thalia was clearly getting her second wind, assuming she'd ever lost her first one. She showed us the diagram she'd drawn of the great room, with clear X's for the poinsettias, and we got to work. No, we didn't get it right the first time, but Thalia was right there to make sure we put the flowers where she thought they needed to go. With her yardstick, of course.

By lunchtime, I was more than ready for a break. Thalia had an appointment at noon, although she promised she'd be back by one-thirty at the latest. She said we could go on working without her, but no one took her up on it. After spending two and a half days working on the barn, we were all eager to do something else for a while.

I needed to bring over the cases of wine jelly wedding favors so they could be placed on the tables. I decided I'd have lunch at the cabin and then load everything up in the wagon we used to transport stuff around the farm. By then, most of the most recent snow had melted, although the resulting mud presented a new problem, particularly for a heavily loaded wagon. Nonetheless, after I had my sandwich and glass of milk, I tucked an apple in the pocket of my parka and loaded up.

I had on my heavy-duty boots, but it was still a challenge to keep my footing in the slippery mud as I tugged the heavy load toward the barn. The last thing I wanted to do was to go down in the slop. Thalia would bar me from the barn if I did, and for once, I'd be on her side.

Fortunately, I made it to the barn with minimal slippage. My boots were coated, however, and I left them at the front door to dry. I also cleaned off the bottom of my jeans before I stepped inside.

Apparently, I was the first one to make it back from our lunch break, which gave me a chance to check things out without having Thalia at my elbow. The barn really was lovely. Thalia knew her stuff, no matter how annoying she could be.

I wandered to the back of the great room, then took the staircase to the loft. The construction company had done most of the work up there, since Uncle Mike wanted to make sure the loft area was structurally sound. They'd done a beautiful job, installing a large window across the wall where there had once been an opening for lowering hay bales. The loft itself spread across the end of the great room, then fanned out into ledges extending partway along the sides. The construction crew had put in railings along the ledges, but they hadn't yet put a railing across the end of the room because Madge and Uncle Mike hadn't decided on a final style. There was around a twenty-foot drop to the great room below, and

I kept well away from the open end. We'd block off the loft on the night of the wedding to prevent anyone from venturing up and dropping off the edge.

I stepped a little closer to the open end so I could get an aerial view of the great room. It still looked good, even from overhead. Thalia had brought in white tablecloths, but she'd also brought in a few that were bright colors, so the room had pops of color here and there—mostly red and green, which were Madge's favorites. I folded my arms and let myself bask in temporary satisfaction. We'd done good.

"Well, well, patting yourself on the back?"

I started so violently that I had to grab hold of one of the benches along the side of the room to make sure I didn't go over the end. I twisted to see who was behind me. Beverly stood at the top of the stairs from the great room.

I put a hand on my chest and took a deep breath. "I didn't hear you come in."

"I got here before you did," she said. "Just waiting for you to show up."

"Oh." I paused. "Thalia had an appointment. She's supposed to be here around one-thirty."

"I know." Beverly moved forward a bit. "I was there when she got to the office. She wanted me to get the final RSVP list from you so she can run through the arrangements one more time. Technically, I'm not working this week, but since I was around…."

"Okay, let me find the list, I think it's downstairs somewhere." I started for the stairs, but Beverly didn't get out of the way. Something about her presence made me uncomfortable, but I wasn't sure what.

She stepped forward again, brandishing a sheet of

paper. "Is this it? I found it on the dais."

I glanced at it. "Yeah, that's the list. Do you need anything else?"

"I guess not." She sighed. "You caused a lot of trouble at the office today."

Given that I hadn't set foot in Thalia's office for a couple of weeks, I wasn't sure what she was talking about. "You mean something about The Wedding?"

"Chief Fowler showed up, asking questions about Mom's information packet, whether we had any copies at the rehearsal dinner. Of course, we didn't. We had nothing to do with it. I hear you told him one of his clues was linked to Mom's promo. So I guess that's why you were taking pictures of the placard at the museum dinner."

"I recognized the font. Fowler showed us a scrap of paper he found under Pollack's body. It had the same printing." I paused, considering something that hadn't occurred to me before. "He must have shown it to you, too. Why didn't you recognize it?"

She shrugged. "I didn't look at it that closely. Why would I?"

"Because it was evidence in a murder investigation?" Granted it was blood-stained, but I didn't think Fowler would have let her get by with a half-assed glance at the evidence.

"Emerson Pollack was a jerk. A criminal. Why should anyone care what happened to him? Why did you?" She gave me a piercing look, and I rotated my shoulders, trying to relieve a sudden tightness. It was a question I hadn't really confronted.

"They suspected Thalia," I said. "Didn't you want her to be cleared?"

"I have no idea if Thalia killed Pollack. If she did, more power to her. He treated her like crap, holding that loan over her head and making her cancel her December schedule for his stupid daughter. He was asking for it if you want the truth. I certainly wouldn't do anything to help the police make a case against her, like identifying that font."

Beverly was beginning to sound more than peeved, almost like she was genuinely furious with me. I wondered if I'd made things tough for Marla, too.

"Did Fowler question your mom again? I didn't think she had anything to do with Pollack, beyond the wedding, that is."

Beverly gave me a sour smile. "Mom isn't much of a businesswoman. It wouldn't occur to her to get backing from somebody like Pollack, even after she went bankrupt in Frisco."

Okay, new information. I'd known Thalia had gotten Marla to come to Shavano, but I didn't know she'd gone out of business before she'd decided to leave Frisco. "Your mom's an artist. Maybe she'll do better here."

"Maybe. Artists don't always make enough to pay the bills. But the overhead's certainly lower in Shavano. And if she can pick up a few investors, she'll be fine. But having people in town think she was involved in Pollack's murder won't help." She gave me another of those piercing glances, but I was getting sick of this conversation.

"I recognized the font, and I passed it on to Fowler. I didn't draw any conclusions, and neither did he. He said your mom already had an alibi."

"Mom did." Beverly's mouth twisted in a grimace. "I didn't. I had to spend a lot of time convincing your pal

Fowler that I wasn't involved."

"That event space was full of people who hated Pollack. There must be a dozen suspects." No doubt now including Beverly.

"Everybody hated him. He was an awful man." Beverly sucked in a breath as she stepped closer again. I thought about backing up, but I didn't want to get any closer to the open end of the loft than I already was.

"You should have just stayed out of it," she said, her voice rising. "It had nothing to do with you. You weren't a suspect. Neither was anyone else you cared about. You should just have ignored the whole thing."

That wasn't entirely true since I definitely cared about Thalia, and she'd definitely been a suspect. But I didn't want to argue about it right then. Or at any other time with Beverly. More and more she seemed like someone with an anger problem. "Maybe you're right. But I wasn't involved in the case. I just recognized the font, and I passed it on to Fowler. That's it."

"That's a lie," Beverly snarled. "You found out what kind of business Pollack was in, and you told the chief. I heard you."

That was a surprise, but I wasn't about to let her know it. "If you heard our conversation, then you also heard that I didn't tell him anything he didn't already know." I took another deep breath and tightened my hold on the bench. "Why were you sneaking around the café, anyway? That was a private conversation." Beverly must have been behind the boxes next to the table. Otherwise, I would have seen her.

"I needed to know what you were up to. You're the great amateur detective." The sour smile had returned. "And I was right. You were making trouble."

I stared at her for a long moment. "Are you the one who tried to run us down that night?"

Beverly's jaw firmed. "It was a warning. You needed to know people were watching. Like I said, you needed to back off, but you didn't get the message."

"You could have killed us." I grasped the bench so tightly my fingers hurt.

"If something had gone wrong, maybe. But it was meant to be a warning. And it didn't work. You didn't back off. You told Fowler about the font."

I gritted my teeth. "Nate wasn't involved in any investigations. He didn't deserve to be run down." Neither did I, but the idea she'd go after Nate was a real sore point.

"Collateral damage. His problem. If he hadn't gotten involved with you, he wouldn't have had any trouble."

Beverly narrowed her eyes, then took another step closer. I stood my ground.

"Did you kill Pollack?" I asked.

"Oh, fuck you," she said. "You don't get to hear any confession. You just go over the edge and out of the picture."

And that finally did it. This whole surrealistic conversation was nonsense. Beverly was a freakin' murderer, and she didn't get to make the rules. And she sure as hell didn't get to push me off the loft. "Well, screw you and the horse you rode in on, toots. I'm not diving off the loft, if that's what you're planning. And if you try to push me, I'll fight like hell, which will mean you'll go over with me. I will definitely not go down quietly." Beverly was no petite damsel, but I was still bigger than her. And we were equally pissed by that point.

"I didn't think you would." Beverly stuck her hand into the pocket of her coat and pulled out an eight-inch chef's knife, probably from Marla's kitchen. "Either you back up, or you get punctured. Your choice."

Some choice. As I pulled myself up straight, I felt the apple I'd put into my pocket for dessert. As a weapon, it was pathetic, but you use what you have. I yanked it out and threw it as hard as I could at Beverly's head.

The apple bounced off her forehead, surprising her more than hurting her. But I didn't wait around to see. I pushed her out of my way and ran for the staircase.

She was after me in a moment, yelling, "You bitch, I'll fucking kill you."

That was what I was trying to avoid. We both thundered down the stairs. I wondered if she still had the knife, but I didn't want to take time to find out. As my feet hit the floor of the great room, I started running for the door. But then, almost magically, the door opened, spilling sunshine across the tables.

Thalia stepped inside. "Beverly," she called, "there you are!"

I dodged to the side, behind one of the pillars, and watched Beverly skid to a halt in front of Thalia. If she still had the knife, I didn't see it.

Thalia stepped toward us with her usual energy. She didn't seem to notice that both of us were panting, and Beverly was still snarling in fury. I was poised to start running again. "I need you to get me the estimates for the Iredale wedding," Thalia continued. "I just talked to Danielle, and her folder isn't in the drawer for March. I need to know what we told her about the flowers."

Beverly and I stayed frozen in place, although now

I saw the handle of the knife sticking out of her pocket. "What?" Beverly asked. She looked a little dazed.

Thalia raised her voice. "The Iredale estimates. Come on, get a move on, dear, chop chop. I know you know where they are in the system, but I can't find them. You're the one who had the initial interview with her, so you know more about the file than I do."

Thalia leaned forward to take Beverly by the arm then pulled her toward the door. "I'll be in the office around four. See if you can find it by then. You don't have to stick around. Just leave me a note."

Beverly stared at her blankly, and I was afraid she was going to try attacking both of us with the knife. But even she must have realized that wouldn't work. She started toward the door. By the time she got there, she was trotting, and she made it outside at something like a dead run.

I stood still for a moment longer, trying to get my knees to stop shaking. And then I dropped down on a chair at the nearest table. I was probably disarranging Thalia's set-up, but it didn't matter. I couldn't get up.

After another moment, Thalia pulled out a chair and dropped down beside me. "Are you okay?"

"I guess so. Did you…were you downstairs during some of that?"

"Most of it," Thalia said. "I wasn't sure what to do. I was going to text the police, but I thought you needed a faster intervention of some kind."

I nodded, but it was shaky. "Definitely. Definitely needed an intervention. Thank you."

Thalia took another survey of the great room. "I couldn't have her messing up all our lovely work, could I?"

Realistically, she was right. A body falling from the loft would mess up the arrangement of the room. To say nothing of spoiling the wedding. And me, too, of course.

"Did you send her here to pick up the RSVP list?"

"Absolutely not. I have that list on my phone. Why would I need paper?"

"Why, indeed?" I wasn't sure my knees would hold me up yet, so I stayed where I was.

"Chief Fowler stopped by to check on the font. Beverly seemed quite angry about that. She stormed out of the shop, which struck me as ominous."

I closed my eyes. "Very ominous."

"She's always had a problem with losing her temper. At one point, I know Marla wanted her to take an anger management class."

"Anger management," I repeated. I had an absurd urge to giggle, but I suppressed it.

Thalia dug into her purse and pulled out her phone. "And now I'm going to call Chief Fowler. I assume Beverly won't check on the Iredale account, but she might still be around town if they search for her."

"Right."

Fowler needed to be notified, but I was relieved to have Thalia doing the notifying. Among other things, I still felt way too shaky to talk to him right then. Plus I thought he'd give me another of those lectures about staying out of things that didn't concern me.

And this time around, he had a point. I wasn't ready to take a vow that I'd never get involved in investigations again, but right now I felt like that wasn't such a bad idea.

Chapter 22

I walked to the cabin rather than sticking around the barn for the last bit of decorating. Thalia said she'd cover for me, which was nice of her since she might have been as traumatized as I. On the other hand, she'd always struck me as the type of workaholic who overcame any anxiety by getting back to her job.

I was hoping Nate wouldn't be there. He was filling in for Marigold at the café so that she could get off her feet for a couple of days. The Braxton-Hicks contractions had subsided, but she still felt a little shaky. I thought he might stick around to get started on the chili after lunch was done, but when I stepped inside the cabin, I smelled something terrific coming from the kitchen. It was either Nate or elves, and it didn't seem like an elf kind of day. I dropped down on the couch and tried to push my expression into pleased exhaustion.

It didn't work. Nate came out of the kitchen and stopped cold when he saw me. "What's happened?" he said. "You look like it's something bad."

"Beverly showed up at the barn. She was talking crazy, making threats. Thalia got her to leave, then she called Fowler." That was, of course, the expurgated edition, but I wasn't going to talk about how close I'd come to falling off the loft unless I absolutely had to.

Apparently, I absolutely had to. "Threats? What kind of threats? Did she threaten you?"

"Yeah. She was mad at me because I identified the font on Fowler's scrap of paper. And she said she was the one who chased us on Thanksgiving night."

Nate dropped down beside me. "Whoa. Does that mean she killed Pollack?"

I nodded. "I think so. She came close to admitting it."

Nate stared down at his hands, taking it all in. "Do you think she's still around?"

"No. She ran out the door. She must know we'll tell Fowler what she said. I think she'll try to get as far away from here as she can as fast as she can." At least I profoundly hoped that's what she'd do. The thought of Beverly hanging around the wedding made my shoulders itch.

"This is nuts." Nate shook his head slowly. "Why on earth would she want to hurt you? You'd already told Fowler what you knew. Silencing you wouldn't help her."

I took a deep breath, trying to loosen all the tension in my body. "I don't think she wanted to silence me. I think she was pissed at me. She just wanted revenge." I took another breath. "Which is nuts, as you said. But maybe so is she."

Nate leaned back and put his arm around my shoulders. I snuggled against his chest and tried some yoga breathing. "Does this mean Fowler's on his way?" he asked.

"Probably. I'm not sure. Thalia talked to him." For which I was profoundly grateful.

"You want a drink? I think there's some whiskey."

I thought about it. I did, in fact, want a drink. But I'd be talking to Fowler soon, and that required a clear head.

"Maybe some tea."

"Tea it is." He pushed himself to his feet, and I slid down to rest my shoulders against the couch.

I hoped Uncle Mike and the other workers hadn't heard anything about this. Uncle Mike would be upset, and he didn't need that when he was getting married in a couple of days. But Thalia was capable of keeping a lid on things, and she understood better than most the need to keep wedding prep on schedule and wedding participants in good spirits.

Fowler arrived as I was finishing my cup of tea and contemplating something stronger. He narrowed his eyes at me. "You look like somebody threatened to throw you off a balcony."

"It wasn't a balcony. It was a loft. In the barn. And I let her know that wasn't going to happen." I handed Nate my teacup and made a quick decision. "Could I have a beer, please?"

"Sure." He glanced at Fowler. "Want one?"

Fowler sighed. "Oh, hell, yeah." He was in uniform, but maybe he was off duty. Or maybe he'd decided he didn't care, and I wasn't about to question his judgment. He was the chief of police, after all.

He took a seat opposite me, leaning back in his chair. "Now, I've heard Ms. Rosenberg's version of what happened. Tell me yours."

"Okay." I ran through it again, trying not to emphasize the being-thrown-off-the-loft aspect of things.

Fowler held up his hand about halfway through. "Hold on. She said she was the one who tried to run you down?"

"She said she'd heard me talking to you. I guess she

was annoyed. She strikes me as the type who gets annoyed easily and stays annoyed for a while. She said it was a warning, but I think it was more than that."

"I'd say it was considerably more than that." Fowler took a swallow of his beer. "Keep going."

I ran through the rest of our conversation, what there was of it.

"Did she have a weapon?" Fowler asked.

"Yeah. She had a chef's knife in her coat pocket, and she took it out when I told her I wasn't going down without a fight. She threatened me with it. But I threw an apple at her, so she was distracted, and I ran downstairs. Then Thalia came in before she caught up with me."

Nate didn't look happy, but I couldn't help that. I hadn't paused to consider how much danger I'd been in until after Beverly had trotted out the door. Now all I wanted to do was sit and drink my beer. "Did you catch her?"

Fowler shook his head. "She drove out of town without stopping by her place to pack. We've got an APB out on her car. With any luck, somebody will spot her."

I took another swallow of beer and decided to ask the questions that had been bugging me, not that I expected Fowler to have many answers. "Why did she kill Pollack? Was she trying to protect her mom?"

Fowler gave me a long look, then shrugged. "I've been going through Ms. Freedman's personal papers, courtesy of a friendly judge and a search warrant. She wasn't so much helping her mom as selling her out, so far as I can see. When we searched her house, we found a proposal packet she'd put together. She was planning to start her own event planning company, with her mother's cake business as the main part of it. That's where the scrap of paper came from."

"She wanted money from Pollack?" Beverly had called him an awful person, but she still wanted him to invest in her own business? Even after she'd seen what he'd put Thalia through?

Fowler nodded. "Looks like it. My best guess is Pollack turned her down. Another event planning business probably didn't interest him much since he already had an investment with Ms. Rosenberg. And Ms. Purdue already had one business failure under her belt. Pollack was a crook, but he was also a businessman."

"He might also have been unimpressed by that cake for the engagement party," I mused. "If Marla had put a little more into it, he might have been willing to consider taking on her business. But the cake really was sort of dry."

Fowler stared at me blankly for a moment. Then he took another swallow of his beer.

"And you think Beverly killed him because he rejected her business proposal?" Nate blew out a breath. "That's…crazy."

"Yeah, well, Ms. Freedman had what we might call 'anger issues,' as she demonstrated this afternoon. Her former husband had a restraining order against her after she broke into his apartment and attacked him with a tack hammer." Fowler gave me a half smile. "She doesn't handle rejection well."

"So she went after Rox because she was mad?" Nate looked like he wanted a beer of his own.

"Partly, but my guess is she was covering her tracks. Nobody saw her kill Pollack, but we ended up with a torn piece of paper and some information about Pollack's business practices. Rox was investigating both, so Ms. Freedman may well have decided she was dangerous. She was frightened, and she was angry. And she clearly wasn't the most stable person around."

"You can say that again," I muttered.

"What about Jennifer Pollack's wedding? Was that some kind of money laundering scheme?" Nate asked. Apparently, he'd decided to follow my lead and get all his questions answered while he could.

Fowler shook his head. "I've got nothing to share about that. If I had to guess, I'd say Alice was probably right—Pollack was setting up a business relationship with Lukens. And he didn't have any qualms about involving his daughter in his schemes. He spread a lot of cash around with the wedding. You should ask Ms. Rosenberg about it the next time you see her. She might have a story to pass on."

That was an intriguing possibility, but my guess was Thalia wouldn't have any time to dish over the next couple of days. Still, I made a mental note to have a long discussion with her at the first opportunity.

Fowler got to his feet then, handing Nate his empty bottle. "Thanks for the beer. And the information."

"Glad to help," Nate said. "You'll be here on Saturday, right?"

"Right. I may be on duty, but I'll take a break for The Wedding." He picked up his hat.

I took a breath and asked my last question. "Do I have anything to worry about? Could Beverly come here trying to find me?"

Fowler stared at the window where another few snowflakes had begun to drift down, probably the harbingers of the next big storm. "She could, but I doubt that she will. She's got a very limited window of time to get away from us. I think she'll take it."

"I hope so." I didn't want to go through another episode of Beverly and her discontent. And I absolutely didn't want Nate to be collateral damage.

"Don't worry," Fowler said. "Everybody around here is on the alert. But she's not likely to come here. I don't think so anyway."

Nate stepped beside me, putting his arm around my waist. "We'll be okay. We've got a wedding to worry about."

He was right about that. And wedding worry took up most of my time after that.

For the next two days, I made cornbread, slaw, quesadillas, guacamole, and tortilla chips. Bobby and Nate took care of the chili at the café, since it was their dad's recipe that they made at the café all the time. I think it took on a kind of special significance for them, and I was absolutely okay with letting them make as many pots as they felt like making.

It was the kind of all-out cooking that's either energizing or soul-killing, depending on your point of view. Right then I came down on the energizing side, particularly when I could see Madge's excitement and Uncle Mike's bliss. I wasn't going to worry about Beverly Freedman when I had so much great stuff to do and so many happy people around me.

Still, I kept my doors locked and my curtains drawn. And I was very careful to check the windows when anybody knocked.

The rehearsal dinner on Friday was a hoot. Since the wedding party consisted of Nate's family and Uncle Mike and me, pizza from Moretti's was a great choice.

Coco invited Marcus and Bianca, which was fine with everybody. They were as close to family as friends could get.

Bianca pulled me aside when I was pouring a second glass of chianti. "Anybody heard anything about that crazy dame?"

"You mean Beverly?" I shook my head. "She's probably long gone by now."

"She is if she's got any sense," Bianca said. "But then I never thought the wedding business called for much sense."

"Thalia's a very sensible person," I said loyally.

Bianca nodded. "Thalia's got her head on straight." She turned toward the dining room where Coco was leaning toward Marcus, her hand on his arm. "Hope that goes somewhere," she muttered and started toward Madge.

New Year's Eve, the day of The Wedding, dawned sunny and cold. The barn was all ready to go and looked terrific. Uncle Mike switched on the baseboard heaters in the morning, so the space would be nice and toasty by the time things got underway.

Coco, Marigold, and I were wearing black as Madge's attendants, both because her dress was burgundy velvet and because who doesn't need another black dress? Even Marigold allowed as how she'd probably wear her dress again—or use it as a tent.

The crowd had settled in by seven, munching chips and salsa, and the Flamers got going on their version of "Home." Judge Solis, a Robicheaux's Café perennial who'd also officiated for Bobby and Marigold, took his place on the raised dais Uncle Mike had constructed to Thalia's specifications. The judge was smiling broadly.

Uncle Mike walked to his place at one side of the dais, accompanied by Nate and Bobby. Then Madge made her way down the narrow aisle Thalia had laid out in the middle of the tables, followed by the three of us. She had a bouquet of white roses and evergreens, and she looked great. We had nosegays of pink rosebuds, and we were passable. Who notices bridesmaids anyway?

It was a lovely ceremony if I do say so myself. I sniffled into a tissue once or twice, and Coco's eyes were a bit brighter than usual. Marigold was mopping tears, but she got a bye since she was hugely pregnant and thus hormonal.

For the procession out, Bobby and Marigold were paired, and so were Nate and I. That left Coco on her own, but Marcus appeared at her elbow and walked out with her, both of them grinning. I found myself agreeing with Bianca—I hoped they were heading somewhere good.

And then it was time for food. We'd hired some servers so Nate and Bobby wouldn't have to spend their evening dishing up chili. Of course, that didn't stop Bobby from fussing around the service line until Marigold took him very firmly by the arm and dragged him to their table.

I saw lots of friendly faces—Harry and Caroline from Dirty Pete's, Susa's assistants Carly and Pip, Spence Carroll from High Country, Donnie, Carmen, and Dolce, Annabelle Dorsey and her daughter Dorothy, Lorraine from the Made in Colorado store, Donnell the legendary waitress, who was off duty for once, Aram Pergosian of the wonderful summer tomatoes, and Susa herself hanging onto Ethan Fowler's arm.

Fowler wore jeans and a leather jacket, so I guessed

he was off duty. "Nice ceremony," he said.

I agreed with him. "Did you get some chili?"

"In a minute." He paused. "I've got a wedding gift for you."

"For me?" My eyebrows went up. Was this some kind of subtle dig at Nate and me?

Fowler nodded. "Just wanted you to know we picked up Beverly Freedman late this afternoon."

I hadn't realized until then how tense my shoulders had been. I hadn't expected Beverly to show up at the wedding, like the bad fairy in "Sleeping Beauty," but I couldn't rule it out. "Where was she?"

He paused for a long moment, then shrugged. "Turning down the drive toward your cabin. Fortunately, we were waiting for her."

I stared at him for a long moment. "You said she wouldn't come back."

"I said I doubted it. A rational person in her position would have been long gone."

I shook my head. "She wasn't rational."

"No, she wasn't." He shrugged again. "Which is why I had people watching your place. Just in case she was crazier than I thought."

For once I couldn't come up with a single thing to say.

"I guess she had some plans," Fowler went on. "We found a gun in her purse. That'll add to the charges against her."

I closed my eyes, trying to block out the image of a vengeance-minded Beverly with a gun at her disposal driving down the road toward my house. "Well, I'm glad you caught her."

"So am I."

"Thank you."

He gave me one of his dry smiles. "Anytime."

Susa stepped up to pull on his arm. "Come on. I want some of Nate's chili before we're stuck with vegan."

Fowler smiled his goodbye as Susa dragged him toward the food line.

I spent the rest of the evening talking to all the friends who'd shown up to wish Madge and Uncle Mike well. After a while I started to feel a little more relaxed. After all, it was good that Beverly was under lock and key, even if she had been planning another attack, and that's what I decided to concentrate on. I'd think about what might have happened later. Much, much later.

As usual, Thalia was everywhere, making sure the whole affair ran smoothly. She didn't have to worry much because things were bumping along nicely. Seeing her reminded me of what Fowler had said about her "interesting story," so after a while, I maneuvered her into a chair at the side.

"Fowler said you knew something about the Pollack wedding, about whether it was some kind of illicit money laundering scheme or something else illegal."

Thalia blinked up at me. "It was some kind of illicit scheme. That's for sure. I'm not sure what he was planning, but Emerson wanted me to do some invoicing that didn't seem right to me. So I went to Morris, my accountant, and asked his opinion."

Morris was everyone's accountant, including Uncle Mike's. "What did he say?"

"He said what Emerson was asking me to do was not on the up and up, so he got me in touch with some people who could help."

"Some people? What people?"

"The FBI." Thalia smiled brightly, "Honestly, I talked to the nicest agent. His daughter may be getting married next year. His wife is going to call me."

I paused. "You worked with the FBI?"

Thalia nodded. "I did for a little while. Until Emerson died, that is. After that, there wasn't much point, although I'm sure they're going over his records with a fine-tooth comb."

"Right, I can see that. Do you think he was using his daughter's wedding to launder money?"

Thalia sighed. "Possibly. He was trying to do something shady, and poor Jennifer was just a pawn. She's better off without him although that sounds harsh, I know. Of course, she'd also be better off without that Trent. He's a nightmare, believe me."

"I agree." I didn't remember Trent, the drunken bridegroom, fondly. "Thanks for all you've done here, Thalia. It was a lovely wedding."

"It was, wasn't it?" Thalia smiled. "A barn wedding on New Year's Eve. I'll definitely put it in my picture book."

I wondered if Thalia had ever been a serious suspect, given that she was a government informant. I guess that depended on whether the FBI had shared anything with Fowler. They must have eventually since he knew Thalia's story. On the other hand, I suppose being a government witness doesn't necessarily mean you can't also be a murderer if provoked.

I wandered on to the other guests, telling myself the whole Pollack thing was over now and I needed to just let it go. I wanted to do that, but I wasn't having the best success in accomplishing it. I still felt vaguely guilty, and I wasn't sure why. I'd gone into finding information about Pollack with the best of intentions, but somehow, I was coming out of it feeling like I should have minded my own business.

After a while, some of the guests with young children began to leave. The Robicheauxs and Constantines were going to stick it out until midnight, but not everyone was ready to spend the rest of the night with us. I said goodbyes to some of the guests and got hugs from others. It had been a great ceremony, and I knew I needed to stop being such a downer.

I grabbed a piece of Marla's cake—I hadn't been sure we'd have it, given all the drama with Beverly and our involvement in it. But she'd done a very pretty sheet cake, which was what Madge wanted. It tasted better than the one she'd done for Pollack, which was reassuring.

Maybe Marla hadn't appreciated her daughter's efforts to sell her business to a crook. I'd have to ask Thalia about it sometime.

I sat at one of the empty tables, nibbling on my cake. Nate was in the food service area, making sure we had enough food to last until midnight. We even had some quesadillas in reserve that we could bring out after everyone had had their midnight kisses, and some extra champagne to go with them.

Someone sat down beside me, and I turned to see Uncle Mike. He'd taken off his tuxedo jacket and loosened his collar. He looked relaxed and happy and like someone who'd gone through a lot to get to where he was.

"That was a lovely ceremony," I said. "Congratulations." I leaned over and kissed his cheek.

Uncle Mike's cheeks flushed. He wasn't used to

compliments, even from me. "It worked out, didn't it? You guys and Thalia did a great job."

"Thanks. We had lots of help."

Uncle Mike sat smiling at me, until the smile became a slight frown. "What's the matter, honey?"

"Matter? Nothing," I said quickly. It was his wedding night, and I wasn't about to spoil it with philosophical musings.

"Yes, there is. I've known you since you were three, and I know when something's bothering you. What is it?"

I took a breath. Might as well put it in words. "Well, I keep thinking about this Pollack thing. About Beverly."

Uncle Mike's face darkened. "Heard they caught her. Not a minute too soon."

"I agree." I stared down at my hands, trying to work through everything I was feeling. "But when she was yelling at me up in the loft, she said Pollack was an awful person, that I shouldn't have gotten involved with trying to solve his murder because he was such an awful person." I took another breath. "And I guess I sort of wonder if she was right. He *was* awful. And the world seems better off without him. And I didn't really accomplish much by getting involved, plus I put Nate at risk along with me."

"Pollack was a bad guy, that's true," Uncle Mike said slowly. "But I don't know that I want someone like Beverly deciding who gets to live and who has to die. A jury should do that. Pollack should have ended up in prison for the rest of his life, and a jury might well have sent him there if the FBI had been able to keep on investigating him. Beverly didn't do anybody any favors by deciding he needed to die instead."

"But if I hadn't gotten involved…"

"If you hadn't gotten involved, Beverly might not have gotten caught. And frankly, I don't like the idea of somebody like her running around loose."

I paused, thinking. "There is that. I hadn't thought about it."

"Of course, there is that. And now I need to go find my bride. It's almost midnight." He patted my shoulder. "Go find your fella. You don't want to be sitting here all by your lonesome when the countdown starts."

I watched him step away. Then pushed myself to my feet. He was right about a lot of things, but mostly that I needed to find my fella.

Chapter 23

My fella wasn't that hard to find. He was in the makeshift kitchen we'd created in one of the storage rooms, putting the finishing touches on a platter of quesadillas and guacamole dip. He grinned when he saw me. "Hey, babe, I was just going to come for you. It's close to midnight, you know."

"I do know. Uncle Mike just told me I needed to find you for kissing purposes."

Nate's grin got a little hotter. "Glad to oblige." He bent me over his arm and gave me one of those Hollywood kisses that usually don't work out as well in real life.

This time it did.

It took me a minute to get my breath back. "Want some help getting the food out?"

"Sure." We carried the platter of quesadillas and another of chips and salsa out to the serving table. The empty pots of chili had already been removed, and as soon as we set the rest of the food down, it started to disappear.

"Come on, everybody, gather round." Aram Pergosian was standing in the middle of the great room, surrounded by half-empty tables and grinning guests. He was slightly buzzed and remarkably cheerful for a farmer during the slow time. "Time for the countdown."

I grabbed Nate's hand, and we hurried into the great

room, followed by Coco and Marcus. Susa and Fowler emerged from one of the darker corners at the side. Fowler looked rumpled, possibly the first time I'd ever seen him when he was in less than total control.

Aram held a large gold pocket watch in his hand. "My great grandpa bought this watch when he stepped off the boat from Armenia. Still keeps great time."

I believed him, but I noticed a lot of the guests were checking their cell phones. I resisted the impulse to do the same myself.

"Five," Aram announced, "four, three, two, one. Happy New Year, everybody!"

Nate spun me around and gave me another Hollywood kiss. From somewhere behind us I heard a champagne cork popping. Probably Uncle Mike getting the last few bottles ready to go.

"Happy New Year," I murmured when I was on my feet.

He grinned. "Right back at you."

We ambled over to the cabin around two. Most everyone had gone home by one or so, but we stuck around to straighten up a little, knowing that we'd have to return and do the lion's share later. The air was crisp and cold, well below freezing and inching toward zero. We should probably have been trotting, but we both felt too happy and relaxed to put out that much effort.

"That was a helluva good evening," Nate said. "Everything worked. And if anything didn't work, nobody cared."

"It was the best. I'm so glad we got it done right." I rested my head on his shoulder for a moment as he fumbled for his key.

Inside, the house was dark, but I heard Herman's

questioning *woof* from across the room. He was sleeping with us tonight since this was technically Uncle Mike and Madge's wedding night. They weren't going on their honeymoon until after Marigold had had her baby, but they deserved a couple of days of privacy all the same. I dropped onto the couch, switching on the lamp next to it.

"Want something to drink?" Nate asked.

I thought about it. I'd had enough champagne to last me for a while. "Maybe some fizzy water."

Nate grinned again and reached into the refrigerator for a bottle of club soda. Herman clicked across the floor to bump against my knee. Just another evening of domestic bliss.

Nate sat down next to me, handing me my glass of water. Herman switched his attentions to Nate, and it took a moment to convince him there wasn't room for a third between us on the couch, particularly when that third had a lot of Great Dane in his family tree.

I leaned back, closing my eyes. In a few minutes I'd be asleep.

"Do you ever think about it?" Nate asked.

I decided not to open my eyes. "Think about what?" Although I had a pretty good idea what he was talking about.

"Marriage," he said. "Us. Married."

I blew out a long breath. "Sure, I've thought about it. I don't know exactly how I feel, though." I looked up at him, trying to judge his mood.

He nodded. "I know. We've got a good life here. I'm happier now than I've been since before I came back to Shavano. Maybe even since before Las Vegas. I don't want to mess it up."

"No," I said. "We don't." I waited a beat, then

sighed. "But…"

"Yeah," he said. "But…"

We sat in silence for a moment longer. Then Nate took my hand. "I love you, Roxy. I want to spend my life with you. And I sort of think that means marriage."

My shoulders tensed a bit, but I let it go. "It could well mean marriage."

"If it did, would you say yes?"

My heart was hammering, but I wasn't going to back down. "I would only say yes to you. But I would say yes to you. I would."

Jesus, could you be any more roundabout than that?

Nate chuckled. "Well, that's a relief. "

"What about you?" I said quickly. "Would you say yes?" Because this was a two-person thing.

He turned his head to look at me. "Yes. I would say yes. Like I said, I want to spend my life with you."

My heart was hammering again. Had we just reached an agreement? "What does this mean?"

"I guess it means we want to get married," Nate said slowly. "I guess you're not ready to talk about when and where, though."

I bit my lip. "Not yet. Not when we just went through the whole thing with your mom and my uncle. I need a little breathing space. We both do."

"Right. Breathing space is good." He pulled me closer, resting his cheek against my hair. "But we'll come back to this later, right?"

"Right." I snuggled down to rest against his chest. "Happy New Year, Nate. I love you."

"Happy New Year, Roxanne." He kissed my temple, then rested his head against mine.

Tomorrow might be a panicky day, but I was ready

for it.

It was likely to be a very happy new year. And a very interesting one.

A word about the author...

Meg Benjamin is an award-winning author of romance and cozy mysteries. Along with her Luscious Delights series for Wild Rose Press, she's also the author of the Konigsburg, Salt Box and Brewing Love series. Her other work includes the paranormal Ramos Family trilogy and the Folk series. Meg's books have won numerous awards, including an EPIC Award, a Romantic Times Reviewers' Choice Award, the Holt Medallion, the Beanpot Award, the Carla Crown Jewel of Books, and the Award of Excellence.

Meg's Web site is http://www.MegBenjamin.com. You can follow her on...

Facebook (http://www.facebook.com/meg.benjamin1)

Pinterest (http://pinterest.com/megbenjamin/)

Twitter (http://twitter.com/megbenj1)

Instagram (meg_benjamin).

Meg loves to hear from readers—contact her at meg@megbenjamin.com.

http://www.MegBenjamin.com